SIMMER

GATE SERIES BOOK 2

MARIE BOOTH

This one's for readers who love jelly beans,
music, Italian food...
and second chances.

Thank you.

1

_____

"**C**hef. Someone to see you. Says it's important." Gio leaned in close and spoke in softer tones. "Don't let him in. It's bad news."

"How do you know it's bad news?" I placed a hand on my lower back, stretching to ease the ache.

"Mrs. Krieger chased him down the block with a rolled-up newspaper."

Mrs. Krieger and her husband owned Krieger's Delights, the deli on the corner, although most of us just called it Krieger's. A rolled-up newspaper was always within reach in that establishment. "Please, Gio. I'll speak with him." Gio was my head maître d', a loyal employee but moody as hell. He had a spooky knack for knowing when something bad was going to happen and I wouldn't have been surprised to find Gio had Roma blood.

"Yes, Chef." He marched toward our visitor, mumbling something about me being sorry.

Crossing his arms, Gio pointed toward my table, his ferocious frown thankfully ignored by the pleasant-looking victim of Mrs. Krieger's ire. I gave the man a cursory glance as he ambled toward me. When I realized who he was, I gulped down another mouthful of coffee. My usual customers didn't wear hand-tailored suits, shiny leather loafers or carry folders branded with a cheesy company logo that looked as if it were designed in the 1950s. This guy was from the fancy rental agency that managed a lot of the buildings in the area.

An icy chill speared my spine. Maybe the guy was only carrying a notice stating my rent was going up and not something much worse.

The young man extended his hand and smiled warmly. "I'm Samuel Flint from Mission Management."

I shook the hand but couldn't force my face to fake a smile. "Sloane Gabrielli."

I indicated the chair on the other side of the table, then shuffled some papers, stacking and putting them aside. I'd been tying up a few loose ends after the lunchtime rush. Running a restaurant was a 24/7 job.

"Thank you, Ms. Gabrielli." He maneuvered his wide-ish body and sat. The chair creaked as if the restaurant were protesting his bad news mission.

"Call me Sloane. I'll have Gio bring water and coffee." I wasn't in the mood to offer something stronger.

"Just water, thank you." He tugged at his collar. "It's warm today. Perhaps we could talk for a few moments so I can explain the situation and answer all your questions?"

"Explain what?"

He slid an envelope across the table. My hands trembled as I opened it, fumbling with the flap. The gold-embossed Gate of the Bay Realty logo was splayed across the top of the page in a fancy font. Mission Management handled the rentals, but Gate of the Bay Realty was the owner of the building and held all the power. The ostentatious name and font fit them to a tee. They'd been messing with my neighborhood for months, evicting longtime residents, tearing down buildings with history and character and constructing spaces that fit into their skewed model of a nice community.

Total crap.

I read the letter twice, only slightly conscious of my stomach dropping past my toes, through the floor and into the wine cellar. Here was my worst fear in black and white. I might as well have been reading my obituary. "You're not renewing my lease?"

"I'm sorry, but no."

Gio placed a pitcher of water and two glasses on the table, then moved aside. He was wearing a panicked expression. I kept my voice steady as I met his eyes. "I'm going to take care of this. Please don't spread any rumors with the staff."

He straightened, nodding. "Yes, Chef. You can count on me." After giving our visitor a decidedly evil eye, he returned to work, managing to switch gears, smile and wish the couple leaving the restaurant a very pleasant day. I had to admire the guy.

Maybe if I played the hostess I'd get to the bottom of this debacle. It might be a mistake. I was the perfect tenant. "Would you like something to eat?"

"No thank you. I've already eaten." He perused the obviously Italian décor. "In Chinatown."

"Woo Young?

"No. Yat Sum."

"Try Woo Young next time. Tell them I sent you."

He smiled. "I will."

Why was I being so damn nice? I'd just begun working on my list of ingredients for next week's menu when he'd shown up. Now I didn't even know if I'd be open next week.

I slapped my notebook closed hard enough that Flint's eyebrows rose in surprise. The timing couldn't be worse.

Over the last few weeks, good reviews had appeared in the *Globe* and the *Standard*. Yelp reviewers seemed to love us and I'd even gotten four and five star reviews on Trip Advisor from tourists who'd visited the San Francisco Mission District. We were so busy I'd hired another two servers—college students who needed the work to survive, like so many of my employees.

Shit! How was I going to tell my employees? I sipped more coffee to clear my head. It wasn't working. I needed answers. "I pay my rent on time. What's this about?"

"You have been an exemplary tenant, but the firm has decided to revitalize the entire block."

"Revitalize?" More bull.

"As you know, the space next door was renovated for Mrs. Granger and is now a successful art gallery and studio, pulling in a wealthy clientele. Gate of the Bay Realty intends to renovate the remainder of the storefronts on this block to fit in more with the ambiance The Graham Gallery has created."

"Doesn't Damien Granger have some connection to the realty company? Cassie never said a word." Cassie Granger had become a good friend in the few years she'd owned the art studio. I'd even catered their wedding, an extravagant affair at an exclusive resort.

"Mr. Granger is close friends with the son of the owner, but I doubt Mr. or Mrs. Granger know anything about the senior Mr. Hanley's decision. Mr. Hanley's lawyer and brother, Mr. Andrew Hanley, called our office regarding his brother's decision. Property values have skyrocketed in this area and the company wants to take advantage of this trend."

"I see." I glanced down at my hands, shocked that I'd crumpled the letter. I smoothed it out again. "I have... I have sixty days before I have to be out?"

"Correct. That's when your original lease is up. The company is calling in a structural engineer to do an inspection sometime in the next few weeks. I'll let you know when you can expect him."

I winced and rubbed my belly. It was as tight as a fisherman's knot. Taking a deep breath to calm my nerves, I glanced at my phone to check the time. This didn't end here. "Is Mr. Hanley in his office?"

Mr. Flint had been tucking papers back in his folder, but I had the man's attention now. "I believe Mr. Hanley usually leaves for the day around three, but he arrives at his office quite early. Even on Saturdays."

"Where is his office?"

"At The Gate Club in Marin County."

How nice for the rich bastard to be finished with work by three. What did Andrew Hanley do with himself for the rest of the day? Float in his pool at The Gate Club while his brother thought up ways to ruin hardworking people's lives?

I knew where the owner, Mr. Frank Hanley, was cooling his heels, and it wasn't in the club pool. He was in a prison cell somewhere in California. I'd read a couple of articles online about his case. He'd pled guilty to manslaughter and grand theft and had taken a deal.

Mr. Flint had finished his first glass of water and was pouring another. He wore a way too happy expression. Mission Management: Executions with a smile. If he could read my mind right now he'd be backing toward the door.

I forced my body to calm as I smoothed the crumpled letter one more time. Flint was only the messenger. Mr. Frank Hanley and his brother Andrew were the villains. I allowed my mind to wander. Strangling came to mind, but I'd probably have to stand on a step stool to do it. At five foot one and a half inches my reach was limited. Poison was tempting but completely out of the question. It would ruin my reputation as a chef. Maybe I could knock him out with one of my cast iron frying pans, *then* strangle him.

"I've already notified number 2232." Mr. Flint broke into my lovely fantasy.

"Krieger's?"

He nodded. "The thrift shop was closed."

"Silvi and Sophie Garcia are gone for the weekend." They were attending a wedding in Oregon. "What about the families in the upstairs apartments?"

"They have yet to be notified. The owner will most likely be tearing down the building, Ms. Gabrielli." My scowl told him how much I'd enjoyed his patronizing tone. "Forgive me. This must be difficult for you."

"Difficult is when you're late for an appointment and you have a flat tire."

"I understand."

"You can't possibly."

My neighbors and I had officially become victims of the gentrification movement in the San Francisco Mission District. Until now the situations other businesses had faced had only floated around on the back of my radar. Now it was real. "The local papers will eat this up. Gate of the Bay is tossing the owners and employees of three essential neighborhood shops plus a group of residents out with the trash."

"The company will be offering the neighborhood a set of businesses more in line with their specific needs."

"Will this space be a restaurant?"

"That's the plan, with offices and apartments above. I've seen the drawings. It's going to be lovely."

Yeah. Mortared in blood. "And the new rent?"

"Will be commensurate with the value of the renovated building."

In other words, five times what I was paying now.

"Mr. and Mrs. Krieger have owned and run that deli for over thirty years. The neighborhood residents buy their milk and bread and eggs there. The deli draws in a great crowd at lunchtime from the nearby businesses. Her potato salad is to die for. Have you spoken to Silvi and Sophie Garcia? The thrift shop tenants?"

"Not yet."

"I wouldn't go in there alone with this news."

He frowned. "Oh?"

"What's going into those two spaces?"

"A spa and a wonderful boutique grocery."

Exactly what most of the residents of the Mission needed–mud facials and free range pheasant. "How long will the renovation take?" If it wasn't too long maybe I could still keep the lion's share of my customers. I lifted my cup for another swig of caffeine. I'd need a whole pot today.

"Over six months. Probably more."

I froze, placing the cup slowly back on the table so I wouldn't be tempted to throw it in the guy's face. *Only the messenger. Only the messenger.* "This restaurant has been in my family for forty years."

"I understand the food's quite good here." He lifted the menu and nodded approvingly as he read down the list of dishes. "I'm sure you'll get your customers back no matter where you end up. Who's your head chef?"

I rose and removed the menu from his grasp, making a great effort not to bop him on the head with it. I handed it off to Gio. "I am the chef de cuisine, Mr. Flint, and have been for the last five years. Gio will show you out."

Gio waited stony faced until the representative of Mission Management rose, tucked his seat under the table, picked up his folder and nodded his goodbye, not seeming at all upset. Maybe he was used to being thrown out of places. Out of the corner of my eye, I caught Gio moving his foot forward, probably planning to trip the guy, then apologize profusely. I cleared my throat and shook my head. We didn't need a lawsuit on top of everything else.

The Garcia sisters wouldn't be taking the news as well as I had. Visions of flying clothing racks brought a smile to my face. Those girls didn't take shit from anyone.

Neither did I.

I stormed up the stairs to my combination office and emergency bedroom, slamming everything but my laptop down on the desk hard enough to be heard in the kitchen. Grabbing up a legal pad, I rushed to the window in time to see Mr. Mission Management get into the back seat of a waiting car. Off to ruin someone else's life.

One thing about being from a large family meant you had a brother, sister, or cousin in just about every sort of useful occupation you could think of. I emailed my police detective older sister Katherine the plate number, then emailed my oldest brother—Tony Jr.—a software designer and tech whiz kid, asking him to find out anything he could about Mr. Frank Hanley, Mr. Andrew Hanley, Gate of the Bay Realty and The Gate Club. One of my twin brothers, Angelo, was a PI who'd taught me it was always best to approach your enemy armed.

My answers came through an hour later, but I was already into dinner service and couldn't read their reports. The Friday night rush came to an end around midnight when I sat the staff down to tell them the news, knowing it was better to be honest than try to keep secrets. The word would be out soon enough and I wanted them to hear it from me first. I'd grown to care for my employees and I absolutely would not allow a wealthy, selfish, greedy man to force them to scrounge for work in a very slow job market. I had a loving, generous family. I'd survive. But Lori, my head bartender, Gio and some of the others had left their families and friends behind when they moved to the San Francisco Bay Area. Several of them shared an apartment. Where would they go if they couldn't pay their rent?

"When will we know for sure what's happening?" Lori sat at the bar, too anxious to continue her clean up routine until she heard what I had to say.

"I'll have to start looking for another job right away," Chandra, one of my line cooks, was on the verge of tears.

I reached for her hand. "I'm going to help you. All of you. If we have to leave, I'll contact everyone I know to get you jobs. I promise."

Chandra nodded, biting her lip.

I scanned the other worried faces. "We'll get through this together."

"Thanks, Sloane," Lori said, looking hopeful again.

"I'll be discussing this situation with our landlord, Mr. Andrew Hanley, bright and early tomorrow morning." I wasn't sure the lawyer was the one taking over, but that made the most sense. I'd only have a few hours' sleep, but it had to be done.

To get from my apartment in the South Beach neighborhood, I'd have to walk to the Ferry Building, catch the ferry to Sausalito, then take a ride share from there. But it would be worth every penny if it meant Bel Cielo could stay open.

We closed up and I jumped on a BART train and walked home from the Embarcadero Station. It was only a half-mile, and tonight I desperately needed to clear my head after the unexpected and gut-wrenching news I'd had to digest. When I made it through the door of my apartment it was almost one thirty and I was beyond beat. My clothes ended up in a heap and I groaned as I set the alarm for five thirty, forgetting all about opening my email to read the reports my siblings had sent me.

Those Hanleys didn't have a chance in hell against a Gabrielli on a mission.

"Where were you yesterday afternoon?"

"Not here."

Uncle Andrew's strident voice cut through the ending bars of the song I'd been working on for the last few nights. He'd found me in my usual position, eyes closed, shoes off, feet on my desk, guitar in lap, leaning back in my ergonomically perfect desk chair.

"Sit up. We have business to discuss."

I pried open one eye and squinted. "Too bright."

"Victor!"

Forcing my body forward, I slid my feet to the floor, wrinkling my nose. When had I changed my socks last? I blinked, trying to focus, but the world was spinning in unnatural ways. "What couldn't wait? The sun's barely up." And I was more than a little hungover.

"It's 7:05 and you're in the office. That means you're open for business."

"I was in the office at three and four and five and six too."

"An office is a place to work, not collapse after a night of heavy drinking."

"If you're having me tailed, Unc, you'd know I haven't gone in for heavy drinking since college."

Andrew shook his head, the usual disgusted expression plastered on his weaselly face. I turned in the chair, leaning over to place my acoustic Les Paul carefully in the case, then spun back to open a desk drawer and fish out a bottle of pills to help with the headache. I hadn't had a hangover in years, and the four shots of whiskey I'd enjoyed with the band after the news Shereen's latest hit had garnered me a Grammy nomination had thrown off my system.

I'd composed "Why Now?" after listening to her belt out an Aretha Franklin standard, and I'd known right away what style she was meant to sing. She'd tried several genres, but bluesy rock would have people swarming to buy her albums. She did sexy like no one else on the market right now.

I moved too quickly and winced. My head throbbed like a bass. I should know better. And Andrew wasn't helping things by continuing to talk.

"The evidence tells a different tale."

"Last night was an exception." I didn't bother mentioning the award nomination to an uncle who'd always tried to get me to give up my music. "Drinking interferes with my creative energy." And my sleep. Nightmares came with heavy drinking. "Early mornings in the office give me a couple of hours to sip my coffee in peace and clear some of that shit off my desk without being bothered by people showing up uninvited." I pointed to the three piles of work I'd spent hours organizing, then glanced toward the office door. "Why didn't Steven stop you?"

"If he wants to keep his job, he won't get in my way."

Andrew made himself comfortable in one of the large chairs facing my desk. "I visited your father yesterday. His request."

"I don't want to hear a fucking thing about Frank, so you can turn around and head to your golf game or tennis match. Or are you actually going to your office and doing some work for your clients today?"

"Feeling guilty about turning you dad in, Vic?"

"Yeah, when aliens land in Moffett Field. He murdered my best friend's dad and beat up Mom. He doesn't deserve the time of day." I slipped off my thin leather jacket and tossed it toward the coat stand. It caught and hung perfectly. My aim was good today despite the throbbing head. "Enjoy your day, Unc."

"This is business."

Uncle Andrew's clarinet concerto started up, the background music I'd composed in middle school when my father's older brother started getting on my case for spending too much time at the piano and not at my studies. The piece was dissonant at the beginning, turning into a reedy rhythm, kind of like electronic focus music. Usually easy to ignore.

Toot, toot. Toooot.

Everyone who annoyed or interested me had their own unique soundtrack. Frank's was an organ dirge. My mom's a soulful violin sonata.

I sighed, imagining rolling up my sleeves before the battle my uncle and I were about to have. "I want nothing to do with Frank's businesses."

"You can't hide from responsibility your whole life."

I'd heard this tirade so many times I had it memorized. Usually the toots rose to a staccato crescendo around the words, "mistake to allow you to attend Cal," then eased off to a lethargic buzz around "disappointment."

"I've done a lot of work as a consultant for Franklin Software."

"When was the last time they called you in for a job?"

"I've got things running smooth as butter over there. They're good on their own."

I moved to the corner counter and eyed yesterday's coffee pot, scowling at the sludge on the bottom. Was I this desperate? No. Fresh morning coffee was a sacred ritual. I wandered into the small kitchen to wash out the carafe and throw away the filter with the used grinds. Damien's assistant usually made the coffee on Saturday mornings, but my damn business partner had decided to take off on his damn honeymoon and had given his assistant some time off. The least he could have done was leave me some damn instructions. I lifted the top of the coffee machine. There were two places water could go. I had a fifty-fifty chance of getting it right.

Andrew opened the cabinet above the sink and removed the bag of filters. "Are you truly this incompetent? You can design software that can bring a corporate board to orgasm, or hack into their systems while they're discussing whether their security needs an upgrade, yet you can't work a coffee maker?"

"Put me in a kitchen and I'll set the house on fire, no problem. It's a gift." I rubbed my temples, hoping to quiet Thor's hammer.

"Fill the carafe with water up to the top line. Then pour it in the hole."

"Which hole?" I glanced at the machine warily.

"Either side."

"Okay. I got this."

"Do it."

I followed his directions as ordered, although it went

against the grain to do anything my asshole uncle wanted. Besides being my dad's brother, he was also a corporate lawyer—two strikes against him. But my need for caffeine was reaching the point of dire. I was ready to call up the local coffee bar to see if they could deliver a few large cups of their strongest brew. A whole box sounded even better. I moved to rub my throbbing temple only remembering at the last minute I was holding a pot full of water. No reason to give Unc another reason to mock me.

My studio session had ended at midnight, but Jake and I had been strumming out some great riffs and I was falling into the music the way I loved—forgetting the shitstorm my life had become. The shots of single malt had helped, although my head disagreed.

"Why don't you purchase one of those pod coffee pots? Children can operate them."

I made the finger in the mouth gagging motion. Andrew shook his head. Our usual conversations often ended like this. Andrew brought out the worst in me. He was wearing the stubborn expression perfected by all Hanley males, determined to give me the info he'd come about no matter how much I whined. He set up the coffee while I watched, then tilted his head toward one of the enormous Chesterfield chairs my dad said would look perfect in my office. They were ugly as shit and I had plans to donate them to some charity at the first opportunity.

"Sit." Andrew pointed.

I smiled without a touch of goodwill and leaned against my desk instead. He glanced at the chair. If he sat I'd be in the dominant position and that was unacceptable. Hanley males of my father's generation preferred to lord it over people, particularly their own family. But I knew every game and how to play it.

He threw a folder onto the desk. "Frank has gifted you his half of The Gate Club, as well as your house in Larkspur. As for the rest, he's designated you Special Trustee for Gate of the Bay Realty Group and Franklin Art Acquisitions. You'll be paid a generous salary from a private fund."

I didn't even glance at the folder. "Not interested."

"We sold the software company to cover Frank's legal costs and to pay back taxes. The employees were informed and given their severance pay."

"He sold Franklin Software?"

"Yes. Focus, Victor." I narrowed my eyes. "And drop that hostile expression. These changes are in your best interest."

"Pfft. When have you ever done anything in my best interest?"

He ignored the question. "You will meet with me on a biweekly basis to ensure that you are exerting due diligence and following the direction Frank wants the realty and art acquisitions companies to take. I suggest you have your lawyer friend, Bob or Bill, look over the paperwork immediately."

"Blake."

I let him rattle on, staring at the coffee pot and willing it to glug faster.

He waved his hand in the air as if batting away a fly. "Blake. Frank has signed over ownership of the main house in Larkspur and the surrounding property, along with fifty percent of all profits from his remaining two firms, to your mother."

"But Frank's alive." I placed my palm over my chest. "He planning on killing himself?"

I often pictured him sitting on a cot in his stark accommodations at the federal penitentiary. Hopefully with some huge roommate named Bubuh. Although, with the wealth

Dad had socked away in offshore accounts, he probably had the pen's version of a private suite, eating king crab every night and getting conjugal visits from the local *ladies*.

"Call your lawyer buddy now. This has to be taken care of immediately."

The tooting background music was getting harder to ignore. I clutched the edge of my desk so hard my knuckles turned white. "I'd appreciate it if you'd use Blake's name when you refer to my lawyer. He's been my friend since I turned eleven and you sent me off to the third circle of hell private boys' school."

"The school had an excellent record."

"I'm sure many of the former students also have records."

"You should have kept your business within the family and not hired an outsider."

"Really? I'm shocked, Uncle. Maybe you feel that way because he attended Stanford Law instead of Harvard?"

"You're being ridiculous."

"It couldn't possibly be because he's mixed race, could it?"

"I won't grace that question with an answer."

"I didn't expect you to."

He smiled his snaky smile. "Call Blake now, Victor."

"Oh, are you finished, because I'm not. I have no intention of taking on the trustee job. Find another minion."

I filled a mug with coffee and downed half, wishing I could inject it directly into my brain. Putting me in charge of two companies I had no interest in running was all about Dad kicking me in the ass one final time. I'd been a huge disappointment to him, never taking an interest in the corporate world or the empire he built. The Gate Club was the only business I enjoyed managing, but mostly because I shared the responsibility with Damien, another childhood friend.

"Frank trusts you to run them. He believes you'll do the right thing by your mother. Elaine is in for fifty percent."

"He's never trusted me before."

"Frank's been sent away for twenty-five years. It's the least he can do after what he's put you and Elaine through."

I laughed. "Are those your words or his?" Andrew didn't comment. "I'd say he owed our family and Damien's quite a bit more than twenty-five years in prison." I'd never forget the bruises on Mom's face and arms or the look in Damien's eyes at his dad's funeral. "You've said yourself, Frank will be out in ten, maybe less. He'll find someone to bribe with the money from those secret accounts I'm not supposed to know about."

"Vic…"

"I don't want the job. Find someone else."

"Read the paperwork. You can't delegate authority."

"I won't sign."

"Don't be stupid. If you won't take the job he'll sell the companies and hundreds of people will lose their jobs. Think of Elaine and the income she'll lose."

Fuck.

"Mom can always sell the house. It's way too big for her."

"You know she'll never do that."

"Why are you the messenger?" Andrew and I tended to avoid each other. He and my dad had been on my back to go into law since the day I could read *One Fish, Two Fish*. When I'd shown an interest in computers, he started pushing software design as an option. Only Mom had ever encouraged my music.

"I thought the information would be easier to coming from me."

"Your plan crashed and burned." I walked to the large window and turned my back, hoping Andrew would take the hint and leave. No luck.

"Is it because you'll actually have to take on some responsibility instead of hiding in your office humming songs? No more long lunches and quickies at the Carlton."

I fisted my hand, but Andrew wasn't worth the effort. He was as shady as Frank, he just hadn't been caught yet. "Why didn't he leave it all to you? Make you trustee?"

"You're his only son."

"Yes. The son who turned him in to the police."

"His actions got him where he is. He knows that. He's hoping you'll visit."

"Yeah. Right." I snatched the folder out of his hand and did a quick scan, leaning back against the desk. "If I take this on, I'll only meet with you, not Frank."

"So, he's Frank now?"

"He lost the right to be called Dad."

Andrew rubbed one of his shoulders. It always gave him trouble when the weather changed. "I stopped by your mother's yesterday when I couldn't get ahold of you. She's planning to visit Frank tomorrow."

I pushed off the desk and took a step toward him. "There is no way Mom is going to that prison. Ever."

"Your mother is an adult with the right to do as she pleases. It was her idea. I'm going along."

There were some battles it didn't pay to start. He was right. My mother would never sell her house and I doubted I could convince her not to go to the prison. I'd give it my best shot, but I wasn't holding out much hope. I shook my head and walked around the desk, grunting as I landed hard in my comfortable chair.

Andrew moved to sit across from me. "I know you're upset, but—"

"Miss! Miss, you can't go in there!"

My office door flew open and a tiny blonde female strode inside, making it to my desk in record time despite her four-inch heels. Her dark eyes were narrowed, her full lipped mouth turned down. I expected her to start snarling any minute. She waved around an envelope.

"I insist on seeing Mr. Hanley or whoever makes the decisions at Gate of the Bay Realty."

Her voice was husky, her wavy hair windblown, her olive toned cheeks pink from the cool morning air. There was something familiar... Did I know her?

"I'm sorry, Mr. Hanley." The guard wasn't sure whether to grab her and drag her out or let her be. I was glad he chose not to manhandle her. It would have been his last day at The Gate if he'd touched her.

Yeah, she was pissed about something, but what harm could this perfectly petite female do?

I remembered my manners and stood, scanning her body from head to toe in the process. She was angry enough to be dangerous. I kept my smile on the inside. It was possible she had a bomb strapped to her beautifully shaped chest, or maybe to her inner thigh. The formfitting dark blue dress she wore under her open raincoat was short. Maybe I should pat her down, just to be certain she wasn't carrying a weapon.

She slammed the envelope down on my desk and it scattered the stacks of items I'd just finished sorting yesterday. Half the pile ended up on the floor, but I managed to ignore the reports from the various boards, the requests to attend political fundraisers, the invitations to family events from relatives I barely remembered. Nothing in that mess was important enough to convince me to take my eyes off...

Sloane. Sloane Gabrielli. A fellow student at Cal Berkeley. She'd worked in the library. Majored in business. Wanted to go to culinary school.

Sloane stared at me as if she were witnessing the end of days. Guess she hadn't expected to see me either. I'd always thought I might run into her sometime, but here in my office at The Gate Club? I walked around the desk and extended my hand. "How are you on this fine morning, Ms. Gabrielli? Please sit, won't you? Would you like coffee? It's fresh." I smiled but she still looked shell-shocked. "It's great to see you again, Sloane."

She hesitated, glancing back at the door for a moment then straightening her shoulders and meeting my gaze. "I'd like the lease on Bel Cielo renewed. Today. Five years. Same rent."

"Ah. I see this is a business call. Would you mind waiting a moment? My uncle was just leaving." I helped her off with her coat, remaining in place until she was seated in the ridiculously large chair. She looked like a child in the arms of a giant, her feet only touching the floor because of those sexy heels. I hung the jacket on the hook next to mine and walked Uncle Andrew to the elevator.

He laughed softly. "I see the Hanley charm is in good health."

"Very funny. Give me fifteen minutes and I'll have her eating out of my hand."

"Or on her knees." He chuckled.

"Despite Frank's best efforts, I've never learned to treat women like chattel."

"Please. Your bedpost is scarred beyond recognition."

"I treat the women I see with respect, which is more than

my father can say." My jaw tightened hard enough to crack. Uncle Andrew loved to pull my chain. I shouldn't let him get to me. "My private life is none of your goddamn business."

"You can pretend to be a gentleman all you want, but there's more of your father in you than you'll ever admit."

A sick feeling churned in my gut. "You're wrong." We reached the elevator. "If you speak to Mother, tell her I'll be calling this afternoon."

"You won't talk her out of visiting Frank."

"We'll see."

The elevator doors closed on his smirk at the same time his theme song faded out. I quickly stepped back to the room where Sloane waited. The security guard was still watching her. "You can go back to your post. Thank you."

"Yes, sir." He nodded and left.

From the side, all I could see of Sloane were her crossed bare legs and bright blue shoes. The kind you wanted your woman to leave on as you stripped her of every other item of clothing. Her top foot was wiggling impatiently.

"Mr. Hanley?"

"Mmm?" God, those shoes. Maybe she's like me to help her slip them off.

"We have my restaurant to discuss."

She slid forward in the chair so more of her attributes were visible. Her dress rode up, giving me a better view of her thigh. "Of course." I swallowed hard and moved fully into the room.

"Your security guard was watching me like a hawk. Did he think I was going to run off with your laptop?"

"This is a private club. You're armed and angry. My customers come here to relax."

"Angry, yes, but armed?"

I indicated the shoes with a straight face. "Sharp."

Sloane smiled full-out and my cock stirred in response. She'd had this same effect on me during my undergrad days at Cal. As a music major, I'd had no interest in most of the academic subjects I was forced to take to graduate. My only option was to head to the library where I'd be forced to study and stay away from the studio or practice rooms. Dropping out wasn't an option, so I'd gritted my teeth and done the work.

The first time I saw Sloane she'd been helping some jock find a book he was supposed to have read before the semester started. He'd asked for the Cliff Notes. The library didn't carry them and someone else had checked out the book. When he couldn't get what he wanted, he decided he wanted Sloane instead, getting a little physical with his requests. I was about to take care of the asshole when she whispered something in his ear. He frowned and stormed out.

During the next few days I couldn't stop thinking about her, so I looked for help where I usually did. Blake, who knew everyone everywhere, was able to get her work schedule from another library employee. It cost me a ski weekend in Tahoe, setting Blake and his girlfriend up in the most expensive resort, but it was worth every grand I spent.

I arrived at the library at the beginning of her shifts, making sure to settle at a desk in the sections she worked the most often.

I took a moment to look at the updated version of Sloane. God, she was even more beautiful. Her wavy golden hair and expressive brown eyes gave her the look of a temptress out of one of those Grecian myths. In the library her actions were quick and efficient, self-assured and always thought out. But when I'd seen her walking on campus, she'd greeted friends with warmth, strangers with kindness, sharing her incredibly sexy smile with each of them.

I'd wanted that smile directed at me. I'd needed that kindness and warmth.

After some urging on my part, we'd become good friends, but I hadn't pushed her to go farther than that. Sloane was meant for a man who was worthy of her, and that man wasn't me.

Her turned-down mouth and narrowed gaze couldn't hide her beauty. The young Sloane had turned into a gorgeous woman, the fire in her eyes waking places in my body that shouldn't get involved during a business meeting.

I shifted the position of the matching chair so I could face her before I sat. A little put off by my sudden closeness, she uncrossed her legs and tucked her feet under the chair, knees together, ankles crossed.

"Tell me what I can do for you."

"Renew my lease."

"Can you explain the situation? I've just been put in charge."

"Your company is kicking me out of my restaurant. My family has run this restaurant for forty years. How can you treat your tenants like this?"

"Gate of the Bay is owned by Frank Hanley. He made the decision to evict you."

She stood. "Then you're not the person I should be talking to."

"I think I am. Why don't you sit?" She stayed where she was. "Please. I may be able to help."

"Fine." She lowered her body back into the ugly chair. If anyone could make that monstrosity look good, it was Sloane.

"You're the owner of Bel Cielo?"

"And the executive chef. What exactly is your position with the company?"

"I've been appointed trustee. Give me a minute." I stood to retrieve my laptop and the folder on Gate of the Bay Realty that Andrew had slid across my desk. It contained general information on upcoming projects, along with relevant financial information and passwords. I signed in and looked at the calendar. "Are you located near the Graham Gallery?" Cassie had named it after her dead brother. He'd been her best friend and business partner.

"Next door."

I nodded. Frank was a businessman first, last and always. When Damien had decided to renovate the empty space next to Cassie's art studio and turn it into a swanky art gallery, Frank's minions had taken a closer look at the rest of the block. "According to this report, that entire strip of stores is going to be renovated to match the gallery. Possibly torn down and rebuilt if the inspector advises we take that action. I'll make sure you're offered a new lease when the work is done."

"In six months."

"That's an optimistic estimate, but I give you my word you'll have the first option to lease the new restaurant."

"Your word." She didn't seem mollified. Sloane was looking at me as if my word meant shit.

Time to change the subject to something she might enjoy talking about, a ploy that usually worked with pissed off women. I smiled. "Do you cook French food?"

"My specialty is Northern Italian cuisine."

She'd spoken as if I were a child. I suppose her last name should have clued me in, but she didn't exactly look a hundred percent Italian, with that gorgeous blonde hair. And I would have bet the royalties from my next song that her particular shade of blonde was not from a box and maybe could be found...

I needed to get a grip.

"My family has cooked Northern Italian cuisine in the US for over fifty years."

"Isn't Northern Italian similar to French? I've never been a huge pasta fan. It sits in my belly like a rock."

"Have you ever eaten fresh homemade pasta?"

"Pasta's pasta."

"Not at all." She bit her lip. I might have believed she was flirting because it was such a sexy thing to do, except her eyes held a dangerous glimmer. She could be planning to poison my coffee. I clutched the mug to my chest, then realized it was empty. "Are you certain you wouldn't like coffee? I made it myself." Sort of. I washed the carafe and filled it to the line. I was pretty sure I'd ace it the next time.

"If my restaurant is closed for six months I'll lose my customer base."

"Not if your food is as good as people say. Damien and Cassie rave about it."

"Have you eaten at Bel Cielo?"

She'd pronounced the second word like cello, the stringed instrument. "No. Bel Cielo?" My version came out pretty close to hers. "What does it mean?"

"Google translate works wonders."

"Ah. I'll get right on that."

"Closing a restaurant in this competitive climate is a death sentence. If I'm lucky, maybe half my customers will come back when I reopen. That's not enough to sustain my business. I'll also have the added expenses from packing up my equipment and storing it somewhere, then moving it back and setting up all over again. The kitchen appliances are mine, so we're talking about ovens, stovetops, freezers, not to mention dinnerware, glassware, cutlery and linens."

"Gate of the Bay might consider absorbing some of those costs." At least I would consider absorbing them.

"How kind of you."

I leaned forward, pretending to ignore her sarcasm. "We had some laughs back at Cal. You remember that couple you caught behind the military history section?"

"Yes. I remember everything." She'd drawn out that last word.

"Are you pissed off about something other than the eviction?"

"I don't want to be the one to dredge up sludge from the past."

"Our friendship was sludge? That's pretty harsh. I remember talks over coffee. Take-out picnics on the quad. You even listened to me play some of my first real compositions. You seemed to like hanging with me. I sure liked—"

"I do not want to discuss our brief college acquaintance." Sloane stood and walked quickly toward the window, her face flushed. She snagged her heel on the edge of a rug and her ankle turned in a funny way, making her wobble for a moment before recovering. She turned without missing a beat, her expression more determined than ever. "When will I know the company's decision?"

Not a gazelle, but a lioness. My body came alive as she rested one hand on her hip, the other fisted at her side, the perfect stance for a local warrior about to do battle against corporate America. Sloane wouldn't take crap from anyone and never had, especially me. And here she was again— same strength, same spirit.

Give me her brand of fangs and claws any day.

Her sexy outfit enhanced curves improved with time and

those too spiky heels made her legs look delicious. I'd always imagined nibbling up the inside of her thigh, where her skin would be silk, her intimate scent a call to action for a guy who loved to take his time pleasuring his lovers.

My gaze was glued to her determined expression as she stood with her back to the large window, the towers of the Golden Gate Bridge looming behind her. Where was a photographer when you needed one?

"If you do this, I'll lose everything I've worked for."

Aaand... I was a world class ass. She was scared she might lose her business and all I wanted was to look at her and think dirty, wonderful thoughts. We needed to get out of this office and talk her situation over in a less stressful atmosphere. "Could we discuss this over dinner? Maybe check out the competition." I winked.

Her expression told me I'd said exactly the wrong thing. "I'll be *cooking* dinner tonight, Mr. Hanley. At *my* restaurant, Bel Cielo. The restaurant you want to close in sixty days."

"Fifty-nine."

"I beg your pardon."

"The letter was delivered yesterday." She opened her mouth to respond, but I interrupted her. "The close is temporary. I'll even pay for you to move everything back in when it's finished." I thought that was a generous offer. I mean, I hadn't made the decision to tear down the building.

"Are you also helping the resale clothing store or Krieger's deli?"

"You're being ridiculous." Shit. I sounded like Uncle Andrew.

"Well, are you?"

"I'm helping you, an old friend. We have a history."

She sauntered closer, not sitting but resting her hand on

the top of the chair. Her eyes shining with passion. In this case, anger.

"We do not have a history." The words were spoken in a low tone, each word emphasized. Her staff must shiver when she used that tone. My reaction was even more visceral.

Didn't she remember what happened at the party? After the party?

I stood, keeping a smile plastered on my face, despite the irritation I felt over her obvious blackout. Even though I towered over her, she stared up at me with a fierceness I'd never seen in a woman before.

I'd always hated drama. Confrontation where women were concerned, but this woman... I had to know. "You don't remember the party?"

"My memory is as sharp as ever, but I'm not in the mood to chat about old times."

"At the frat party, you told me I was the first man you'd ever kissed." I stepped closer, yearning to reopen the connection we'd shared. No one had made me laugh harder than Sloane during those days of constant arguments with my father. With all that was happening in my life recently, a dose of Sloane might bring me some relief. And it wasn't like I had a choice. Her feisty passion, her outspoken honesty, her determination to do the right thing sang a perfect song.

She scowled but didn't step away. "We were both drunk. Your memory is skewed."

"So, it wasn't true? I wasn't your first?"

"You were definitely the first boy I ever slapped."

I rubbed my cheek and smiled. "I was twenty—more man than boy."

She laughed. "Being old enough to shave and hold a job doesn't make you a man."

"What does?"

"It's a little late for you to learn that lesson, don't you think?"

"You willing to give me lessons?"

Fire flared in her angry eyes. She tilted her beautiful face toward mine in challenge. Never an ounce of fear, no matter the circumstances. Her scent filled my nostrils, sweet and spicy. "You're still the same reckless, impulsive guy."

"I remember everything about you." I touched her cheek with the tips of my fingers, smoothing them down to her chin, then lifting her head with the gentlest of motions. Sloane's skin was as soft as I'd remembered. Perfect for kissing.

Sloane's eyes widened at my touch, but she didn't move away. Against all reason, I pulled her close, tilting her head and kissing her.

I was gentle, hoping she'd respond the way she first had when I'd kissed her at that party. The attraction between us had grown with every meeting as students, so even though I'd been drunk, a kiss had seemed like the obvious progression. Now my body wanted to pick up where I'd left off all those years ago.

Her lips softened, her body relaxed into mine. I smiled against her mouth.

It lasted ten seconds.

Sloane pushed against my chest and I released her, already partially regretting my impulsive move. I sensed movement. Horrendous pain shot from my balls to my brain and back again, bending me over at the waist. A moment later, something hard banged into my nose with enough force to send me collapsing into the chair. I cupped my groin with one hand, my nose with the other. My eyes filled with tears.

"Fuuuck!" I didn't recognize my voice, strident and hoarse, as if someone were holding my throat in a tight grip.

"Oh, god. I'm sorry. My brothers gave me self-defense lessons. It was automatic. Are you okay? Can I get ice or something?" She talked so fast I could barely understand her, not that I was really listening. My world had narrowed to one excruciatingly painful cluster of nerves.

I was an idiot. "You've...done enough." My stomach churned. My throat burned as bile threatened to rise.

"You wouldn't be in pain if you hadn't kissed me. Just like at that fucking party. Have you ever asked for permission first?"

"You...slapped my face at the party. You didn't try to kill me." I coughed and leaned to the side, pulling a potted plant a little closer just in case. "Most women like...like my kisses." I coughed again and cupped my crotch. "Shit!" Everything hurt. I wanted to tear off my clothes to make sure she hadn't kneed my junk into my lower intestines. My eyes watered as blood dripped onto the carpet. "You use a... a hammer?" My balls must be black and blue. They throbbed in rhythm to my aching nose. Another sharp twinge. "Fuck!"

"Stop cursing." She rummaged through her purse. "I never did it before."

"'It' meaning take away my ability to sire an heir?"

"You're not a damn duke." She handed me a wad of tissues. "Your nose is bleeding."

"Not...the area...of most...concern." But I pressed the tissues to my nostrils anyway. Security was going to flip when they saw me.

"You deserved it."

I'd been impulsive and stupid. "I... Sorry." I panted. "Not...happen again."

"There is no need for us to see each other after today."

And why the fuck did that thought irritate me so much? I mean the woman was a loose cannon. Her knee was a dangerous weapon. And what had she hit me with? My nose was sore but nothing could compare to the tsunami of hurt happening between my legs.

"Please call me when you get an answer from the person in charge."

"Ung." I couldn't even stand up to see her to the door. A feeble wave in the direction of the exit was all I could offer.

At least she was looking guilty. "I'll hear from you soon?"

"Ysss."

Steven arrived and made a move to stop her from leaving, probably thinking I wanted to call the cops. I motioned for him to guide her downstairs. "Get her a ride home. On the club."

"I can manage." She bristled.

"Please. Ferry schedule is crazy." I'd forced my back to straighten, despite the lightning strikes threatening to bring me sliding to the floor. Blood pounded in my ears, matching the throbbing and hammering going on everywhere else in my body. A percussion of pain.

A metal melody, screamer included.

Thank god the keyboard bench was padded. I had more music to work on.

A few minutes later, Steven was back. "Do you need medical attention, boss?" He took a closer look at my nose, then left, returning with ice and a damp cloth. "It's not broken." Steven, the head of security, knew when to keep his mouth shut and when to tease me unmercifully. I'd been coming to the club since I'd turned toddler and he'd treated me like a little brother from the start.

"Another part of me may be broken."

He glanced down to where I was cupping myself. His eyes widened. "You should go home."

"Maybe, when I can walk to the bike." I rode my Scrambler on weekdays when I commuted between Marin County and San Francisco. I'd tried using my car, but the traffic made me crazy. I pulled out the Tesla or the Land Rover SUV only on the weekends.

"You're not going to be riding that bike today," Steven said. "Someone will drive you home."

Kissing Sloane Gabrielli had jumped onto my Top Ten Most Dangerous Activities list. Most dangerous and most enjoyable. Her lips had been soft and yielding, actively demanding more. For a few seconds at least. I tried to laugh, but it hurt too much. I wasn't angry, because she was right, I shouldn't have kissed her. But that didn't stop me from wanting to kiss her again, no matter the consequences.

I winced as my balls throbbed with every move. But then I'd always been told I was an impulsive idiot. Might as well embrace my true nature.

I huffed and waddled toward the window. Sloane was just sliding into the ride share. God she was glorious: rounded ass, perfect breasts, and eyes that made you never want to look away. She'd walked into my office waving that notice around, glowing with anger and showing no fear. So fucking hot. Sloane was just what I needed to get my mind off Frank and the latest mind-numbing news that I'd be running two businesses, leaving me with even less time to hit the keys or compose.

I could back out. But then most of those employees

would lose their jobs. I should try at least. Try to do the right thing for them and Mom.

The pain in my groin was letting up. I poked at my face. "Am I bruising?" Steven nodded. "I'm going to ask for your discretion."

He grinned. I considered Steven a friend as well as an employee. "It was horrible the way you walked into the edge of that shelf, then tripped and fell awkwardly against the corner of the desk. You really shouldn't text and walk, sir."

I laughed, groaned and glanced at the clock. The day was just beginning and sore or not, I'd have to spend most of it reading over the paperwork Unc had handed me. Tomorrow, I'd treat myself to a good meal.

"Steven. Make a reservation for me at Bel Cielo for tomorrow afternoon. A late lunch." He turned to do just that. "And for every day this week and next."

"Two p.m. sir?" His grin was irritating.

"Two will be perfect." I couldn't wait to see her in her chef hat.

3

T he day had been a good one for a Sunday. A party arrived a little late for a celebratory luncheon, but we managed to get them seated and eating without too much disruption in our schedule. I hated that we didn't have space for a large waiting area. All we could do was put out a few chairs by the wall and outside on the sidewalk. The awning offered shade and respite from the rain, but hungry people weren't always patient. And to be honest, I loved that we were packed with people willing to wait to taste what my staff and I had cooked today.

Grandma Geneva would have loved it.

"Excuse me, Chef. There's a man here who says he wants to compliment the chef. He knows your name. Says you're old friends." Gio was like a younger version of my twin brothers. Protective and certain he knew what was best for me despite the fact I was five years older.

"Is he blonde and built like a center for the 49ers?" asked Poppy, one of my sous chefs.

"No. He's dark-haired with light blue eyes. Think Steph Curry. Just as hot, but not as tall." Gio was pretty hot himself, and Steph Curry would have been just his type if Steph wasn't straight. Gio always seemed to be in the middle of a new romance. One cute guy after the other.

"Really? I'll investigate." Poppy handed her spoon to another girl and ran around the counter and through the swinging doors. She was back a few minutes later. "He is soooo nice. His name is Vic and he loved the food and he asked me my name and I told him I wasn't the exec chef or anything, but he still thanked me for my expert culinary skills." She waved her hand frantically under her chin as she panted. "And hot does not begin to describe that healthy hunk of manhood. Holy crap. Although he looks like he had a run in with some gangster. Are you really old friends?"

"Like ex-lovers or something?" asked Donna Marie, one of the servers.

"Would you like to know who Vic really is?" They nodded, eyes wide. "He's the acting landlord who is kicking us out of this building in fifty-eight days."

Their joyful expressions turned dark. "That creep. I'm never serving him again." Donna Marie was one of the few who had parents in town and would always have a home to crash in if things got bad, but Poppy was in the same boat as Gio and Lori. They'd moved far away from their homes and barely made the rent on their shared apartment.

"You will serve Victor Hanley as we would any other patron. He's connected to a lot of wealthy families and the last thing we need is bad word of mouth," I said firmly, taking off my chef jacket and hat. "I'll handle him personally."

"Yes, Chef." Donna Marie's eyes widened. "He's the guy who ratted out his own dad, right? The murderer and kidnapper?"

"Don't forget the art thief part. His dad is a real piece of work," Poppy said.

"I hope his hot son doesn't go down that road." Donna Marie sighed looking dreamy eyed.

"I still want to poison him," Poppy said.

"Quiet," Gio spoke up. "We do as Chef Sloane says. We don't have to like it, but we do it." Gio gave me a look that pretty much told me I was an idiot for even talking to Victor. "He's moved to the end of the bar to free up a table. He didn't complain about it so I didn't kick him out."

"Thank you for your generosity, Gio. You can return to your station. Please see to your other diners, Donna Marie. The rest of you, back to work."

"Yes, Chef," came the group reply. Donna Marie disappeared through the door and it only took one serious glance before the rest were busily tidying up or prepping for dinner, all thoughts of this particular *healthy hunk of manhood* hopefully replaced by creamy sauces, spiced soups, and speck risotto, one of tonight's specialties.

"I'll see what he wants."

As much as Victor infuriated me, I had to agree with Donna Marie's assessment. Victor Hanley had the bad boy looks that stirred my libido in dangerous ways. When we'd kissed in his office, I hadn't instantly pushed him away, a mistake I'd probably be paying for in one way or another. My body had been all "Oh yeah. The drought is over." My more responsible mind and my years of defensive training had kicked in big time. I'd been attacked in college, and that training had kept me sane and secure for many years.

But I'd overreacted. Even though the kiss was unexpected, I hadn't felt unsafe. Never with Victor. He and I had laughed over gallons of coffee and months of chats at Cal, sharing our dreams and worries, our friendship growing quickly from fragile to firm. Our ending had been a shock, but it was ten years ago. Too long to hold onto disappointment.

He wasn't the only one who needed to apologize over what had happened yesterday.

Victor sat on a stool at the end of the bar with his laptop open. I'd seen him sitting just like that in the Cal library many times, only he hadn't known how often I'd been watching him. Just like now.

Tall and dark haired, his body was lean muscled and limber. He was slender in college, sometimes forgetting to eat, but he'd filled out in all the best ways since then. "Mr. Hanley." I leaned against the bar, an empty stool between us.

"Sloane. Or should I say, Chef Sloane?"

His smile lit up his face and my belly flipped, warmth cozying up to my heart. A hundred people called me chef, but hearing Victor speak it in his rich baritone was pure pleasure. As Mom would say, I was in a stew around Victor Hanley—a mishmash of feelings seasoned more sharply with time.

"In the restaurant, chef is fine."

I shouldn't have smiled. I should have encouraged him to leave. I should have refused to see him. Victor was running the company about to ruin my life, yet my body was trying to get me to ignore the facts, jut out a hip and smooth down my hair. When had I lost control of my libido?

"Where's the outfit?"

"I don't often wear it in the dining room."

"You're ruining a lot of guys' fantasies."

I had to laugh. Couldn't hold it in. "I'm shocked to see you here."

"Why shocked?"

"Our last encounter wasn't exactly civilized. I didn't mean to hurt you and I'm sorry I did."

"I'm just happy you weren't packing a cleaver. Should I pat you down to see if you're carrying or am I safe?"

"I'm serious." Although the corners of my mouth were twitching despite my express orders to behave.

"I'm sorry too. And that um...move was pretty impressive. Are your brothers in the military?"

"The twins were in the Marines."

"Ah. Well, you can rest easy. I'd like to have kids one day, so surprise kisses are off the menu."

I flashed on Victor picking up a child, a boy, swinging him onto his shoulders, tickling the little guy until they collapsed on the floor, wiping their happy tears with tee shirts and shirtsleeves. One day, Victor would teach his son to play the guitar. His daughter too.

I glanced away. "My brothers will tease me for months if they find out what I did to you."

"You're going to tell them."

"I won't mention who I...you know."

"Unmanned."

I laughed at his word choice. "Did you grow up in Victorian times?"

"You can take the kid out of the fancy boarding school but..." He trailed off, his eyes losing their shine.

I'd forgotten. The bullies in that school had beaten him down until he'd made friends with Damien and Blake. The dynamic trio. They'd fought them off as a team, eventually gaining enough supporters so they were left alone. "They taught you Latin and Greek, I suppose?"

That quick smile was back, his blue eyes glittering with mischief. "Only the very dirtiest words. Perfect song lyrics."

"For rich old men who speak those languages."

"I was thinking the English translations."

"Oh." A shiver tickled my spine. "You write dirty songs?"

"For fun. When I'm bored."

"Do you perform them?"

"Only in the bedroom."

I squeezed my thighs together and shifted position. Ten years. Ten years and he was still making me feel like a horny teen. With only a sexy glance and a few words, he'd turned my focus from saving my restaurant to all the dirty things he might do if we were alone together.

I pulled up some anger, my first line of defense. "Why are you here? We're prepping for dinner."

"I'm sure they can live without you for thirty minutes or so. Climb up. I kept this stool open."

He spread his long fingers on the seat, brushing the wood the way he might stroke a woman's thighs. He looked innocent enough, but Victor had a charm, a charisma that beckoned to females everywhere. Before his father's recent arrest, Victor had been the typical playboy, dating a different woman every season. Not that I'd kept track. He'd hung out with some of the bands he wrote songs for, sometimes getting into fights. A man not opposed to taking risks and celebrating when he survived.

But after the arrest, a lot had been written about how he'd turned in his father, an ultimate betrayal according to some. Others thought he may have been involved in the crime but had escaped prosecution, probably by paying someone off.

And here he was sitting on a bar stool, still making my heart beat faster. This had to stop. Right now. Gio and Poppy and my other employees needed my help. In this moment Victor wasn't a hot guy with a delicious mouth. He was the face of Gate of the Bay Realty, dangerous to my business, my community and my livelihood.

Victor pulled up a program on his laptop. "I thought we could chat about the renovations. How would you like the new restaurant to look?"

I shook my head in disbelief as my body cooled to its normal temperature. "So as a tradeoff for throwing my employees onto the unemployment lines and me out of my restaurant, you're going to allow me to pick a color palate and suggest a pleasing interior design for the new restaurant owners?"

He twisted his mouth into a lopsided frown. "I made it clear the restaurant is yours when it's done, as is the upstairs apartment, if you want it."

"And the rent?"

"What?"

"You know, that fee I pay on the first of every month without fail."

Victor rubbed the back of his neck, sending an unexpected jolt of sadness to my chest. He used to massage his nape when he was studying for a test in a subject he hated. Once or twice I'd massaged his neck for him, easing some of his stress. He'd thanked me, taken me for coffee, invited me for lunch on the quad, but that was it. He'd never come onto me. Never asked me out. Never even flirted.

Until the frat party.

"The rent will be commensurate with—"

"I heard that spiel already."

"What you pay now is way below the market rate. This is an emerging neighborhood."

"Emerging." I'd added as much disgust as I could to my tone. "You sound like you memorized some YouTube video on how to convince people it's great to be evicted. The term is gentrification. People who've lived here their whole lives are forced out simply so wealthy couples and singles can say they live in a cool *emerging* neighborhood and building owners can cash in on their vanity. The Mission District is not a toy you rich kids can play with."

"There's anger on both sides. Most of the people who choose to move here do so because the Mission is a vibrant mixed community. They'd fit in fine if they were given a chance."

I shrugged. "I don't dispute that, but it doesn't change the fact firms like yours are pricing us out. My Italian grandmother and grandfather rented the apartment upstairs for forty-five years, the restaurant for almost forty. I'm proud to be carrying on their legacy, although you'd know nothing about that."

Victor's expression hardened and I winced. My tone had been sharp and my words hurtful. He was going through his own trauma right now.

"Look, I didn't..."

He shook his head and held up his hand. "Let's stay on topic." A coldness had crept in, erecting a wall where a minute ago there was none. "According to the file, Damien Granger approached Andrew about this topic first. He was concerned by the number of homeless on the nearby street."

Oh sure, let's throw someone else under the bus. "Cassie wouldn't want us evicted." She and I often grabbed sandwiches at the deli and shopped at the thrift shop. I'd catered their wedding. She'd invited me, but I hadn't been able to come.

"I said Damien, not Cassie."

"They'd discuss it together."

"How well do you know Damien?"

"Not well."

"Damien is not the discuss-it-together type."

"According to Cassie, he'd give her the moon."

Victor smiled. "He can almost afford it." He closed the laptop, sighed and brushed a clump of dark hair behind his ear. "I'll keep trying to find a way—"

"I'd like to make something clear. Even though I grew up in Marin, I think of the Mission as my neighborhood. I've worked here for over eight years and visited my grandparents at the restaurant for almost thirty. The other shop owners and I are not going to stand around while your father's company molds our block into something superficial and flashy. My restaurant, the resale shop and the deli are useful and important to the long-time residents as well as the neighborhood workers. We allow plate sharing during our lunch hours, we don't turn our noses up at giving people doggy bags, and we bring all our leftovers to the shelter two blocks down Twenty-Fourth Street. Nothing is wasted. Bel Cielo has value here."

Victor huffed out a short burst of air. "I hear what you're saying. Your restaurant is more than a business." He looked over the menu again. "Your prices are reasonable for the size of the portions and the exceptional quality of the food."

I arched a brow, not expecting the sincere compliment. "Thank you."

He closed the menu and shoved it aside. "But how are your profits?"

I hesitated. "I'm paying my bills and business is picking up."

He looked around the room. "Some of the new residents you were just putting down have already become your customers. These people know good food. They'll bring in high paying customers. With a larger, more modern space, you could be doing a lot more than just paying your bills."

"You're talking about the future, but I have to concentrate on the present. How would you feel if you had to shut down In the Zone for six months? Or sell it? What would happen to the musicians you hire or the engineers?"

"You know about my studio?"

"I do my research."

"I'd bring the musicians to The Gate. I have a studio there."

I frowned, losing patience. "I don't have a second restaurant I can offer up as an alternative." I turned to walk away. The arrogant lord of the manor couldn't see past his black Amex card.

"Please wait." He rubbed his nape. "I get it, I do. This is your passion like music is mine."

"Yes, but Bel Cielo and the people who work here are my responsibility."

"Whether I like it or not, Gate of the Bay Realty has become mine. If I refuse to do my job, Frank will sell the company. Forty-seven employees will lose their jobs."

I huffed out a breath. How many times had I heard him on the phone with his dad, arguing about changing his music major to business? Victor had called Frank the dream crusher, a man focused only on making money and wielding power. I doubted Victor ever had the kind of affection and approval a boy needs from a father. My parents had loved my sister, brothers and me from the moment we'd voiced our opinions about being forced into the world. Even during my most bratty moments I'd always felt loved.

But Victor was thirty. Time to grow up. "Sounds like he's manipulating you just like he always has. When are you going to live your life on your own terms?"

"You don't know anything about my life." Victor raked a

hand through his thick dark hair, his brows pulled closer in anger.

"You're right. We don't know each other. College was a long time ago."

"I'll do whatever I can to help the other businesses find new locations."

"The Kriegers are elderly and can't travel far from their apartment. The sisters can't afford—"

"I can't work miracles."

I turned away, examining the familiar polished wooden floors, the wooden tables with their small vases of fresh flowers and cream-colored tablecloths, the mocha shaded walls where pictures of former customers and their families hung alongside folksy traditional items crafted in Italy. One of Cassie's paintings held pride of place near the bar, a landscape of Italy she'd painted from photographs I'd given her when she'd first moved into the studio. The fireplace in the back kept the restaurant warm on rainy winter nights and made the customers feel at home. Tables in that section were reserved a month in advance.

"You know what I think would be a wonderful motif for the new restaurant?" Victor wisely remained silent. "A mural of all the families who will have to move away because of your renovation. I could bring them in for a sitting with Cassie. Oh, and don't forget to include a portrait of yourself, the conquering hero."

I turned back toward the kitchen, but Victor caught hold of my arm. I spun around and spoke through gritted teeth. "Let go of me, Mr. Hanley."

"Tell me about what's happening in the area. Maybe—"

"Ever read a newspaper?" I left him there with a shocked expression and stalked back to the kitchen, my weaker side urging me to turn around and go back. My arm had warmed where he'd touched me, along with a few other spots I had no business thinking about at work.

I would not let this man under my skin or into my heart. It had happened once. Never again.

I washed my hands and plunged into dinner prep, pouring all my frustrations into preparing the delicate sauces that would be accompanying the smoked trout and the saltimbocca specials while my staff worked on prep for the regular menu.

Gio came in. "He paid and left."

"Good. Thank you."

"He has a Scrambler." Gio sounded a lot less antagonistic. I might have even noticed a note of awe.

"A what?"

"A BMW Scrambler. An awesome bike."

"Figures." I'd wondered why he was wearing leather pants, but I'd heard rumors he played in a band and so he could have been performing later. He'd looked damn good in those pants.

"Did you see the tattoo on his neck? I wonder where else he has tattoos."

"Were you checking him out?"

"I'm human and gay, so yes." Gio grinned. "He's got the hots for you, Chef."

"You're impossible."

"He's back Tuesday."

"What?"

"He has a reservation every day at the same time."

"After our conversation I'm certain he'll cancel them. I've seen the last of Victor Hanley."

"Why don't you let me cancel them?" He watched for my reaction.

I hesitated. "I... I don't think that would be a good idea."

I wanted him to come back. I was losing my freaking mind. Gio wiggled his eyebrows. For some reason it looked adorable and not creepy when he did it. "Get back to work and try not to flirt with the customers."

"Those techies in the corner—definite threesome."

"Shut up!" But by this time the entire kitchen staff was laughing. Gio had a way of making people laugh. He also had a way of making us want to tear our hair out. Depended on the day.

When I finally had a break, I took the stairs to my office and finished my shopping list for the week, always giving myself several options. I based my specials on what I found to be the freshest ingredients when I shopped at the fish market and butcher. I usually took Poppy with me. She had a quick and creative mind and her skills in the kitchen were excellent, perhaps leaning more toward avant-garde cuisine than I was comfortable with. But I allowed her a few original dishes every week, just to see how the customers enjoyed them. Sometimes it took her five or six tries in the kitchen to get it right, but that was the norm for an upcoming chef.

Before long Chef Poppy would have her own restaurant and staff. I was as proud of her as I was of my own siblings' accomplishments. I'd made Bel Cielo a safe place for my head sous chef to try out new ideas, for my young employees to feel secure in a steady income, and my regular customers to have a great meal at a reasonable price. I wasn't the only one who thought of Bel Cielo as a refuge.

Thoughts of telling my staff the bad news brought me back to reality. I'd have to tell my family about losing my lease, but not just yet. I sighed, my body slumping in my desk chair. My grandparents would tell me it wasn't my fault. My parents too. But I couldn't help feeling responsible, as if I should have done something more. Should have fought harder. Should have hired a top lawyer to make sure my lease offered more protection.

After taking the first sip of my half glass of Sangria, a ritual before the dinner rush started, I slipped my tongue along my bottom lip. The fruity tartness of the mixture brought back the drunk kiss Victor and I had shared at that horrible party, our mouths and breaths tainted by whatever wine had been handy at the time. I'd wanted to kiss Victor and that wide mouth two weeks after I'd met him at the library. I'd wanted more, but he'd only allowed friendship. Kept his distance.

The drunk kiss hadn't been anything like what I'd dreamed about, not because he wasn't a good kisser. He was. But because he'd kissed me as a last-second decision. I was there and he wanted to kiss someone. Why not Sloane?

And the worst part—after the initial shock, I'd kissed him back. Just like in his office.

The sight of Victor sitting behind his desk in his fancy office at The Gate Club had been a mind fuck of the highest level. Why it hadn't occurred to me that he'd be the one I'd have to deal with, I didn't know. His dad was in prison. He had no siblings. I'd known this, only I'd envisioned dealing with his uncle or maybe some unknown board member.

And then that kiss.

He'd moved me into position like some kind of Viking chieftain, owning me, pressing his lips against mine, claiming more than my mouth. My body had warmed, glorying in the taste and the scent and the feel of Victor. For just a moment I'd wanted to move closer, to press my aching breasts against his hard chest, to open my mouth and explore. His lips had been firm, his mouth demanding.

Shock had moved me to action. My violent response was

born of anger with myself as much as with Victor. But he shouldn't have kissed me. Not like that. It had been too much like the kiss at the party.

Impulsive. Unexpected. I'd had no way to prepare myself for his rash action.

I'd wanted him to dream about me the way I'd dreamed about him. To plan each move to win me over. A kiss without forethought was easily shaken off. No biggie. But the kiss at the party had haunted my dreams for years. Now those dreams were back full force all because he'd kissed me unexpectedly. Again.

I downed my drink, trying to shake off the vision of his full lower lip, his cool blue eyes, his broad shoulders and panty-melting smile. He'd tasted of mocha coffee, his mouth a sweet warm lure, urging me to open. His hands stroking my arms had burned yearning into my skin, sending liquid fire to my core.

What the hell was wrong with me? How could I want a man whose life view was so different than my own? I'd never been attracted to bad boys, and Victor definitely had that streak. Rumors around school had spread that some of his money came from stolen art, but he'd never been arrested or charged with anything. He'd dated girls who gave attractive, wealthy guys what they wanted, then parted ways without the emotions of a couple who really cared. As far as I knew, he'd never been in a serious relationship at Cal or anywhere else.

My blood boiled with his talk about renovating the neighborhood to make it better. Everything was perfect the way it was, the way it had always been. My life was orderly and safe. I knew who I was, what I wanted and what I had to do to get it.

This wasn't over. I'd dig in my heels and fight to keep my

family's restaurant open. I'd done it before—when my parents took over after my grandparents died and decided a few years later we should close it when business fell off. But I'd known I could make it work, and despite their advice, I had taken over the lease. When they'd seen my determination to make a go of Bel Cielo, my family had become my biggest support team, applauding every success. I'd had to fight hard at first, spending every penny I made to keep it going, even working odd catering jobs to pay salaries.

Victor Hanley was about to find out I wasn't someone to mess with. If only my boiling blood wouldn't start to simmer when he was near me.

I laid the pen on my half-written list and buried my face in my hands. I should be thinking about running my restaurant and not the man who'd haunted my fantasies since I was a seventeen-year-old college freshman. The man who was currently doing his best to wreck my life was the same guy who'd saved it ten years ago.

I'd left the party alone, too drunk to hear the footsteps getting closer and closer. The two frat boys had been just as drunk, knocking me around when I told them no. Pushing me to the ground, straddling and slapping me when I tried to rise. I'd curled into a ball, but one of them forced me onto my back, pinning me to the ground, his knees between mine while his buddy held my hands over my head. Number one punched me in the ribs a few times for good measure. I sobbed and begged as my blouse was ripped open, my short skirt pushed up. Rough hands grabbed my breasts, then disappeared along with the rest of him.

I'd curled up again, part of me wanting to die, another urging me to crawl away, to pull myself to safety.

"I'm here. I'll take care of you. You're going to be fine, I promise. Just hold onto me."

Victor's gently whispered words had kept me conscious, kept me hopeful despite the pain. I found out later he'd brandished a knife to get them off me, then punched the first boy in the nose, breaking his pinkie with the effort. Victor carried me half a mile to the clinic, unsteady and stumbling a little while I'd bled all over his shirt and moaned in his ear.

"Don't leave me."

"Shh. I promise. I'll stay."

But he hadn't. He hadn't even stayed at Cal.

I shook off the useless memories and forced myself to go back to work, determined to keep Bel Cielo running on schedule with the same high-quality food right up to the last day. If I had to go down, I'd go down with claws out and chin held high. But first I'd do everything I could think of to make Gate of the Bay keep their hands off my restaurant, my block and my neighborhood. Gabriellis didn't back down. Our ancestors had survived since ancient Greece and we were not about to take shit from a Hanley, that was for sure.

Later, as I waited for the BART train, I punched in Caty's number, my youngest sister. She wasn't answering my calls, which was always a source of anxiety. The family took turns driving her to the doctor and looking after her son, Chad, when he wasn't with his lowlife father. When no one picked up, I called Mom.

"Any word from Caty?"

"No. Could you stop by her apartment?" Mom couldn't hide the tension in her voice.

"Sure."

"Thanks, honey. I'm sorry so much falls on your shoulders."

"Mom. It's family. It's not too much."

"How are things at Bel Cielo?"

"Great. Everyone loved my saltimbocca."

"Yours is much better than your father's, but don't tell him I said that."

"I heard you!" boomed a familiar voice.

"Oh dear." Mom and Dad laughed as a rustling sound ensued.

"How's my *bel fiore*?" Dad's warm, deep voice filled the empty place in my heart reserved for family times. I should visit Monday. I could use a hug from Mom and a quiet talk with my father.

"Great, Dad." He'd called me his beautiful flower since the day I'd gone with him to the San Francisco Conservatory of Flowers. I was seven and he'd taken only me—a Father/Daughter outing. I kept asking him which flower he thought was the most beautiful.

We'd been surrounded by the most spectacular blooms. *"You're much more beautiful than any of these sad seedlings."*

For a second I thought I might cry. All these years and Mom and Dad were still as much in love as ever, happy with their lives and their family. Proud of what I'd accomplished. How could I tell them I was going to lose the restaurant?

Now definitely wasn't the time.

Instead of taking BART, I called a ride share and twenty minutes later I was in front of Caty's apartment building. I knocked using the code and Caty appeared at the door, looking as if she'd been sleeping.

"You okay?"

"Ya gotta stop coming by just 'cause I don't answer the phone."

"Answer the phone and we'll leave you alone. Better yet, give us a call once in a while."

"Okay, *Mom*."

"Ha ha. Look, I know I can be an overprotective ass, but I love you. So deal."

"I'm doing fine. Come inside. You can heat up dinner. Chinese."

"You ordering fast food Chinese again?" I accepted her offer and stepped inside. The studio apartment appeared neat and organized, not like when she was too sick to take care of anything, especially herself. Some of my tension drained away.

"I like Chinese food and it stays down."

Couldn't argue with that. "How's my nephew?"

"Ugh."

"That good?"

"He's a devil disguised in a thirteen-year-old body."

"The twins weren't angels either."

"Couldn't he have taken after Tony Jr.? Or Dad?"

"I hate to burst your bubble, but Dad was a hellion too. Grandma used to tell me all about the crazy shit he did. That's why he doesn't flip when one of us goes a little wild."

"You never go wild."

"That's not true."

"You get angry, but you never go wild. You never let loose."

"I have responsibilities."

"Hmm. And how's your dating life going?"

"I'm not dating at the moment."

"Or the two billion moments before this one."

"That was cold."

"C'mon, there's gotta be someone. When was the last time a guy kissed you?" I hesitated. "I knew it. There is a guy. Tell me who."

"I don't think I should."

"Why?"

"Because you might flip."

"Spill."

"Victor Hanley."

"What? *The* Victor Hanley? The jerk from college who never contacted you again? The guy who turned in his murderer father?" I nodded. She tilted her head in thought. "The... The billionaire who writes Grammy-winning songs and looks like someone any sane woman would want to rub her naked body all over? That Victor Hanley?"

"Very funny."

"That bad boy simmers with sexual tension. If there were any man on the planet to get your wild on with, Victor Hanley would be the guy."

"I'll go heat up the Chinese food." I started to stand.

Caty grabbed my wrist, but she didn't have the strength to pull me back. Her arms had gotten so thin. I sat. "C'mon," she said. Caty had always liked to gossip. "I'm living vicariously through you."

I told her everything, from how it felt to be kissed by the man I'd thought I loved so long ago, how I'd kissed him back, then attacked him. She laughed at that part. I explained how Victor was involved with the disaster happening at Bel Cielo and how I wasn't sure if he was being sincere when he said he was trying to help.

"You still want him."

Caty held a precious place in my heart, if only I could give her a piece of mine. She'd just gotten on the transplant list, but it could be years.

I smiled at my baby sister, spilling my secret to only her. "I want him more than ever."

"Then take him and let him take you. It doesn't have to be a forever thing. Let your body feel what it's supposed to feel. Get wild, Sloane."

4

Sloane's brush-off on Sunday hadn't surprised me, but my plans to enjoy her company every day at Bel Cielo were still on. I'd been disappointed to find out she was closed on Mondays, but I spent that time working on a proposal to keep the rents reasonable and the time frame short. I added a clause that first refusal should go to all the former tenants, even the apartment dwellers. I had Blake give it a few tweaks, then sent it to Uncle Andrew so Dad could approve it when Unc visited.

I was trying to be optimistic. It wasn't easy with my family.

The only snag was the engineer's report. I wouldn't cancel the inspection. The building was old and the last inspection hadn't been thorough. If the report came back stating the building should be torn down because of structural damage, my hands would be tied. And if that were the case, Sloane should be glad to move her restaurant to a building that wouldn't collapse with the next major earthquake.

It would be tough at first for her to close the doors on a

place where she practically grew up, but Sloane and her customers and employees would be much safer in a building that followed the strict building codes the state of California had in place.

Gio was already scowling at me before I made it to the host's podium. He snatched a menu from the stack and seated me at a table near the front of the restaurant.

"I'd rather sit at the bar, if that's all right."

"It's not all right. Chef wants you here for some reason I can't fathom."

The restaurant was packed, even though it was three thirty on a Sunday, not really lunch or dinner. Families and couples filled the room—more of the neighborhood crowd. "Wouldn't you rather someone else has this table?"

"I'd rather you walk out the door and never come back, but this is where Chef wants you and this is where you'll sit if you want to eat."

"Gio!" The bartender, Lori, had placed her hand on his arm and was tugging him away.

"No worries." I sat. "Who am I to argue with the chef de cuisine?" Gio shook off Lori's arm, grunted and tramped toward the kitchen, probably to report my arrival. Donna Marie took my order of caponata bruschetta and pistachio crusted salmon with mixed roasted vegetables accompanied by a glass of their special sangria—Sloane's favorite.

I'd just gotten through the delicious caponata when the door to the restaurant opened and a TV crew walked in. The blonde woman in front of the group was someone I recognized from the local news channel. Glancing toward the kitchen, I noticed Sloane standing there wearing an impish smirk. She figured she had me by the short hairs, but after the shit that went down with my father, I was a shark when it came to fielding reporters. I smiled back, wiped my mouth as I sent out a quick text and stood to greet the reporter who seemed to have every intention of interviewing me.

"Mr. Victor Hanley?"

"Yes. And you are?"

"April Smithson. Channel 9 News."

"It's a pleasure to meet you." I smiled, adding a little of what Mom called The Wilson Charm. Wilson was her family name. Hanley males were mostly lacking in charm.

April smiled back. "May I ask you a few questions regarding the destruction of this restaurant and the two vital neighborhood stores next door?"

"I'll give you all the information I have on the subject, which isn't much."

"Thank you." She checked with her crew who were already set up. I wouldn't be surprised to find out they'd come in earlier to scope out the room. The director counted down with hand motions. Five, four, three, two, one.

April's smile was suddenly brilliant. "Hello! This is Neighborhood Watch. Today I'm in the Mission District with Mr. Victor Hanley, owner of Gate of the Bay Realty, a company that's been in the news quite a bit lately because of their move toward gentrification in this neighborhood. Good Morning, Victor."

"Good morning. It's nice to have a chance to talk to you, April. But I'd like to correct your earlier comment. I'm the trustee of the company. Not the owner."

"I see. Nevertheless, our watchers have a few questions regarding your latest plans to take down Bel Cielo Restaurant, Krieger's Delights and S & S Resale Shop—all neighborhood favorites." A few of the patrons in the restaurant booed. "First of all, why is the building being destroyed?"

"The building will be thoroughly inspected sometime in

the next few weeks. If the report finds extensive damage, we will rebuild. If not, we will renovate."

"So you refuse to promise the tenants that the building will not be torn down?"

"If the engineering report comes back with proof the building is unstable, it's to the benefit of everyone in the neighborhood to take it down and build something structurally sound to replace it."

"I see. And would this new building have retail stores and apartments?"

"Yes, and also offices. The current plans are to add another two floors."

"But what about the history of this particular site? I understand the restaurant has been owned by the same family for over forty years, isn't that so, Ms. Gabrielli?"

Sloane had slinked over when I wasn't watching. "Yes, that's true. My grandparents started this restaurant from scratch four decades ago. My parents ran it before purchasing another restaurant closer to where they live."

"And now it's yours?"

"Yes. I'm also the chef de cuisine. Bel Cielo has become my home and my customers are family now. The Gabrielli clan are a part of the history of this district. Immigrants coming to make a better life. I can't believe anyone would be so heartless as to kick us out after all these years."

Oh, she was good, but I was better. I smiled directly into the camera. "I've drawn up a proposal to allow the original tenants to move back in when the work is done if they choose to do so. They'll have the right of first refusal. I was going to discuss this with Ms. Gabrielli today, but *neither* of us expected your arrival, April." I slid a sideways glance toward a guilty-looking Sloane, then met the reporter's gaze.

"That's wonderful news, Mr. Hanley, but will they be able to afford the new rents?"

"I'm hoping there's a way to make it affordable. The company has to wait to hear from the engineer before we can make any definite decisions."

"When you say the company, you're referring to the owner, Mr. Franklin Hanley, your father, correct?"

"Yes. My father is the owner of Gate of the Bay Realty." My body stiffened, dreading what would come next.

"He's currently serving time in the federal penitentiary for manslaughter, isn't that true?"

"I don't see how this is relevant to our discussion."

"He's the owner of the company that plans to disrupt a peaceful neighborhood with unneeded construction."

"I explained—"

"Your father is responsible for the murder of your best friend's father, isn't that true?"

"I agreed to answer questions regarding the renovations planned for this building and nothing else."

"But Frank Hanley—"

"Excuse me." Blake elbowed his way through the crowd at the door. "April, you've gone completely off topic and my client will not be answering any more questions." He handed the reporter his card. "C'mon, Vic." I glanced at Sloane. She stared at April, her eyes wide.

"You'd better go," she said, taking a step toward the reporter.

I allowed Blake to usher me out the door. "Thanks for showing up, Watson," I joked.

"Sure, Sherlock. What's a buddy for?"

We'd played mystery games as kids, trying to puzzle out what neighbor's dog had pooped in the yard or who'd stolen the kid next door's bike. It was a game that kept us occupied when life at home wasn't so great.

"So who was that babe?"

"Who? The reporter? She's a bitch."

"That wasn't who I meant. April isn't respected by anyone in the business. I was talking about the hot blonde standing next to you. The cook." He started to make a curvy motion with his hands. I glared at him and he stopped.

"You mean the executive chef and owner of Bel Cielo?"

"Great things come in small packages."

"There's nothing small about Sloane. She's got more spirit than a case of top grade single malt."

"But she called in the reporter."

"She's fighting back."

"She looked upset when April started nailing you about your dad."

"She was more likely gloating." Her little set up had pissed me off, especially after I'd taken the time to put together that proposal.

"Nah, you're wrong. She was not happy with April. Did you and Sloane know each other before this?"

I hesitated. Blake was sharp when it came to reading people and could be merciless when he got his lawyer's claws into something. "We have a history."

"From where?"

"Cal."

"Is she the one who ran around na—"

"No." I'd never told anyone about Sloane. "Stop grilling me. You're not getting any info."

"We'll see."

We parted ways with a pat on the shoulder and I strolled to the garage to pick up my Scrambler, then back over the bridge to the club, still hungry since I'd never gotten my salmon. After parking, I dropped the proposal in my office, took care of a call the secretary had marked as urgent, then talked to a few members about the possibility of opening up club membership to women. Two of our younger members seemed fine with adding women to the roster, as long as the male members were able to find time on the courts or the golf course. They weren't averse to mixed doubles tournaments or even occasional family days. The older member was not as enthusiastic, but he told me he'd wait and see what our decision was.

I picked up the recording I'd made last night, then walked a couple of blocks to Marin Munchies, intending to order a grilled steak sandwich, fries, and a couple of pieces of fruit to eat later at the studio. The club kitchen was still open, but I was a firm believer in supporting local businesses whenever possible. Sloane wouldn't believe a word, but the O'Connors would back me up. Plus, they stocked my favorite jelly beans in all the best flavors, and I could use a sugar rush.

Sian was behind the counter. "Vic, what's up? You look like you've been run over by one of my delivery trucks."

"I plead the fifth."

"Ah, woman troubles." He bent over the counter to whisper. "Don't I know how violent they can get." Sian had a hint of an Irish accent, adding melody to the warm tone of his voice.

"Shut up, you lazy dog. Go in the back and dig out Victor's stash. Can't let the boy go into sugar withdrawal, can we?" Katrina, the tiniest female I'd ever met, had one of the loudest voices. She rose to her toes and pecked her husband of thirty years on the cheek, then sent him off with an affectionate slap on the butt. He laughed and bowed to the love of his life, disappearing through the storage room door a moment later.

"So talk to me, sweet thing. What warrior woman bruised your face like that?"

I grinned. "One almost as beautiful as you."

"Oh. That explains it. I'm surprised she didn't bruise other areas." My expression told the tale. "Ah. She must be Irish."

"Italian, but maybe there's some Irish in there too."

"Close enough. Spirited. Passionate. Worth the trouble." She winked.

"I hope you're right, because trouble or not, I think she's the one."

"What? How long have you known the girl?"

"In total? A year and a half plus four days."

"You're keeping track. That's a good sign."

"She's mad as shit at me right now."

"That means she cares."

"Or it means she's going to murder you. One of the two." Sian was back carrying two bags of gourmet jelly beans. Coffee Mocha and Cappuccino.

"You staying off the nicotine?" Katrina asked.

"That's what the beans are for. I'm cool."

Sian made my sandwich and fries, while Katrina packed up a bag with fruit and packets of nuts, placing them on top of the beans. "Eat these first. The candy will rot your teeth."

"My teeth are iron. I see a dentist twice a year and never have a cavity."

"Good genes," Katrina said.

I winced. "I'd argue with you there."

She hesitated, then reached over to pat my hand. "How is your mother?"

"Fine." I really didn't want to talk about Mom. Some

might think my mixed feelings were irrational, but Frank had continued to abuse her and she'd continued to forgive him. I'd been the one calling the doctor when I'd found suspicious bruises, the one to hold her as she cried. It was as if she'd given up trying to find herself again. I was frustrated and angry, but at the same time, I loved her. Adored her. She'd brought me to music, given me an outlet for my deepest feelings. Mom understood what I needed better than anyone else.

She needed me now, but it was so hard to face Mom without bowing down under the weight of my guilt. I should have protected her from the monster I used to call Dad. I'd failed her, like I'd failed myself.

"She's a lovely woman, Vic. We've known her as long as we've known you," Sian said.

"She loves you very much." Katrina stroked my arm.

"I know. Thanks." They were trying to help but thinking about all that shit hurt way too much.

I paid at the register. They hadn't charged me for the fruit or the nuts. "You're too thin," Katy called out as I left the store. I waved, sucking in a deep breath of the foggy sea air, anxious to be in the studio. Everything fit in my side bags, and I hopped on the bike and tore down the road, heading for the highway that would take me to the Golden Gate Bridge.

The fog cooled the warm air, making visibility bad, but this was my hometown and I gloried in the journey. I shook off all thoughts of Frank and Gate of the Bay Realty as I rode, cutting between lanes of traffic that had slowed because of construction. I grinned when a female driver gave me a thumbs up as she admired my bike, then laughed when another driver flipped me off. Few things could turn down the volume on the joy of tonight's ride over the bridge and into my favorite city. The stress of the day shimmered off my body like the last of the sunlight on the bay.

I hummed a few bars of a new riff, taking the sharp turn after the tolls, heading to the studio I'd designed and built with money I'd earned composing. The only thing that would have made the ride better? Sloane behind me, her arms tight around my waist, her chest pressed against my back. I smiled when I saw the turnoff for my street, imagining her laughter as we pulled into the small parking lot. In my heart I knew she'd love the ride the way I did—the bite of the wind, the taste of sea air, our senses alive in a way you couldn't experience shut inside a car. She might seem guarded, even distant, but her kisses told me she had a side she hid from the world. My challenge lay before me. Step one: another kiss.

Bright and early Thursday morning, my phone blasted out the Duke Ellington piano piece I used for my two friends. Damien was out of town so... "What is it, Blake?"

"Vic. You need to hear this."

"Give me a minute." He was using his "lawyer tone" which meant the news wasn't good. I angled my chair in front of the enormous picture window so I could take in the view of the city from Marin. I loved my town and this view in particular always calmed me. Unfortunately, the San Francisco Bay was still fogged in and I couldn't even see the top of the bridge. Typical summer in the city. "What's up?"

"I got a call this morning from Sloane's lawyer."

"Uh huh." All had been quiet on that front for a couple of days, even though I saw her bustling around her restaurant when I showed for my lunch reservations. She tended to avoid me when I was there, as did everyone but my server and the friendly bartender.

"She's threatening to file two suits."

"Two?"

"One is for unfair eviction. She doesn't have a leg to stand on there, because her lease will be up and the company didn't write in an auto renew clause, but the other..."

"Tell me."

"Look out the window."

"What? All I see is fog."

"Go to the window that faces the entrance."

"Hold on." I walked to the end of the hallway and glanced outside. At least a dozen females were standing together chatting. Most wore red tee shirts with some kind of slogan and a few of them carried signs. Sloane seemed to be the ringleader. "I see them."

"She wants The Gate to admit women. She's gotten a permit to protest outside the club from nine to five today. She's contacted some of the wives and mothers of the members."

"How the hell does she know who the members are?"

"Isn't she from this area?"

Fuck. I'd forgotten. "She grew up a few miles away from Mom's house. Her parents own that great Italian restaurant we love in Sonoma."

"Abbiocco?"

"Yeah, that's the one. They work as chefs Thursdays thru Sundays."

"That food is to die for," Blake said.

Just thinking about it was making me hungry. "I think hers might be better."

"Don't tell me you went back to the restaurant after she pulled that dirty trick."

I wasn't about to tell him I hadn't missed a day. "Yeah, I went back." Silence. "I'm working my way through the menu. Great specials."

"She's hot, I admit, but isn't that stalker-ish behavior?"

"I want her to be okay with the move."

"You mean the eviction. And why do you care? Wait... Is she the girl from Cal who—"

"No!" What happened after our drunken kiss at the frat party had been my fault, and I wasn't ready to discuss it with anyone, except maybe Sloane. As my lawyer and my friend, I trusted Blake with my most sensitive information, but relationship shit was off the table. He had a past tragedy he wasn't sharing, so we were even on that score.

"I have a plan." At least I was hoping to come up with one really soon.

"Apparently, so does she."

"Does she have a leg? We have a right to keep it all male, don't we?"

"Legally, that's absolutely true, but in this political climate and in this particular part of the state of California, you might want to rethink your policy, especially if the media or gods forbid, Twitter gets involved. I see it this way. You and Damien are like-minded. You have an opportunity to make some changes. Why not talk about your vision for the future of the club?"

I groaned and leaned against the wall, staying behind the curtain so the women outside wouldn't see me if they glanced up. The sort of changes Blake was talking about took money, time and energy, but all I wanted to think about was hitting the studio again. Since Sloane had stormed into my life, my music was flowing, taking me places I hadn't explored.

More women arrived. They seemed to be discussing something serious, probably how to make my life miserable.

Blake was fighting to hold in his laughter. "I can see it now. Hashtag: The Gate. Hashtag: misogynistic blight."

"If we change our policy we'll lose members."

"And gain back just as many, if not more. I'd be willing to share the locker room, no problem."

"Get serious. Dame and I would have to build a whole new wing with facilities for women."

"C'mon, Vic. You have money to pay for twenty wings and more, not counting your inheritance from your grandfather. You're probably a fucking billionaire." I didn't reply. "Are you?"

"A lot of good it's done me."

"Boo-hoo. I feel so bad for you. Is this hissy fit all because of Ms. Gabrielli?"

"No! I'm not discussing her with you."

Blake laughed. "We should meet later."

"I'll be working. Trying out some new music."

"You're still playing at Sessions?"

"Nando, Jake and I play after hours. Sessions has the best acoustics and a friendly crowd."

"Isn't composing enough?"

"Isn't choreographing numbers enough for you? Do you still have your dance studio?"

A pause. "Touché."

"Composing keeps me sane. Playing keeps me happy. I have some new music to work through at the studio tonight before we hit the club tomorrow." I glanced at my guitar case, making a note to take it to the studio. Every guitar had a different sound, and my Les Paul had a clarity I loved.

"Enjoy it while you can. You'll be cutting back on extracurricular activities when the corporate world needs your attention."

"Fuck you."

He was laughing full-out now. "Don't worry. I've got your back. I'll meet you at the studio tonight at one. You may decide you need a drink." He ended the call.

Women were chanting right outside the window. I pulled the bag of jelly beans out of my pocket and popped a few in my mouth. I didn't crave alcohol, only cigarettes, although only in high stress situations. Like today.

One of the member's wives waved a sign around that said, "Open the Gate to Women!" Shit. I was going to have to go outside and deal with this before the members started complaining. Of course, I'd also be dealing with Sloane, a woman I'd like to bend over my knee and spank until her cheeks turned pink, or better, over my desk so I could fuck her into the next century.

Holy shit. Was my mind really going there? Not cool. As annoying as Sloane was turning out to be, she deserved my respect. I narrowed my eyes, watching the women chant and glare at the members just entering the building. She also deserved a throw down after what she'd done at Bel Cielo. My turf. My rules.

I backed away from the window, smoothed down my hair, threw my leather jacket on over my ratty white tee shirt and glanced around the room. My gaze landed once more on my guitar case and I smiled. Oh, yeah. Sloane Gabrielli would not be leading this group for long. I draped the guitar strap over my shoulder, allowing the Les Paul to rest against my back. I'd be civil and levelheaded, but Ms. Gabrielli would learn I was not the pushover she imagined me to be.

When I left the building and moved toward the

protesters, they quieted quickly, some of them looking me over with interest. Pulling out a dose of Wilson Charm, I spoke to the entire group and ignored Sloane's smirk.

"Good morning. I'm Victor Hanley, one of the owners. Is there something I can do to help you?" A sudden burst of pride warmed my chest. The Gate was truly my club. Mine and Damien's. Finally, Frank had given me something I wanted.

A couple of the women pumped their signs up and down and called out a half-hearted boo, but another stepped forward—tall, maybe around twenty-one, with green-streaked, short dark hair. I recognized her as one of the club member's daughters. "What happened to your face, Vic?" she asked.

I'd forgotten about the bruise. "I had a run-in with an Italian ninja, but I'll live."

The young woman laughed, then pointed at the guitar. "You workin' on your music?"

"Always. Never stop." Her name came to me in a flash. "How are you, Dina?"

"I'm great." She had her sign resting on the ground now, as she leaned on the handle. "Did you write the new song by Sanity?"

"Yep. Do you like it?"

Some of the other women in the group whispered excitedly, their protest forgotten for the moment. "It's already on my playlist for when I work out." Dina had positioned her body at just the right angle to show off her assets. As lovely as they were, I wasn't interested in this particular female. I snuck a glance in Sloane's direction.

If looks could kill. She moved in front of me, brushing against my arm. My entire body came online. "We're here to discuss The Gate's all-male policy, not the latest bubblegum music."

I barked out a laugh. Dina put her hands on her hips and started rattling off some of my more popular song titles, including a few Grammy winners. I held up a hand to stop her. "Thanks, Dina, but I believe Sloane is right. I'm open to any and all discussions on the club's all male policy. If you'll make an appointment, I can accommodate all of you in one of our larger meeting rooms. Damien is out of town, but I recommend he also be in attendance.

"Some of you may not know this, but we do have limited hours for women to use the courts for doubles matches and the spa on Sunday mornings and Wednesday afternoons, as long as the member who signed them in is somewhere on the grounds."

I scanned the small crowd, positioning my body in front of Sloane's this time. I recognized two of the more mature women. "Your husbands are in the club. Would you like to watch their match? I believe it starts in fifteen minutes." They were tennis partners and participants in a regular competition we held at the end of the summer.

"They know we're here," Susan Walkerton answered, a hand on her hip. She smiled at her companion, who nodded. "They're in favor of the change."

"Umm hmm." More likely the husbands were being threatened with dire consequences if they didn't agree. I'd have to speak to them privately.

"Why don't you tell us something about The Gate Club's history, Mr. Hanley?" Sloane asked with a catlike grin. "Explain to us why it has never admitted women."

I shrugged. "The Gate has been in existence for over one hundred and twenty-nine years, founded by my great-great grandfather, Carlton Hanley, and his closest friend,

Davidson Granger. They were musicians as well as patrons of the arts and wanted a place for other artists and those who supported the arts to feel at home. It started out small, but over the years has been renovated several times. Owner-ship has always been passed down to the first-born males of each generation. I can't say why they excluded women when the club was formed, other than to say that was the norm for its time."

"You and Mr. Granger are living in the past. This is no longer the norm."

"Our club still serves a purpose, Ms. Gabrielli. In addi-tion to the usual services found in most clubs, we offer rehearsal and studio space as well as networking between artists. New works are born within these walls every season."

"Do you do all your composing here, Vic?" Dina asked.

"I own a studio in the city, but I have been inspired to write here on occasion."

"What kind of inspiration do you need?" She shifted her hips.

I glanced at Sloane. "I'm working on something now that has to do with misunderstandings and the loss of love."

"Sounds pretty bland," Sloane said.

"You'd be surprised."

"Not much about you would surprise me, Mr. Hanley. This is California. An exclusion of this sort can't be legal."

"We are a private club in every sense of the word, funded entirely by our members' yearly dues, private donations and bequests. Legally, we are within our rights to set the para-meters for membership as we choose."

"Clubs such as these create an atmosphere of mistrust and resentment within the community and between the sexes. Admitting women and gender neutral citizens would not harm The Gate's reputation or standing in any way. In fact, we believe the reputation of your club would flourish and be very well received. The Gate would set a precedent and perhaps other male-centric establishments would follow your lead."

The women cheered. I leaned in close, whispering, "You could have come to me or Damien with these concerns. Your protest implies we are against change when you haven't even given us a chance to respond."

"You and your families have had over one hundred years to respond."

The sound of a car horn cut off her next sentence. Members were trying to get their cars in the parking lot, but the women were blocking the entrance. "Would you please move to the side so our members can park?"

"We have a petition for them to sign." Susan lifted a clipboard.

"No petition signing is allowed on our property."

"We have a permit!" Sloane shouted, holding it up for all to see. The women cheered and Sloane turned to me, smirking. When my grin wasn't what she wanted to see, she started the chant I'd heard earlier. It had a pretty good rhythm.

I shifted my guitar and played along, adding a couple of cool chord progressions the crowd seemed to like. They quieted to listen, their chanting fading away as I worked the notes and rhythms to come up with something resembling a melody. I hummed and the crowd moved closer, fascinated by the process.

When my chords grew loud, they began to clap in rhythm.

Everyone but Sloane.

Oh, she was fuming, but I was having the best time

watching her fume. Sloane's skin was glowing in the sunshine, her golden hair tossed around by the breeze off the bay. Her forehead wrinkled as she tried to push the wild strands behind her ears, only to have them find their freedom with the next gust.

She was here to bring me grief, that was clear. I had no doubt she had other tricks up her sleeve, but today's plan was backfiring in a big way. Sloane's determination to save her restaurant, her employees and even her neighborhood was something I'd never encountered before. My world was mostly populated by entitled wealthy jerks, people who thought about their own happiness before anything else. Not one of them would have cared about the residents or even most of their employees.

Not so for Sloane Gabrielli. Why she'd decided to take on this cause was obvious, but it didn't make her words insincere. Her arguments were sound, and I was more than willing to take the matter up with Damien when he returned from his overly long freakin' honeymoon.

Her passion for justice drew my spirit as music stirred my soul. Adrenaline shot through my bloodstream in waves, melodies warring for attention, words for space on the page. Before Sloane had come to my office, composing had lost some of its joy, become a task I was good at, but not inspired by. I couldn't remember feeling more alive than I did standing right here in the middle of this chanting group of women led by a small dynamo with passion enough for an entire city.

I softened the tones, singing a few lyrics that popped into my head. The protesters laughed at my terrible rhymes, even shouting out words that fit better. I stopped and tried their versions and everyone cheered when it worked.

I glanced at Sloane. Not cheering.

She was stubborn. Stubborn, tenacious, with a heart the size of the neighborhood she loved. I wanted her, but I wanted more. When it came to relationships I'd tried to avoid drama, but maybe drama was what I needed. Maybe I was ready for the kind of drama Sloane Gabrielli would bring into my life. Off the charts energy, life with a purpose outside of my own happiness, and a sexual tension my body screamed for.

Sloane had made it clear she wasn't interested, but a few seconds after I'd kissed her, she'd yielded. Even kissed me back. She was more than interested. She just didn't want to admit it. I grinned as I played my last notes. The more Sloane defied me, the more I wanted to have her—on my desk, on the rug by the picture window—wherever was closest. As long as she wanted me back.

I'd have to find a way to kiss her.

She waved the permit in my face and I snatched it away to read it over before she bopped me with it. "This permit states you have to hold your protest outside my property lines." I rolled it into a tube and pointed toward the road. "In case you weren't sure, that means outside the main gate on Winnow Road."

"The road is dangerous." She retrieved the paperwork, scowling as she smoothed it out.

Cars were speeding by at good clip. The last thing I wanted was anyone getting injured. I nudged her aside the same way she'd done me. "Ladies," I announced. "You can stay..." I glanced around, "...over there under those trees where it's shady. Wouldn't want to be sued for promoting sun damage." Some of the women laughed. Sloane looked ready to growl. I winked at her. "Just trying to be reasonable."

"You're making a serious subject a joke."

"Would you rather I called in some reporters? Maybe we can use your connections with April. She did such a good job interviewing me. Or there's always the cops." I turned away, pissed she wasn't seeing that I was doing my best. "I'll have tables set up and cold drinks brought outside." The fog was clearing and it looked like the day would be warm.

"How about a tour?" a woman in a long blue dress yelled.

"Sorry. Tours have to be arranged in advance."

"Will you play for us again?" Dina asked, moving closer and laying a hand on my arm and squeezing. I'd gathered a small following when I played locally, mostly people who knew I'd composed some of the bigger hits of the last two years. Once in a while I'd sing one of those songs the way I wrote it, reclaiming it as mine.

Young women would sometimes ask for autographs or a picture to post on Instagram. I was cool with that, but Dina was edging toward crossing a line I didn't cross. Fans never became lovers. Ever.

"I think I saw your dad on the north side basketball court playing horse with Hank Fraser. Does he know you're here?"

She pulled away. "What I do with my life is none of his business."

"You paying your own college tuition now?" She stormed off. Sloane narrowed her eyes, her gaze suspicious. I shrugged. "She likes the wrong kind of attention. It's gonna get her into trouble one day."

"You know your members pretty well."

"They're family. I grew up here. Ran around like a hellion when Frank was busy. Played with the members' kids when I was young. It's one of the only places I'm comfortable."

Some of the crowd had begun moving toward the spot I'd indicated, but Sloane huffed as if I were telling her group to huddle in some cold, dark cellar.

"We're staying right here. Come back!" The troops reformed, looking fierce once more. "We insist on a hearing."

A private meeting was oh so tempting. This close, she smelled of honey and cinnamon, a confection I wanted to lick up and swallow down. My dick was on board, taking over all the spare room in my jeans.

"What happens if we don't stand aside?" Susan asked.

"If you block the entrance, I'll be forced to call the police. It's a fire hazard."

Sloane jutted out her jaw and turned toward her supporters. "We won't be seen under the trees. We're staying right here by the entrance!"

"Go Sloane," someone yelled. "You tell that misogynistic pig we're not giving up!"

"Open The Gate to women!" The chanting had begun again.

"Will you meet our demands?" asked Sloane, moving closer. Her nipples were poking into the thin material of her tee. Her eyes had darkened.

"You can present your...*argument* in my office."

"Susan and I—"

I moved closer, so close we could kiss without taking another step. "A *private* meeting. Send the rest home. You and I can work this out to our mutual satisfaction." We locked gazes and my body leveled up with lust, the sexual tension ramping to molten levels. Her breathing was rapid, her nipples hard little buds. She was feeling it too.

"I hate you." Her voice was a husky whisper.

"Good."

Pretending to be as cool as the breeze off the bay, she spoke to her followers, assuring them she could *handle me*. Some seemed a little disappointed, but most were only too glad to hop back into their Beemer and Benz SUVs and head out. They had their own private clubs and spas to visit. Sloane lifted her chin and marched inside, ignoring my heated expression, part pissed off—part turned on. She nodded at Steven who was wide-eyed as his gaze followed her progress up the stairs.

He turned to me. "Should I call a doctor now or wait until she bops you on the nose or...you know."

I handed him my guitar. "Keep it in your office until I call for it. No bopping today." My blood was on fire. I had plans for this woman. Delicious, despicable plans.

5

I walked straight into his office, my heart beating heavily in my chest, my nose taking in the delicious scent that hung in the air of Victor's private space. In college, he'd always smelled like the cologne he'd used too much of, but here the room was a miasma of Victor. Fresh coffee and fine wool suits, crisp cotton and a male scent impossible to ignore, like everything else about him.

Rather than walking to the side of the room where I might have some space to maneuver, I headed straight toward his desk, turning and leaning against it the way he had a few days ago. This was a position of power, and I would not be relinquishing one smidgeon during our negotiations.

He seemed calm and in control as he entered the room, not at all as furious as I thought he'd be. As I'd hoped he'd be. The click of the door closing and locking didn't surprise me. We had more than just the protest to discuss. He was ten feet away, but that wouldn't last.

Good. Let him come closer. My fingers itched to shake some sense into him—make him see that a men's club didn't belong here, just like another spa or high-end grocery didn't fit into the Mission.

Victor's light-eyed gaze raked my body as he allowed his soft leather jacket to slide down his arms and onto the back of the couch near the window. "Sloane."

Victor's husky tone brushed over my skin and vibrated low in my belly, forcing me to clutch at the edge of the desk. Holy fuck. I was supposed to be in control of this meeting. "Victor." I'd tried for a kick ass and confident tone, but what came out sounded needy and vulnerable. How could he still have this effect on me?

"You used to call me Vic at Cal."

He smiled, slow and sexy, and suddenly all I wanted was to pull him closer until there was no space between our bodies. To allow my hands and mouth the freedom to explore this man in all the wicked ways I'd imagined night after night. Victor had been a regular visitor in my bedtime fantasies since the first time he'd accidentally brushed up against me at the Cal library. Pathetic but true.

Instead, I folded my arms. "I'm here to..." He took another step toward me. "To negotiate."

He had the nerve to smirk at me. "That may be one of the reasons. But first I have a few things to say."

"What?"

"Your stunt at the restaurant was beneath you, especially since I'd opened up and told you what it was like for me and Mom when the reporters hounded us."

"I didn't give her permission to talk about your dad."

"But you gave her permission to malign me."

"She didn't—"

"She said I was responsible for the decision to evict you when you know that isn't true."

My face heated. He was right. It had been a stupid move.

I met his gaze because he deserved my full attention. "I shouldn't have asked April to come to the restaurant or put you on the spot. I apologize, but—"

He held up his hand. "You staged a protest just to pull my chain. Interfered with the running of the club by making it difficult for some of my members to get into the lot. I'm not saying the cause isn't worth looking at, but there could have been an accident on Winnow if the traffic had backed up."

I took a sideways step, trying to put more space between us. "You don't sound like yourself." More like a responsible business owner than the impulsive, doesn't-give-a-shit guy I'd drawn him as.

"I'm an owner now. Liable if anyone gets hurt, including your group." He rubbed his neck. "You've made irritating me your pet fucking project."

"That is not true and you know it." I pushed away from the desk and moved toward him, pissed that he thought he knew me so well. Victor Hanley knew nothing about me.

"If it looks like trouble and acts like trouble it must be goddamn trouble."

"You don't understand what this eviction will mean."

"I don't understand? I've listened to every word you've told me on the subject. I'm turning cartwheels trying to help. Writing proposals, dealing with my uncle when I can't stand spending even five minutes in his presence. If it were up to me, I never would have served the eviction notice."

I moved quickly, putting the chair between us, but he circled around, a wolf on the prowl. I took in a breath and started again. "Gate of the Bay Realty is owned by your wealthy family. A family that thinks nothing of dumping on marginalized groups or neighborhoods as long as you're getting richer in the process."

"I am not my father. That statement is discriminatory and false when applied to me."

"What are you claiming?"

"From the start you haven't given me a chance to tell you where I stand. Why is that? We used to be friends. Are you afraid you may start to like me again?" He inched even closer.

"Not much chance of that, is there?"

"My lawyer is working on rescinding the contract I signed. Soon someone else will be in charge and you won't be able to use me as a scapegoat anymore."

"Typical of you to run away. You could do some good in this new position. Change things for the better instead of destroying lives. Stop the eviction."

Victor switched direction and grasped my wrist, yanking me against his body and holding me there. "When did I run away? I saved your ass after that party."

"Yes. Thank you. But you dumped me with the doctors and disappeared." I shoved his chest but he didn't move. Angry tears were pooling in my eyes.

He leaned so close his breath warmed my cheek. "I did you a favor. I was a fucked-up mess back then. A lot of shit was going on you knew nothing about."

I wiped away the first tears that wet my face, then thumped his chest with my fist. "Why didn't you talk to me, you idiot?"

"I wanted to, but you deserved better."

"I never wanted...b...better." Shit. Why did I have to show weakness now? Our mouths were so close—close enough to lean in and bite or suck or...

Before I could decide, Victor crushed his lips into mine, clutching at my hair and my hip, pressing my form so hard against his body it was almost hard to breathe. If I was going to pull away, now was the time, but my gut was an angry stew of emotions, all of them filtering down to one thing. I wanted him in the most primal way. His body using mine for pleasure as I used his.

His tongue licked and teased and I opened my mouth, joining his erotic dance. His scent, his touch, his soft moan liquefied my muscles. But he held me up, protecting me as he had that night at Cal.

I tried to force my sense of reason to regain control, to move away, to negotiate as planned, but the only kind of give and take my body had in mind was the sort that brought mind-blowing pleasure.

Our mouths came apart and Victor nuzzled my ear. "You taste so good." His hand trailed over my ass and squeezed. Hard.

I leaned against his chest and closed my eyes, forcing away dreams and facing reality. The last thing I would ever survive was Victor making love to me. I'd lose myself to hope only to have him leave again with some new excuse. Heartbreak was not a special on my menu. Not again.

That didn't mean I couldn't enjoy myself. I clutched his shoulders and met his gaze, hoping he'd see the invitation in my eyes. Today would be a get him out of my system one-time fuck, a drop the past and get back to the important shit fuck. I needed him inside my body, but I'd never allow him a place in my heart.

I pushed against his chest and he backed away. We were panting, turned on to the point of pain.

"You drive me crazy." His voice was rough and sexy. "You provoke and demand, pull all kinds of smart-ass moves to confuse me, then kiss as if you want me as much as I want you."

I pulled the red tee shirt over my head. Victor's expression turned feral. After tossing it onto the chair, I rested my hand on the chair back and lifted my leg, pointing my boot clad foot in his direction. "Help me."

Suddenly we were pulling off clothing in a mad rush, circling each other like caged beasts. His shirt ended up on the floor by the couch, his pants by one of the large chairs in front of the desk. Shoes were tossed around like tennis balls. With me in my Victoria's Secret panties and Victor wearing only his sexy briefs, he backed me to the desk and placed his hands on either side of me. He bent close enough to nose my hair aside and whisper in my ear, "Good enough to eat."

I picked up my hair and fanned the back of my neck. "I'm hot and sweaty."

He nuzzled my neck, licking my nape. "Hot for sure, but not sweaty enough."

His kisses moved down as he sucked on a nipple and played with another. I moaned and held his head to my chest, all the while terrified he was going to start saying lovely things that would make me cry when I was alone and he'd left for good. I clutched at his hair and yanked him away.

"What?"

"Fuck me."

"Can't I have my fun?" I slid my hand into his black briefs and stroked his cock. "Oh fuck." The panties were off a few seconds later, but when he lifted me onto his desk, bent my knees and spread my thighs, he lowered his head to lick my clit.

"Vic. Please."

"I need you wet." I cried out when he finger fucked me, fast and hard, until I was spasming around his hand in a glorious orgasm, my howls loud enough to be heard by the guards. I hated the power he held over me.

I loved the power he held over me. God, I couldn't let him know, so I yanked on his hair.

"Ow. What?"

"Fuck me, you insensitive tycoon." This would be my one chance to have Victor inside me, and I wasn't going to waste another second.

He laughed. "Hold that thought." He fished in his top desk drawer for a condom, took off the wrapper and handed it to me. He must have known right away I hadn't done it before, so he showed me, guiding my hand as we slid it on together, then lowering his lids as he brought my hands back up and down again, tightening our hands around the base.

"Feels so good, babe." He pulled my legs around his waist, then thrust inside, pressing my ass even closer so he was buried deep.

"Oh." I closed my eyes and forced my body to relax. He was large and the fullness was incredible.

"Am I...hurting you?" He grunted out the words, struggling with control.

"No. You're... I haven't... Long time."

He kissed the top of my head then took my mouth in a searing kiss. "I'll go slow."

My heart melted a little, but no. Melting was not allowed. No sweet kissing. No tender words. "Don't you fucking dare go slow."

He pulled out and slammed into me.

I cried out. "Oh god. Like that. Again."

He grinned and took my mouth, using teeth and tongue, taking and taking. He broke away and playfully nibbled my chin. "You screamed for me." Another hard thrust.

"Won't happen…again."

Victor laughed as he pulled all the way out swirling his head over my clit, then slamming into me again and again, angling his body so he teased my clit and rubbed against my sweet spot with every thrust. He pulled one of my hands into his mouth, sucked on my fingers and guided them to my nipple. "Pinch." I did. "Harder." So good. "Again."

He rubbed my clit with fingers soaked in my own juices and slowed the rhythm down. I was getting closer. "Harder."

"Let go, Sloane. Give yourself to me."

"Vic…"

"Do it."

He pounded faster, deeper. My flesh ached for release. He pinched my clit and I cried out, the pleasure-pain so incredible I thought I'd come apart. He pinched again and I came all over his hand, my pussy tightening around his cock.

"Yes," he hissed, picking me up when I'd calmed, turning me around and pushing me down on the desk face first, my feet on the floor, my legs spread wide.

"You. Ass."

"You asked for this, babe."

When he plunged back inside, I groaned, but not from pain. He was wild, his tight balls slapping against my inner thighs, his hands cradling my hips, keeping me from shooting forward on the hard desk. I wanted to laugh at the irony of the situation, scream at myself for giving in, for being weak, but his cock felt so good, filling every inch inside me, rubbing all the perfect places, driving me closer to coming apart.

How long had I wanted this man? My eyes welled with tears, but I blinked them away. Stupid girl. Now was all that mattered.

He stilled, his entire body vibrating above me as he came. He groaned with pleasure, then pushed my hair aside to kiss my nape, my shoulder, my back. "God, your skin is beautiful."

I smiled, then tensed. No. No, no, no. I was an idiot. I was letting him get to me.

"Mmm." He pulled away and disposed of the condom, then returned to lift me in his arms. He was grinning like the Alice in Wonderland cat.

"Put me down."

"Not ready." He sat in one of his large chairs with me on his lap and covered us with a throw blanket he'd grabbed off the couch. "This is cozy."

"You're sitting in this chair bare assed naked."

"I want to get rid of them anyway."

"Why? They suit you."

"How?"

"Big and ugly."

He smiled a smile that spoke of sated pleasure and mischief combined, then moved my hair aside and kissed my neck. "When I kiss you right here, you stop breathing for a second."

I patted my hair back in place then twisted in his arms. "Let me up."

He kissed my ear, then released me. I rose, tossed the blanket in his face and gathered up my clothes. I cleaned myself up and dressed in the bathroom connected to his office, combing my hair and using lip gloss on my kiss-swollen mouth. I was sore in places that hadn't been sore for a long time, but my muscles were loose and I couldn't stop smiling. He'd been amazing, rough when I needed rough, but never crossing the line into real pain. I didn't regret my decision, because now I'd be completely clearheaded around him. I'd had my fill—literally–and now...

Now I would focus on the facts. His company was kicking me out of my restaurant and keeping women out of this mausoleum of a club. Gate of the Bay Realty was everything I despised—a selfish company unable to see past the bottom line. The fact my body wanted their corporate representative every time we were within twenty feet of each other would now be easier to ignore. Maybe he'd fucked those feelings right out of me.

When I returned to the room, he was dressed and standing near the door holding my shoes. "I'll be at the restaurant at two. We can talk afterward. Maybe in your office?"

"I thought..."

"I'm not sure I'll be able to concentrate on what you're saying. In fact, I'm certain all your arguments will go in one ear and out the other."

"You have better things to think about than our business?"

"I'm finding one thing in particular way too distracting." He squatted down and helped me on with my shoes, then trailed his fingers up to my hips and jerked me against him. "The evidence is damning."

He was hard again and my body wanted a replay of what we'd done in the worst way. My face heated quickly and I stepped out of his grip. I was supposed to be done with him.

"I'll walk you downstairs." He took my hand and I wanted to pull away, really, but... Who was I kidding? I wanted him to hold my hand forever.

"Vic..."

"My territory, remember?"

"Fine."

"I'll see you at two."

When we were leaving the building, one of the club's members was striding up the path to the entrance wearing an angry grimace directed at Vic. I said goodbye on the steps and turned to walk toward my borrowed car, ignoring the male who'd looked at me with disgust. I pulled out of the lot, not wanting to hear what the guy had to say.

6

"You gotta be kidding, Vic." Mr. Howard had been a close friend of my father's, although he wouldn't have admitted to that fact in a million years now that Frank was cooling his heels in prison. Like Frank, this guy was coarse, rude and thought his money entitled him to special services. "You were letting those bitches protest on the grounds? You might want to read over the club rules, boy." His voice was loud enough for anyone within a hundred yards to hear. Did Sloane have her car window down?

He started to push past me, but I stopped him with a hand on his shoulder. "Mr. Howard, I believe you owe Ms. Gabrielli a written apology."

"She can kiss my ass along with the rest of them. If even one of those cunts shows her face around here again, I'll call the cops. I've been a member for forty-four years."

I would not tolerate another bully.

"This is my property, Mr. Howard, and Ms. Gabrielli and her compatriots were here holding a peaceful demonstration. They didn't break any laws."

"I saw it on the local news. Frank is going to flip out. This club is for men and men only." He stormed inside.

"Steven!" My sharp tone brought the security guard trotting over.

"Yes?"

"Please ask Mr. Howard to wait for me in my office."

"Sure, Vic."

"Make sure he doesn't go into any of the members only areas. Get another guard to help you if you need to."

Steven straightened to his full six foot four. "I think I can handle Mr. Howard."

"Don't rough him up. He's in his sixties."

"I'll leave him for you. But he's a foul-mouthed coward, if you don't mind my sayin'."

"I don't. Thanks."

I took the stairs two at a time to my office.

I sat behind my desk, opened my laptop and pulled up a form as Steven and Mr. Howard showed up at my door. I motioned for Mr. Howard to take a seat as the printer went to work. "I'm cancelling your membership."

"You can't do that."

"I'm the co-owner of this club and you have broken rules that have been in existence since my great-great grandfather's time. Harassment and threats are not allowed under any circumstances."

"She's not a member."

"That doesn't matter."

"But I should get a warning."

"I've given you warnings on several other occasions. This was the last straw. Ms. Gabrielli is an acquaintance of mine. She was my guest."

"Oh, I get it. She's your fuckbuddy."

I stood, trembling. "Shut your mouth, Mr. Howard, or I

will toss you out that window and onto the rocks at the bottom of the cliff. The tide is out."

The man's eyes widened. "You telling me if a homeless person walked onto the property and someone told him to fuck off, you'd cancel his membership?"

I met his gaze. "If the club member had received numerous warnings, then I'd do it in a hot minute."

He scowled. "I'm taking you to court."

I laughed. "Get in line, Mr. Howard."

I pushed the form across the desk for him to sign. He read it over. I'd gone into quite a lot of detail, including past incidents and dates. I had witnesses to his misbehavior. "You're making a mistake. Your dad and I—"

"I don't give a shit what either of you think. Sign it."

Instead he ripped it in half. "Fuck you."

"Escort him downstairs so he can pick up any of his personal belongings. Then please escort him out." I turned to Mr. Howard. "You have thirty minutes. If you're found on the property after that, I'll have you arrested."

I stayed at my desk for several minutes, listening to the rushing and waning surf, the wind whipping around the building, the occasional seagull calling for his mate. What had come over me? I'd never threatened to kill anyone before. Certainly not to save a woman's honor. I barked out a laugh. My primal self was starting to see Sloane as mine. This had never happened with any other woman. The fates were thumbing their noses at me.

Maybe I could turn this around and do some thumbing of my own.

I made it to the restaurant right on time and after another amazing lunch, she took me up to her office. It was small, with a cot in one corner and a desk in another. A small kitchenette and kitchen table could be seen through an archway. Shelves with books and knickknacks made it homey, made it Sloane's.

"You less distracted now?" Her sexy, confident smile was sending blood back to a place that didn't give a shit about negotiations.

"I'll keep it to a minimum."

"Coffee?" she asked. "Unless you want something stronger."

"Coffee." She poured two mugs of joe, then sat in the chair next to mine at the table. I took a sip. "It's strong. Perfect. Musicians mostly drink it black. Always on the run."

"I like it strong too."

I flashed back to the sex on the desk episode. She was probably sore, but I was certain she'd enjoyed what we'd done as much as I had.

She eyed my mug. "You used to put whiskey in your coffee."

"I rarely drink alcohol during daylight hours. Hardly ever more than two drinks whatever the hour."

She barked out a short laugh. "Since when?"

I leaned back in the chair and hesitated, but she deserved to know the truth. "Since the night you were hurt."

"After the party?"

"I fucked up that night. I was drunk and shouldn't have let you leave alone. If my head had been on straight, I wouldn't have kissed you. If I hadn't kissed you, you probably wouldn't have run off like you did."

She stared at the coffee mug clutched in her lap, unwilling to meet my gaze. "I was drunk too. Not smart enough to wait or find someone to leave with me. It wasn't your fault. You didn't... You didn't attack me."

"Those two who followed you had a rep for roughing up women. A couple of girls they'd dated had bruises on their arms and faces. One girl left the school. Like everyone else in the frat house, I did nothing about it. Told no one."

"You were twenty."

"A self-absorbed tool." The guilt came flooding back, my stomach a hard knot. "How many other women had they hurt? You were practically unconscious when I found you."

Her face paled, but instinct told me she and I needed to purge this memory together. I wanted to reach out and hold her while we talked, but she'd chosen to keep her distance and I had to respect that.

"Why did you follow them that night?" Sloane asked, her eyes dimmed with pain.

I shrugged. "I had a bad feeling because they'd been watching you. I ended up stumbling around in the dark. It took me twice as long to find you than it should have. If I hadn't been drinking..." I rubbed my hands along the top of my thighs. "I got there too late. I'm sorry."

"They would have raped me. You got there in time."

"You were bruised and bloody."

She shivered. "No permanent scars."

I looked past Sloane's shoulder, my mind traveling to that night. The pain in her eyes. The fear. "Except on the inside."

"What?"

"I'm sorry. I shouldn't make assumptions." I thought to tell her about my past with Frank—my own fears, but changed my mind, instead taking another sip of coffee. "I wasn't sure you remembered me at first."

"I could never forget you, Vic." She smiled. "I think you broke that guy's nose."

"And one of my fingers. I'd never punched anyone before. Only a bag at the gym during training."

"Training?"

"Just the usual sort of thing." He glanced away.

"I heard you had a knife."

"He pulled one and I relieved him of it. I might not have been as aggressive if I'd known about the knife." We smiled at each other, laughing softly.

"You were my hero that day. Carrying me to the clinic and waiting until they called my parents." She frowned. "But after they gave me a room, you just disappeared."

"My dad's lawyers told me not to contact you and like a douche I listened to them." I squeezed the back of my neck, which always got stiff on me when I was stressed. "They told me you pressed charges against those boys."

"Their wealthy lawyers got them community service. At least they were expelled from Cal." She frowned. "Where did you go?"

"I finished up in UCLA. To make Frank happy, I majored in computer science, discovering I had a knack for designing software. When I earned my master's, he had me heading the IT department at Franklin Software, but it didn't last. I wrote a few songs that took off on the charts and quit. Once in a while I'd help them out as a consultant. But that was it."

"I'm glad you didn't give up on your music."

"I played whenever I could find the time. It's been my career for the last five years."

"Still playing guitar. Anything else?"

"Usually a keyboard or piano to compose. Guitar when I play clubs."

"There's a studio at The Gate?"

I nodded. "It's not as high tech as my studio in the city, but a lot of club members use it."

I was itching to touch her again. Kiss those full lips. Squeeze her perfect ass. I shifted forward in the chair so we were closer. "Tell me what you want, Chef."

"This gentleman's club is archaic and misogynistic." She nodded sharply, as if she were punctuating a statement no one would have the nerve to argue with.

I grinned. No beating around the bush with Sloane Gabrielli. I put aside my coffee. "I'm listening."

"Women should be admitted as equal members. Gender neutral applicants as well."

"We don't admit every man who applies. Membership is granted based on various factors. Every applicant is evaluated using the same criteria."

"Evaluated in what way?"

"Everyone is required to give us financial information. The yearly dues are high and we don't offer a payment plan. Occasionally we'll make an exception to help members who fit our parameters but can't afford the yearly fee."

"What parameters are those?"

"The entire point of the club is to offer up a place where like-minded members can congregate."

"How does Blake fit the parameters?"

"His parents were competitive ballroom dancers and he used to compete as a teen. When his partner had an accident, he took up law and stopped dancing. I hired him right after he passed the California Bar Exam and got his license. After a few years, he bought a dance studio and released most of his law clients, except for me. I keep him in those nice suits and that fancy car." I laughed.

"He gives lessons?"

"Yes. Trains kids and older teens who want to compete, but gives kids of all varieties lessons, even if they've never danced."

"I only saw him for a few seconds when he came in to rescue you. Good looking guy." She smiled.

"I'll introduce you soon."

"Besides having the money to pay to join, what are the other requirements for membership?"

"Members have to be residents of Marin County. Men who don't support their local museums, philharmonic orchestras or dance companies need not apply." I shifted my gaze toward the window.

"You advertise it that way?"

"We don't need to advertise. Word of mouth brings them in. The rules were created by our great-great grandfathers, both from wealthy families and both classical musicians. They brought their brand of civilization to the Wild West."

"They didn't make a living with their music, did they?"

"No. They were sent to invest in the west. Carlton made a fortune by building ships and opening up shipping channels to Asia and South America and Davidson bought a lot of prime land and invested in the railroads."

"Women enjoy and participate in the arts. Even back then."

"I can't argue with that."

Sloane glanced at the hand I'd rested on my knee. I'd been beating out a rhythm for one of the new songs I'd worked on the night before. "Sorry. Bad habit. Used to drive my parents nuts."

She placed her hand over mine, calming me in a way only she seemed to be able to do. "I'm sorry about your dad and...and what you and your mom went through. I can't imagine—"

I held up my other hand to stop her. "He's where he belongs. Nothing else to say."

She stared at me for a moment, her expression puzzled. Squeezing my hand in a sign of support, she sat back, removing it quickly along with the warmth of her skin against mine.

"I'm sorry. I wasn't exactly gracious. Thank you," I said.

"You were right. I did come at first to pull your chain. But when I saw the club and spoke to the wives and daughters, I felt the idea had value."

"Are you aware there are clubs in the area exclusive to women? Are you going to protest there on behalf of men?"

"No. If men want them closed they'll most likely be closed. They don't seem to have the same problems gaining support for their ideas as women. We're bitches when we ask for change, but men are innovators." She frowned. "Who was that angry man in the parking lot?"

"Mr. Howard is no longer a member of The Gate Club."

"He gave you a hard time about the protest?"

"He said things about you and the other protestors I couldn't tolerate. I'd given him warnings on other occasions too. I've wanted to let him go for some time."

"Thank you."

"I'm on your side. I hope you know that."

She smiled, blushing slightly. God, I wanted her again. And again. Her nipples stood at attention beneath the thin fabric of her silky short-sleeved shirt, maybe agreeing with me. "How did you get a tee shirt made up for the protest so quickly?"

"Cassie designed it. They're in Florence now but she was able to do it online."

"You contacted Cassandra on her honeymoon?"

"She was happy to help."

"Damien knows about this protest of yours?"

"She'd rather you tell him." Her smile a little sheepish.

"They've been through a lot and deserve some time to themselves. They'll be gone for another month and a half, so no decisions regarding changes in membership can be made until he's back in the office."

"That's bull, Mr. Hanley. A call works just fine."

I grinned, reading over the slogan again. *The Gate Should Open for All!* "I'm sure the members appreciated the catchphrase."

She rolled her eyes. "If their minds run that way."

"Every man's mind runs that way when he's sitting across from a beautiful woman."

"Don't."

"Don't what?" I stroked her face, but she jerked away.

"This is a business meeting. Did you mean what you said about plans to offer the stores their leases back at a reasonable rent?"

"Yes." Although I hadn't heard back from Andrew yet. Probably not a good sign.

"A six month closure for a restaurant is impossible to recover from."

"I'll do whatever I can." I took Sloane's hand in mine and twined my fingers with hers. This time she didn't try to pull away. Warmth sang in my heart, patching the hole I tried to fill with work and music and bike rides. Sometimes it worked. But the hole was usually back the next day.

"Yesterday..." she started, glancing at her smaller desk. "In your office..."

"Yesterday was amazing." I stroked her hair.

"It doesn't change anything." I moved my hand away. "I mean... You were...wonderful. But you have to admit, the sexual tension between us has been out of control. We had to take care of it in order to move forward."

"Take care of it?"

What the fuck?

She stood. "I'm going to find a way to keep my restaurant open. I'm not giving up. You need to know that."

"Do you think what happened between us was about me trying to get you to stop fighting the eviction?"

"Well, no, but—"

"Good. Because for me it was all about wanting you. Only you. Sexual tension can be relieved in a lot of ways, but I wanted to be with you, Sloane. Despite your attempts to drive me crazy. I want you now."

"We lost our chance at that."

"That's bullshit. We never had a chance. Now we do."

She lifted her chin. "Not if you take away Bel Cielo."

"It's my father's decision to make."

"Have you talked to him? Explained what's happening in the neighborhood. Think about the people he's dispossessing."

"My father doesn't give a shit about his own family. Why do you imagine he'd care about the Garcia Sisters or the Kriegers or you for that matter? The best I can do—"

"I'm going to find a way to save my employees and the other families on the block."

She'd gathered up her things and indicated the door with a sweep of her hand. "I'll show you out downstairs."

"I know the way."

"I have to lock up."

No way was today going to end like this. I pulled her into my arms. Her body was stiff for a moment, but when I kissed her forehead, she relaxed. "I'm on your side," I repeated, lifting her chin. "What happened with you, angry sex and all, meant something to me." I brushed my lips across her smooth cheek. "I think it meant something to you too." I kissed her softly, then smiled against her mouth because I couldn't stop myself.

"I don't want this."

"Maybe not today."

"Tomorrow I have to go to my parents' home and tell them there's a good chance I'm losing the restaurant."

"I'm sorry."

"I'm not even... Not even angry with you. I believe you when you tell me you're going to do everything you can to help. Just please, please keep me informed. If I don't know what's going on, it will just be that much worse."

"I promise. I'll tell you everything as soon as I know." My phone sounded. Another text from my mom. I shut off my phone.

Sloane had seen my screen. "What's up with you and her?"

"What do you mean? Nothing's up."

"You can't possibly blame your mother for what happened. She's as much a victim as Mike Granger."

"I don't blame her for anything." Except I did, and it wasn't right and I knew it.

"Bring her to dinner at my house."

"I don't know."

"Is it me?"

"She'd love you. She's always said I need someone who doesn't let me get away with shit."

"Really?"

"She didn't say it like that exactly."

"Then bring her soon. Any Monday."

Why was she pushing me? I'd had enough from Andrew and even Gio. "Look. My family is the last family you'd want to get to know."

"But this is your mother. If you don't want to bring her here, that's fine. Can we visit her at home one day?"

"Why are you forcing this issue?"

"Because I care about you and nothing is more important than family."

"You haven't met my family." I kissed her cheek, backed away and headed for the door. "I have work to do at the studio. I'll see you tomorrow." I left her standing in the doorway and didn't look back.

7

I'd passed this shop a dozen times, but had never stopped in. Music was nice, but I usually used a streaming service and only listened when I was working out. Mom and Dad had always played music when they cooked at home, but I never felt the urge.

A bell rang when I opened the door. I wrinkled my nose. The small record slash used book store smelled musty.

"Good morning. May I help you?" The man behind the counter was middle-aged and bearded, with long brown hair he kept pulled back in a tail. He worked the look pretty well.

"Do you know anything about particular composers?"

"Name?"

"Victor Hanley."

"Oh sure. He writes for Sanity and Desktop Rogues and Cherice. And, let's see, he wrote a big crossover country hit for Harlon Edwards."

"He writes all their music?"

"Oh no. But a lot of their hits. He knows how to write in their style, like he can read their minds or something."

The guy laughed. "I'm a fan, in case you hadn't noticed. He lives in the Bay Area. Nice guy. He's come in a few times, especially when a prospective client wants him to write for them. He'll buy a few of their CDs and study them."

"But he can listen to their music online."

"Yeah, that's another thing. He likes to help out the local business owners."

"Vic?"

"You know him?"

"From college."

"Cool." He glanced at me in a way that broadcast his interest. "You live around here?"

"No. I own the restaurant up the block. Bel Cielo."

"I love that place. The chef is amazeballs."

"I'll tell her you said so. Come by and I'll treat you to lunch."

"Really? But can I get take out? I'm the only one here most of the time."

"Whatever you want." I slid a business card from my wallet, wrote Free Lunch and initialed it.

"Thanks." He placed it reverently in his wallet.

"Can you show me some CDs with Victor's songs on them?"

"Sure. He's got his own CD too. An amazing acoustic mashup."

I paid for Victor's album as well as a few of the other CDs. "Is there any way you can transfer his songs onto a USB drive for me?"

"For a free plate of chicken piccata or saltimbocca, anything."

I gave him an extra twenty dollars and we both ended up happy. When I picked up Caty to head out to Mom and

Dad's, we listened together. Mangia Monday was our family tradition.

"This guy's good," she said as we drove.

"I had sex with him."

"What?" Caty shrieked.

"Ow. Too loud. Driving here."

"Who is he?"

"I knew him in college."

She watched my face as I drove. "It's that guy. Victor."

"Vic."

"So talk. What's been happening?"

I gave her the bare facts.

"You staged a protest at his exclusive club for millionaires and instead of calling the cops he angry fucked you on his desk?" That last part was the piece of info that interested her the most. Same for me.

"I've never been angry fucked before."

"You're smiling."

"Yes I am."

"He's..." She made a motion with her hands.

"Yes, he is."

She sat back in the seat, closed her eyes and sighed. We drove for a few minutes in silence, our thoughts in the obvious places. Mine were ticking off every touch, every taste, every stroke.

"But what about the restaurant?"

"I'm going to tell Mom and Dad and everyone about it tonight. You're my backup. But don't mention the desk thingy and don't mention Victor. I don't want A and J going after him."

"You can count on me, sis. As long as you keep me up to date with all the juicy bits."

"No more juicy bits between Vic and me."

"Have pity. Your life story has become addictive—like a soap opera. Can't you have one more little fling for my sake?" I snorted. "You still snort? No wonder he doesn't want you."

"Oh, he wants me."

"Then what is the problem? Are the pictures on social media a lie? Does he look like cousin Rodolpho?"

"He's over six feet, dark hair, light blue eyes, and a mouth any sane woman would want on every inch of her body. And he's... He's fun. He makes me laugh."

"He's hot, skilled and he makes you laugh. Wow. A disaster waiting to happen."

"Shut up."

"I'm telling you. Go wild. Don't blow this."

"I know." She stared at me. "I. Know!"

Mom and Dad were happy to see us, as always. I gave Mom a swift kiss and Dad the usual hug, then marched straight to the closet to pull out my apron. I figured talking about my messed-up life would be best after dinner.

Only Caty had different ideas. "Slo's got something to tell you. It's not good news."

"Caty!"

Mom and Dad immediately pulled off their aprons and tossed them to my twin brothers, Ang and Joey. "Finish up the dinner, boys," Dad said, taking my arm and sitting me down at the kitchen table so everyone would still be able to hear. A minute later a glass of water and a glass of wine were plunked down in front of me, as well as a plate with olives, marinated peppers, cheese and salami. The homemade bread came next.

Mom made up a plate and handed it to me. "Sweetie, you take your time. We have all night."

Tears filled my eyes. I hadn't thought I'd cry. This wasn't

the end of the world. But my family's kindness always blew me away, especially after hearing more about Victor's mom and dad. I couldn't imagine being an only child in that environment.

Caty slowly lowered her body into the chair next to mine while Mom made a very small plate for her. She didn't have much of an appetite. "I'm sorry, Slo. But holding it in all evening is worse."

She clasped my hand and I began to talk.

8

U ncle Andrew's office was located in the Financial District of San Francisco, only a few blocks from the Ferry Building and Pier 14. After being escorted inside by his personal assistant, I took up my usual position near the window. As a kid I'd never felt comfortable around my divorced uncle, not because he was into little boys—in fact he'd been with a different woman almost every time I'd seen him. No, his dark gaze and permanent scowl had frightened me. He was over six feet tall and had taken a perverse pleasure in looming over me when he spewed his opinions and criticized my choices. Now that we were equal in height, I preferred to stand when we were in a room together. It took away his height advantage and annoyed the shit out of the dominating asshole. A double bonus.

Andrew strode into his office, his eyes gleaming with purpose. "You've asked for a business meeting? On a Saturday?"

Even a neutral question coming from Andrew's mouth could sound as if you'd disappointed him in some way.

Ass.

I took my time and strolled over to one of the comfortable chairs near the fireplace, then indicated he should sit in one of the matching chairs. They looked like a new acquisition. Antiques. He raised an eyebrow but didn't argue. I counted it a victory.

"I'm here about the plans for the Twenty-Fourth Street renovation."

"I'm not surprised." He dusted off his chair with a handkerchief and sat.

"According to the engineers I've spoken with, we can accomplish each interior renovation in a few weeks. That way, the restaurant, thrift store and delicatessen can reopen without much impact to the neighborhood or the owners and employees involved. We'll hire extra workers and space out the work rather than have all three businesses closed at once. After they reopen, we can work on the exteriors of the buildings without interfering with their ability to attract customers."

"You believe the clothing resale shop and the deli will be able to pay the much higher rents?"

I took a pause, my usual ploy before delivering news that might not be met with enthusiasm. "It would be injurious to the community at large to raise the rents."

"In what way?" His tone had dropped, his interest peaked. My dad would have immediately told me I was an idiot, but Andrew loved a good argument.

"The businesses are well-loved and popular, even with the tourists. The deli and Bel Cielo are on one of the Mission District Foodie tours."

"Are you saying we should absorb the loss?"

"We could add a floor or two and rent that space for offices."

"Adding a floor or two would cost more than you might imagine. It would take years before the building made up the loss."

"It would depend on the businesses expressing an interest in that location. Some companies will pay exorbitant rents."

"The Mission is not quite there yet. It can't compare to the Financial District. I've seen the figures. Have you?"

"Yes, but—"

Andrew rose and walked back to his desk, sitting on his *throne*, a chair very similar to the one Frank had in his office at The Gate Club. "Your ideas are not in line with your father's goals for the company." He shuffled a few papers on the desk, not really looking at any of them. "He wants to see you."

"And I want to forget I ever had a father."

Andrew chuckled. "He almost kicked you out of the house and cut you off financially when you decided to go to Cal and major in music. I convinced him you'd come around. And you did...for a time."

"How can you expect me to feel any affection for him? Uncle Mike—"

"Damien's father was not your uncle. I hold that position. All this whining about your father and mother accomplishes nothing. When was the last time you stopped by the house to see Elaine?" I didn't answer. "Are you proud of the way you've neglected her? She's alone."

"Except for the three or four servants who live on property or nearby and the half dozen friends she attends events with. She's constantly busy with her volunteer work and her tennis games. Mom is not suffering."

"You know nothing of the sacrifices she's made for you."

"I've made some sacrifices of my own. I picked up the pieces Frank left behind."

"You'd be happy turning your back on all of us, living in your rented recording studio and playing at making music for the rest of your life."

"I own that studio and the building it's in."

He actually looked shocked. "You do?"

"Why so surprised, Unc? I've grown up with art thieves and shady lawyers. Along the way I've learned what not to do."

"Watch your mouth. Everything you have was bought—"

"Other than The Gate Club and the house Frank gave me, everything I own was paid for with money I earned myself. Frank dragged me into his world when I was a stupid kid and I've managed to claw my way out of it and make a life of my own. I earn more than enough with song royalties to pay for my so-called extravagant lifestyle. I don't need this trusteeship to make ends meet. If fact, I don't need anything my father has to offer." I was tempted to tell Andrew to convince Frank to give over the trusteeships to him, but Andrew would end up gentrifying every building he could get his hands on just for spite.

"Quite the entrepreneur, but you left out my father's will. You wouldn't be where you are now if your grandfather hadn't left most of his money to you."

"Grandfather's monetary bequest has been invested wisely and is making a fine profit. I haven't touched it."

Andrew's expression turned cold as he raked both hands through his graying hair and calmed his anger with a deep breath. Andrew wasn't a hothead like Frank. He knew there was more power in the words themselves than the volume of delivery.

My grandfather had left me, his only grandchild, two thirds of his estate, dividing the rest between Frank and Andrew. Their father's blatant slap in the face had left the brothers stunned and angry. Like either of them needed another reason to be angry with me.

But Grandpa had been a musician and he'd seen the spark in me. He'd convinced Mom to get me that keyboard and whenever I made up another song, he was the first to hear it. He'd given me great advice, advice I followed to this day. He'd died a few weeks before I turned eleven. A few weeks before I'd been sent to that hellhole school.

Andrew cleared his throat, as if to swallow down his bile. "You needn't concern yourself with the upcoming building inspection. I'll give you a copy of the report as soon as I have it. Remember, you are legally obligated to make certain the company remains sound, and whenever possible, to increase profits. Keep that in mind when you're screwing the hot little chef and promising she won't be out on her ass in six weeks."

I stood and moved closer to the desk. "Speak about her like that again and you'll never set foot in the club."

"You can't do that. I'm a lifetime member."

"And - I'm – the – fucking - owner."

I left in a foul mood, feeling guilty about my mother, then forcing the guilt out of my head. I'd done everything I could to help, even calling the cops on my own father to protect her.

Mom had visited Frank three times in the last two weeks.

I'd found her unconscious, bruised and bloody, but she couldn't stay away from the man who'd hurt her. Mom told me over and over she didn't blame me for turning him in, but when I visited, the elephant in the room had grown too large for a comfortable conversation. A trench too big to breach.

When I left Unc's office, I hopped on my bike, my body going on autopilot and driving to Bel Cielo. I was hoping for some comforting food and if I was lucky, some time with Sloane. Nothing melted the ice that formed in my heart whenever I was with my own family faster than time with Sloane.

"Mr. Hanley. You're very early." Gio's classic scowl had become part of the ritual.

"I was nearby."

"Shall I cancel your two o'clock reservation?"

"Yes. Thank you."

His expression darkened. "Please give us twenty-four hours notice next time, or we will be forced to charge you."

He was protective of Sloane, a loyal employee, I got that. But I'd been as sweet as sugar up until now. "Why don't you like me? I'm trying to save your job."

"Are you? Or are you just interested in what you can get before the bomb drops?"

"I'm working on defusing it."

"And we know how that scenario usually plays out, don't we?"

"You're pretty good at hiding your animosity around Sloane."

"My ancestors became experts at hiding who they were. If they didn't they were driven out of town."

"Roma?" He nodded. "We all have ancestors with sad tales to tell."

He looked me over. "Hanley. Scottish Highlander?" This time I nodded. "My grandmother told me too much money will make a man a monster. Are you a monster,

Hanley? Because if you are, and you hurt her, I will come for you."

He loved her as more than a boss or a friend. He thought of her as family. Clan. "I'll never do anything to hurt her. I care for her too."

His dark eyes bored into mine long enough to make me uncomfortable. Finally, he nodded and seated me at a quiet table in the back. Sloane's staff guarded her with the same determination the secret service did the president. But she gave back threefold.

I hadn't seen Sloane alone since our meeting in her office. I'd called, but the calls had gone to voicemail, never a good sign in a relationship. Not that she was one hundred percent on board with us having a relationship the way things stood. Or even fifty percent. But Sloane Gabrielli had rocked my world—throwing me off balance with her feisty ferocity, setting my body on fire with only a gentle touch.

I ordered and pulled out my cell. There were three texts from Andrew and two from Mom. I ignored Andrew's and answered Mom's, bowing out of her dinner invitation yet again. I used the trusteeship as today's excuse. I wouldn't be good company. She said she understood, but if I'd had her on the phone, hurt would have colored her words. One of the reasons I rarely called her.

This Hanley trustee fuckfest was driving me up the wall and I'd spent the last two days speaking to company financial officers, operations managers and a dozen other heads of departments. I'd lost time in the studio, a situation that always put me in a foul mood.

The whole scenario reeked. I was in corporate limbo with my fingers in everything, but no real power to make changes. Talk about frustrating. I put my phone away and glanced toward the kitchen. Sloane was watching me. She wore my favorite outfit, her chef jacket and hat, paired with a short flowy skirt that showed off her bare legs, the ones she'd wrapped around my waist as I'd fucked her.

Would I ever look at those legs and think of anything else? Probably not.

I glanced away and closed my eyes as my cock stirred against my heavy jeans, the sort of frustration that had an easy cure if Sloane...

She spoke to a few of her customers before sliding into the chair across from mine. "I wasn't sure if you'd be back."

"I'm an idiot."

"I've heard that about you."

"I'm sorry. You were just being nice."

"I was. Have you called your mom?"

I smiled. Determined didn't begin to describe Sloane. "We text."

She shook her head, already exasperated even though we'd only been talking for two minutes. "Why are you really here?"

"You know why."

"If it has to do with me and you getting together, that's not going to happen."

"Unless I was having the best wet dream of all time, it already has."

"We had a strong attraction, but we got it out of our systems. Now we can—"

"You are one crappy liar."

"What?"

I took her hand in mine. "Tell me you don't want me."

She stared at our hands, our fingers automatically twining around each other. "I don't want you."

"Look at me and tell me that."

She snatched her hand away. "I don't want to look at you. You cast spells with those blue eyes and that quirky smile."

I laughed loud enough to turn some heads, but I made sure to speak so only she could hear. "You don't want to want me. That's a whole different story."

"And you are an arrogant ass." Only her mouth was tugging up at the corners.

"Give me a chance."

"Why should I?"

"Because I can be fun to hang out with. Because you want to spend time with me as much as I want to spend time with you. Because we both deserve a break." I slid my hand into hers again, threading our fingers more tightly together. "Ms. Gabrielli. Would you go out with me?"

"A date?"

"Exactly. You say I don't understand your passion for the Mission District. That your neighborhood is in trouble. I want to know more about how I can help. You can tell me about your memories of being here as a child and your family's history in this neighborhood. I want to hear how you think things can change."

"Is this BS?"

"No. We'll go someplace fun and enjoy a relaxing meal and talk about whatever you want. No strings."

Not that I wasn't fantasizing about taking her upstairs, stripping off that outfit and kissing every inch of her delicious body. But hope was rising inside me. Hope that maybe Sloane could be more than a friend or a lover. Her sweet generosity, her determination to fix what was wrong, her enormous heart. I yearned to be part of her life more than anything I'd ever wanted before.

She fiddled with the saltshaker. "It's been a long time

since I've dated." She looked up, frowning. "Not that I haven't been asked out."

"I'm surprised there isn't a line out the door." She laughed full-out and my body warmed with a pleasure I couldn't place. It wasn't lust, or at least not only lust. I'd made her laugh and it felt good.

"There is often a line at the door. People hungry for what I can cook and not how well I can kiss."

"I can give you a recommendation."

"Some of my regular customers have posted online that we're together. You're here every day."

"I did see a few tweets after the mess with April. I printed out the picture. You look so hot in your chef hat."

"You always manage to cheer me up, even when I'm angry with you." Her breath smelled sweet, like caramel. She must have eaten dessert. If I kissed her, I'd taste it too.

I quashed that thought. "I've been in the media a lot lately. We'll be discreet so you aren't affected."

"I wouldn't want my family mentioned in any of the posts or tweets."

"I'll protect you from those jerks, I promise."

She smiled so sweetly, the kind of smile that made her eyes shine. I wished I could make them shine all the time. "I know you wouldn't do anything to hurt me."

I craved the sweetness of her sexy mouth—wanted to lose my soul in her soft body. But Sloane was hesitant about our relationship, and I wouldn't do anything to make her uncomfortable. No matter what Andrew said, I was nothing like Frank. "What do you say?"

"I'll go out with you, but it has to be tonight. The staff has given me the night off and the restaurant opens tomorrow at eleven. The kitchen staff and I arrive at nine thirty on a Sunday."

Lori the bartender wandered over. "You can take tomorrow too, Sloane. Poppy has got things well in hand." Lori sent a wink my way before strolling back to the bar.

"Have you won her over to your side?"

"One must find allies where one may."

Sloane giggled softly. "She's a pushover for hot guys."

"You think I'm hot?"

"Sorry, but this restaurant has a no stroking policy."

I grinned and she grinned back, our gazes locked, our eyes crinkled at the corners. My chest tightened as her smile warmed my world. This. This was what I needed. Sloane was who I needed.

"I have a quick session in the studio at one this afternoon, but I should be able to pick you up around four. How does that sound?"

"I can meet you there."

"It's better if I pick you up. Your apartment is on the way."

"I suppose you know where I live."

"I do." She raised her brows. "I was curious. And maybe a little stalkerish."

She rolled her eyes. "Fancy or casual?"

"Wear the hat, the jacket, sexy panties and nothing else."

"Not even shoes?" she teased back without blinking an eye.

"Bring spiky heels."

"Spiky heels make good weapons, remember?"

"I'm hoping you won't impale me if I keep you happy."

"You'd have to keep me very happy." She realized what she'd said and blushed, looking away.

I was tempted to expound on just how happy I could make her, but instead I took the high road. "Casual. Definitely casual."

"The restaurant you're taking me to had better be good."

"The food is always amazing."

"What's the name of the restaurant? Maybe I know the owners."

"Adagio."

"I've never heard of it."

"Bring a warm sweater. We'll be outdoors and indoors. Oh, and since you don't have to cook tomorrow, bring an overnight bag. Jokes aside, I promise—hands off unless you beg me."

"An overnight bag? Now you're pushing it. I have to be back at the restaurant."

"Lori said you can get back late."

"Lori's not the boss."

"You're going to have fun. I promise."

"Camping in the Sierras?"

"Would you like that?" I loved hiking and camping. Anything to get away from the stress.

"Sure."

"Not my plans this time around, but if you'd like, we can plan a trip to Tahoe or Redwood National Park or Yosemite. Plenty of camping in NorCal."

She scrunched up her mouth in a sexy pout. What would she do if I tried to kiss away that expression?

"You're not going to tell me anything else, are you?"

"I'd rather surprise you."

"I'm okay with surprises, as long as I can bow out if I decide I don't want to jump out of a plane or walk a tightrope between two tall buildings."

"I'll save those for our fifth and sixth dates."

"You're an optimist."

"When I'm with you."

"See you later." She smiled and rose, then walked toward

the kitchen, swaying a little more than usual, her skirt brushing her thighs with every swing of her hips. The server brought my meal, only my appetite had shifted to more carnal dishes. I ate what I could and left a good tip, already cementing down a melody to the rhythm of Sloane's exquisite body.

9

Victor arrived at four with a bag in hand. "Here."

I opened it to find leather pants. "What's this?"

"I'm on my girl tonight." He held up two helmets.

"Your girl? Do you mean that BMW monster?"

He laughed. "Shh. You'll insult her. I thought you might get a kick out of taking a ride. A little adrenaline never hurts on a first date. I have an extra jacket. Do you have boots?"

I sighed softly, not wanting him to hear the excitement I was feeling. "Yes." Fortunately, I'd put my extra clothes and toiletries in a backpack and not an open tote bag.

I hadn't been sure about what to wear. An outdoor casual request could mean anything from a romantic picnic to a hike along the windy headlands. I'd dressed more for the romantic picnic with a calf-length, three-quarter sleeved print dress in a warm jersey fabric, flats and a warm sweater. I realized my mistake as soon as I saw Victor's outfit. Black leather pants, long-sleeved form fitting tee and the usual leather jacket.

Too delicious for words. I was in big trouble tonight, but

then what had I expected? I'd accepted a sleepover date with the city's most eligible bachelor.

"Should I change or just put the pants on under the dress?"

"You look beautiful. Just slip on the pants and boots." He leaned against the closed door. "I'll wait."

I turned my back and slid on the pants, then dug the calf-high boots out of my closet. Sitting on the couch, I yanked them on. It was a tight fit over the pants, but they worked. "Where are we going exactly?"

"To see the sunset and enjoy a delicious dinner."

I liked that idea. He carried my backpack to the bike and slipped it into one of the leather bags that hung on the side. "Okay, but I'm only going for the food and the sunset." He laughed. "Why do you call it a she?"

"Have you ever ridden a bike?"

"No."

"More appropriate, really. The engine turns her into a giant vibrator. It's quite the enjoyable ride for most women, I hear. Especially if you lean forward." He laughed at my shocked expression. "Just stating facts."

His smile quirked at the corners as he helped me into the second leather jacket, zipped it much more slowly than was necessary, and showed me how the Bluetooth inside the helmet worked. We'd be able to talk easily as we rode.

The jacket was way too big and smelled only faintly of Victor's delicious scent, as if he didn't wear it as often as the other. He took his seat first and started the engine. When I wiggled awkwardly behind him, I discovered the seat did vibrate, and had to choke back my laughter. I squeezed his shoulders and he patted my hands. "Let me know if it's too much and you want to pull over. I'm here to help you out if you feel the need to—"

"You are a royal ass."

"You have a beautiful ass. I don't believe I mentioned that when I was fucking you on my desk last week. Round and a lovely shade of pink. Not like the salmon you serve, but more like—"

"Can we just go?"

"Whatever you say, Chef." We pulled onto the street and were soon zipping in and out of traffic. I'd started out with my hands on his shoulders, but quickly moved them to his waist. He tugged them a little tighter when we were at a red light. "Just right."

In this position I could sit straight or lean into his shoulder. I would have liked it better without the helmet, but I was pretty sure he wouldn't have allowed me to take it off. He might have a bad boy rep, but Vic had a sweet protective side he pulled out when we were together, except... Maybe not so sweet in the bedroom.

I shivered so hard Vic noticed. "You okay?"

"Really good." The vibration wasn't exactly bringing me to a roaring orgasm, but if I was on the bike long enough, I'd probably be ready for more fun.

And what the fuck was I thinking? Dinner and sunset. Dinner and sunset. Vic was off the menu.

When we crested Nob Hill going a little too fast, I squealed and squeezed him tighter. "You're doing this on purpose!"

"Feels good to have you so close."

"Seductive devil."

"I'm taking that as a compliment." He chuckled and pulled to the side so I could open my eyes and really take a look. "It's spectacular."

"My city. I love her."

"My city too."

"You're one of the reasons I love her. If we weren't wearing helmets, I'd kiss you."

"If we weren't wearing helmets, I'd kick your ass."

A familiar pressure settled on my leg, squeezing it. "You say that now, but the vibrations..." His hand moved farther up my leg.

"Hands on the wheel."

"Have you noticed my bike doesn't have a wheel?"

"Fuck you." But I was laughing so hard and it felt so good.

We got back on the road. "I admit I go a little cave man around you."

"A little."

"You like it."

A statement. "Have I said I like it?"

"You don't have to."

"No?"

"Your body tells me you like it. It sings to me."

"What are you talking about?" I couldn't decide if I should laugh or tell him he was reading me like a book.

He chuckled as he leaned to the left to make a sharp turn. My stomach flipped and I clung to his belt as if it were the only thing keeping me on the bike. When we righted again I breathed a sigh of relief. This was going to take some getting used to. "Tell me."

"Men are simple songs with clear melodies. A woman is a classical aria. Nuanced. Passionate. Complicated yet crystalline. Perfect."

"An aria? Really? What kind?"

"In your case...a song of strength and soul, but also vulnerability."

"Like one of those crazy Valkyries?"

"No, nothing like that. Uniquely you. Courage and heart combined."

His words warmed my heart. A strong urge to kiss him had me leaning forward, only it was impossible with helmets. Good thing. Still... "That was a lovely thing to say."

"I can be sweet with the right inspiration."

"What kind of song are you?"

He grunted in a way that made me think he was frowning. "I don't know. Some kind of racy mashup probably."

I sensed pain in his words. "I'd say more a rock ballad."

"What I write to sing at the clubs?"

"I've heard your CD. Your heart is in those songs."

"You bought my CD?" He sounded so pleased.

"If I'd written a book, would you buy it?"

He laughed. "If it was a romance novel."

"You read romance?"

"I'd read yours, 'cause then I'd know your secrets."

We were close to the Fisherman's Wharf area. Great restaurants and viewing areas for the sunset. An excellent choice for a first official date. This section of San Francisco was alive with tourists, souvenir shops and king crab stands. At a red light I noticed a Mom and Dad in their mid-thirties passing out roasted almonds to three kids, every one of them wearing I Survived the Hills of San Francisco tee shirts. Two of the children were arguing.

"They've got their hands full," I said. The kids were all under eight. When the small bags of almonds and juice boxes had been distributed to everyone's satisfaction, the parents sat on the next bench. Dad snaked his arm around his wife while she rested her head on his shoulder, smiling. He kissed the top of her head.

"You want kids when you find the right guy?" Vic asked,

swerving between tour busses and ride share traffic when the light turned green again.

"I come from a very large family. Most of my siblings and cousins are married. I already have four nephews and an uncountable number of first cousins, second cousins and more on the way. I believe Gabriellis can be found in every state." Vic chuckled. "I'd like to add to the mix one day, but only in a solid marriage and not right away. Couples should take the time to learn about each other before they have kids. What about you?"

"I doubt there's a woman who'd have me. Here we are."

I stared at the back of his helmet in wonder as he turned his Scrambler into a small parking lot. His comment hadn't sounded like a joke. Why would he think a woman wouldn't have him? He was handsome and fun to be with. A little reckless maybe, but a good marriage would steady him. Vic wouldn't go for a woman who'd want him for his money or status. No, Vic would want a woman who could laugh with him, love his city, share his music, ride his vibrating girl through the countryside or the city. Someone who loved racy indie mashups more than a top ten hit.

His hand in my hair forcing my mouth to meet his, the way he'd spun me around and taken me against his desk, the feel of his tongue and his cock... God, I was wet with lust every night. I'd been so sure I could leave thoughts of him behind, but my body still burned when I saw him. Still yearned for more. Vic still pushed my buttons like no one else and my plan to get him out of my system had been a giant fail.

If there was ever a man to get your wild on with, Victor Hanley's the guy. Caty's words danced in my head. *I'm living vicariously.* Her prognosis wasn't hopeful, but she hadn't lost her spark, her snarky wit. Her courage was heroic.

As we coasted to a stop, salt air scented with freshly caught seafood filled my lungs. I'd make a point of buying something off a boat tomorrow, fresh for a fabulous menu special.

"Isn't it great? Listen." Vic had removed his helmet and closed his eyes, taking in the ding of a distant buoy, the swish of water hitting pier stanchions, gulls calling out to the foolish tourists who fed them. A motorboat cut through the peace of the moment, rushing by and leaving a wake that rocked a smaller sailboat, the owner shaking his head in disgust. The sound of the engine had gotten Vic's attention.

"Asshole. That move was illegal." He glanced at me. "Probably a couple of teens. I wasn't let loose on the water until I'd proven I knew the rules."

A colorful sign painted with sailboats and the Golden Gate Bridge held pride of place over a small building to the right. It looked like a place to rent tackle and buy bait. The San Francisco Cove Marina. My heart beat a little faster. I loved boating. Maybe he'd take me to his private island, chain me to his bed and... I laughed as he glanced at me with a puzzled expression. "Nothing. Just imagining what your secret plans might entail."

A guard recognized Vic and waved us into a gated lot. Vic maneuvered the bike into a reserved spot near the main path and parked. A blonde male employee greeted us, holding out his hand to help me off the bike and out of my helmet. His smile was wide and more than friendly. Vic slid easily to his feet and thanked the young man, giving him a look that was all about getting-the-fuck-away-from-his-woman. The man took a few steps back then disappeared behind one of the buildings.

Vic's smile was way too smug. I decided to have some fun. "I get horribly seasick on boats."

He froze, his face falling. "Oh. I should have asked. I wanted it to be a surprise."

I grinned. "Gotcha! I love sailing. Took lessons as a kid on a nearby lake when my family and I went camping."

"You like camping?"

"Yeah, but not with my brothers. The twins would always run off pretending to be mighty hunters and we'd spend half the day looking for them. One day they ran into a moose. Huge animal. That was it. They stayed close to the campsite after that."

"You're older?"

"Birth order: Tony Jr., Kathy, the infamous twins—Angelo and Joey—then me and Caty. I'm only a year younger than the twins."

"But you still had to chase them through the woods?"

"Caty and I were with Dad."

Vic laughed and smoothed down my helmet hair before I had a chance. I closed my eyes for a second, enjoying the soft touch of his hands.

"I'm jealous," he said.

"Of what?"

"Your family."

"They can be overwhelming, but I can't imagine life without them." He did look kind of pitiful. "Come with me for a Mangia Monday."

"Mangia Monday?"

"Yep. We all help cook or barbecue. It's the only time during the week I see my family together in one place."

"You do this every week?"

"I try. I miss them when I can't make it."

"Meeting everyone at once would be terrifying."

"If they like you, they'll torture you."

"Not reassuring at all."

We walked to the marina office where the owners greeted him like a close friend, then practically swore a blood oath to keep an eye on his bike. He left the helmets in their care as well.

I peeked at the expensive yachts moored at the nearby pier, some of them seventy feet long and two masted. "Never sailed on one of those girls."

"We won't be doing the sailing. Not tonight. My cat's down this way. I'll introduce you to the captain and first mate slash galley slave. You'll like them."

"Sounds great. And I'm not allergic to animals."

He laughed. "A catamaran. A beauty of a double-hull. No pussy cats." He scanned my body, his gaze raking over all the key points. "Although..."

"Dirty boy." But I wanted his attention. Every bit of it. Dirty or not.

"You have no idea, Ms. Gabrielli."

My body was tingling. Time to change the subject. "I've never sailed in a cat. They're fast?"

"Yes, and stable too. I wouldn't presume to take it out on my own, but *Adagio* handles amazingly well, even along the rougher coastal waters. It shines in the Hawaiian Islands and Caribbean."

I laughed. "So *Adagio* isn't a restaurant."

"No. But the food is great."

"Well, let's see it." He pulled my backpack out of the side bag, loosening the strap to sling it over my shoulders, then grabbed his own gear. It was cool near the water and the wind had picked up, blowing my skirt around, but I still wore my borrowed leather pants.

So far, we were lucky and the forecast hadn't mentioned

fog. It was August and large fog banks blew in almost every day in the late afternoon.

He held out his hand and smiled. "C'mon. We only have a few hours until sunset." He was excited and happy and I wanted that for him. I took his hand, my heart still walking a tightrope of feelings, my gut telling me to open my arms and jump.

We walked slowly along the dock as Vic pointed out some of the more elaborate features on the other large craft. One had two hot tubs, because one is never enough. Another a twenty-five-foot sailboat mounted on the stern so the owners could leave the enormous cruiser behind and take a spin in a quiet cove. We passed smaller sloops and powerboats, all of them in pristine condition.

The joke was if you liked to sail it was better to have a friend with a boat than to own a boat yourself. The docking fees alone were probably way above my pay grade.

The sailboat at the end of the dock caught my eye, a unique craft when compared to the others. Two men stood on the dock chatting about something, but they turned and smiled when they heard us tramping in their direction.

We came to a halt in front of them. "Permission to come aboard, Captain?" Vic asked.

"Aye, sir. All's prepared for your trip." He tipped his orange and black San Francisco Giant's baseball cap to me, adding a warm smile. "Welcome aboard, Ms. Gabrielli."

"Thank you, Captain." The remainder of his outfit included a basic long-sleeved navy tee, khaki pants, and typical boating shoes. He was a little on the plump side but held himself with the authority one might expect from a sea captain.

I couldn't tell if this was just a show for my benefit or not, but the traditional words managed to pump up my excitement. Vic introduced Paul, the captain, and Drew, his first mate and chief cook. It was obvious from the way they were clasping hands on the dock they were a couple, which made me feel more secure about our journey. I'd never sailed on a cat before and had always associated a multi-hulled sailboat with speed but not necessarily stability. An experienced couple sailing together wouldn't be taking any chances with the weather or the currents. The San Francisco Bay was dangerous at the best of times.

When I mentioned my concerns to Vic, I got the full lecture on how catamarans were much safer, faster and more comfortable than mono-hulled boats.

"Paul and Drew have been sailing cats for over twenty years," he added.

I held up my hands in surrender. "I'm officially sold."

"Stow your gear downstairs in the cabin on the right. Towels are in the closet near the entrance to the head. The shower's in the next compartment. I'm going to speak to Paul about the weather and our trip to Half Moon Bay. We'll be leaving in twenty."

"We're going to Half Moon Bay?"

"Sure, it's just down the coast. Have you been there? It's a great little town, especially when the weather cooperates."

"A long time ago." I'd been a teen, surly and not in the mood to get all sandy. Of course, my twin brothers did everything they could think of to get sand in my hair and inside my clothes. I still had a sea glass pendant Mom made them pay for to make up for my disheveled state. I laughed every time I saw it in my jewelry case.

"You'll like it there." He kissed me on the cheek and turned away, looking as excited as a school kid on vacation. I took the stairs and came to a halt when I walked through the door.

The starkly elegant cabin had everything a seafarer needed, but nothing fancy that took away from the feel of being on an adventure. The bed was an oddly shaped queen constructed to fit perfectly into the space, the headboard being at the narrower section. The walls on either side held shelves with a raised lip on the bottom to hold the books or other items in place when the seas grew rough. The duvet was a blueberry shade, but the brighter throw pillows worked to brighten the room. The head, or bathroom, was elegant in its own way and larger than I thought it might be, as was the closet. I left the cabin and explored a little farther, finding a sitting room slash office at the bow of the boat. I wasn't surprised to see what looked like a keyboard case on a shelf near the floor. Maybe I could get Vic to play for me.

I traded the boots, the leather pants and the dress for a pair of jeans, a tee shirt and a pullover sweater, slipping on pretty flats with straps at the last minute. They had rubber soles and should suit well. No reason to freeze on the ocean, although I wished I'd brought a windbreaker of some kind.

Then I remembered the leather jacket. I held the lining to my nose, breathing in his scent, just noticeable under the faint aroma of his cologne.

I walked upstairs and explored the main level with its all-purpose galley and anchored table surrounded by cushioned seating in the shape of a C. Down three steps was a larger room with a bar, a leather couch, a coffee table and a couple of nice chairs in light tans and shades of rust. The room had small double paned windows on almost every wall, a few of them open and letting in the breeze. The view would be spectacular once we were on our way.

"Do you like it?"

"Love it." Vic grinned and offered me a glass of red wine

as Drew placed a platter of delicious-looking appetizers on the coffee table.

"Thank you." I smiled at Paul's partner.

"I do most of the cooking," Drew explained. "My love does most of the steering. It's for the best." He winked at me.

Drew was slimmer than Paul, wearing dark jeans, a black tee shirt that said something about coffee and a good book, and a dark red button-down shirt in a heavier fabric. He had a cool mustache and barely there beard, which gave him a sophisticated look, even in jeans.

"It's nice not to have to cook once in a while," I said.

"She's a terrific chef. Has her own restaurant," Vic's eyes shone with a possessive pride.

"Really? Where?"

"Bel Cielo. In the Mission."

"Paul and I have eaten there. I had the Valdostano and Paul the...let me see...the Brasato Barolo. Absolutely delicious."

"Thank you. I hope you come back. This time it's on the house."

"Oh, how lovely. We will definitely be back."

"I'm closing in fifty-two days, so don't forget to make a reservation soon."

"What do you mean you're closing? That would be a travesty."

"You might want to talk to the real estate mogul about it." I tilted my head in Victor's direction, then walked toward the door that led outside to the bow. Between the hulls, they'd attached an enormous net which hung over the open water. A couple of lounge chairs were positioned against the main cabin, but I chose a nearby bench. Thinking about my restaurant closing had soured my mood.

A few moments later, Victor appeared, his expression unsure.

"I'm sorry. I shouldn't have put you on the spot like that. I don't know why I did it," I said.

He offered me his hand. "I get it."

"No. It was unfair." I took his hand and squeezed it. "I won't do it again. Today is just us. I'm going to try really hard to let it go while I'm with you."

A slow smile spread across his face. "We're setting off. I have work to do and would prefer you stay in the cabin so you don't get bonked on the head. Once you've taken a few trips with us, you'll be considered crew and I'll put you to work."

"I know my way around a sailboat."

"I'm fairly certain this one is nothing like what you're used to. Next time we'll go out and I'll show you the ropes. Pun intended."

The fresh air had soothed me, so I rose up on my toes and kissed his cheek. "Aye, aye."

Vic's body relaxed as he led me inside. "Here in the salon or in the galley?"

"Wherever the view is best."

"Then here." He led me to a chair near the coffee table in the salon. "It won't take long before we're underway." He kissed my cheek, lingering a little longer than I had, then disappeared outside.

The motor started up with a low roar and Vic jumped to the dock to untie the bow and stern ropes on the starboard side, tossing them to Drew. When he was done he hopped gracefully back on board, his body strong and fit, naturally athletic even though he'd never participated in team sports when I'd known him. On deck he moved from job to job, signaling to Paul with a raised hand or a slice through the air that he was done, the routine one he seemed to gain pleasure from, if his grin was anything to go by.

God, he was beautiful, those light blue eyes slicing into my soul every time he looked at me. Lately he'd dropped his guard and I'd caught a flash of the pain he carried but tried to hide from the world. My family had always been a part of me, a vital presence in my life and in my heart, but Vic had lost his family a long time ago, not by death but from alienation and abandonment. How does a child ever feel safe without a loving home?

An overwhelming yearning to hold him came over me. To soothe him. To show him he wasn't alone. Vic wasn't weak on any level, but like most people, he needed a dose of compassion. A tender touch. Someone to listen when he opened his heart.

Adagio pulled away from the slip, turning into the channel that would take us toward the middle of the bay and heading under the magnificent Golden Gate Bridge. Once we were positioned correctly, Vic and his crew unfurled the mainsail and the breeze became part of our power source. Captain Paul steered us expertly between the bridge's piers and west into the Pacific Ocean.

I'd gone outside on the deck to get a better view, but the cool wind was turning my nose and ears to ice cubes. Vic pushed a knit hat over my hair, making sure it covered my ears, then draped a blanket over my shoulders. I felt like a five-year-old, or maybe a woman whose man cared enough about her to make sure she didn't freeze. He moved behind me and wrapped his arms around my body, pulling me against his chest.

I leaned back even farther, cozy and warm and loved. I stiffened at the thought, then breathed in a deeper breath and relaxed again. Loved couldn't be what I was feeling. I'd lost my ability to think logically when I'd jumped into this date. But I was so comfy and Vic smelled so good.

"This okay?" he asked. "I know you told me hands off, but you were shivering."

"Mmm."

We stayed in this perfect spot on this perfect day for another few minutes. His warm breath tickled my ear. "Hungry?"

"Mmm." I snuggled a little closer.

He laughed. "We should enjoy some of those appetizers so Drew doesn't complain about being under-appreciated. He can be a whiner."

"I heard that!"

"And he's nosy," he whispered.

"I heard that too!"

"And he has super hearing. Paul and I are in awe."

We feasted on grape leaves stuffed with rice and lamb, tabouli with spicy mint, falafel with a delicious dipping sauce and several other wonderful bites. "This is yummy. I was really hungry." Vic was spending more time watching me than what he was eating. "What?"

He popped another falafel in his mouth, chewed and swallowed. "There's something erotic about sitting across from a beautiful woman, watching her scoop up hummus with warm pita, following her hand as she raises it to her open mouth."

He managed to make the words hummus and warm pita bread sound sexy. I stood and walked to the window, sipping my wine. The couch was too close and too inviting.

Victor picked up a napkin and followed me, pointing to the corner of my mouth. "You have tzatziki sauce right... here." He leaned closer as if to wipe it away, but kissed it away with lips and tongue, then patted it dry with the napkin. He waited, wary, watching for any move that I might attack him.

Instead, I laughed. "To be fair, I should clarify a few things about that first morning."

"Oh?"

He'd backed away a step or two, giving me my personal space. "I didn't knee you because you kissed me."

"No?"

"It was an automatic reaction to...to my fear."

"I frightened you?" He took my hand, brow wrinkling.

"No. I was afraid because of how much I liked it."

"You're saying you almost emasculated me because you kissed me back and enjoyed it?" He grinned broadly.

"I'm glad I'm so entertaining."

"You are so much more than entertaining, Ms. Gabrielli."

"Victor..."

"You fight for what's right. Put your heart into everything you do."

"I can't do all that much. I'm not one of the corporate wheelers and dealers. I don't have political connections."

"You've been involved in helping your neighborhood for years, running clothing drives, food drives, helping out at the soup kitchen."

"How do you know that?"

He winked. "I have my ways."

He sure did. Right now, his scent, his closeness, his smooth baritone had me trembling.

"You pour out love and care in all directions, but sometimes..." He brushed my cheek with his knuckles, then slid his hand under my ear and tugged playfully on my lobe. "Sometimes it's nice to be cared for by someone who cares back."

"I'm not a hermit. I go out on dates."

"According to my good sources you go out once or twice, then you dump the poor guy."

"I'm picky." I folded my arms, taking a step back.

"Should I prepare for the worst?"

His eyes were twinkling with mischief, but I could play too. "Don't worry. I'm always nice about it." I poked him in the chest. "Who at the restaurant ratted about me?"

"I have sworn never to divulge my sources. You can try to torture the info out of me. Sexual torture would be my preference."

"I'm a patient person."

"I look forward to our first session."

I sighed and glanced away. "You can't think of this as long term. We're in opposite camps."

His smile disappeared. "Who broke your heart? Tell me where he is and I'll teach him some manners."

I had no intention of answering that question, but maybe now was a good time. I'd never spoken to anyone but Caty about how hurt I'd been.

"I could ask my sources. They've been reliable so far." He'd closed the gap again.

I glanced out the window. The sun was closer to the horizon, the ocean glistening with silver streaks. Pelicans dove with reckless abandon for fish, folding their wings like dragons, giving up caution to get what they wanted most. "My staff wouldn't know."

"Sloane..." He frowned, starting to put things together.

"I was a stupid kid. In love with a good friend who never asked me out. Who changed my life with a kiss, even a drunk one, saved my ass then left without saying goodbye."

"I'm sorry."

"He never called or looked me up, even though we lived in the same city."

"There wasn't anyone else."

"Liar."

"I dated women who didn't want happily ever after. We used each other and said goodbye. It was dirty and fast and all I could risk."

"You must have known I cared about you. I thought you felt something for me too."

"I wanted to ask you out. Wanted to kiss you from the day you put that guy who asked for the Cliff Notes in his place. But not asking you out was something I did right. The shit I was involved in... It would have killed me if I'd put you in danger."

I turned back. "Danger? You weren't dealing drugs, were you?"

"Nothing like that."

"Well, what—"

"Do you know why my dad went to jail the first time?"

"Art theft?"

"He was huge. The best in the business. He trained me beginning when I was twelve. I can pick just about any lock ever made. Even now. Steal from people while we're having a nice chat. I've done it all, the most expensive pieces, all restored and sold on the black market.

"When my dad was arrested for grand theft the first time, not this last time, I went to the cops and they called in the FBI. I figured they'd just lock me up, but I was a valuable asset in their wider investigation."

My high up connections in the music industry got me a lawyer who worked out an amazing deal. No jail time. No house arrest. I'd been a juvenile when it had started and I'd come forward. My lawyer made them believe I'd thought my mom was in danger. That I'd been threatened and coerced the entire time."

"Was that true?"

"Partly, but I loved the adrenaline rush. I turned myself in because I knew they'd come after me once they started to dig deeper. Also, I was afraid I might keep stealing. It was as addictive as the cigarettes. So I took away my choices. The life I knew was over, but there were other people I could keep out of it. When my deal was struck I got more serious about my music. Once it started to flow, I realized composing was what I should have been doing all along. The worst part was the reporters always hanging around. They wouldn't leave Mom alone. Even six months later."

"Or you."

"Or me. The feds took all my profits from the thefts, but I was fine. I had the money my grandfather left me when he died and some royalty money from my first hit."

He sighed and met my gaze. "That was what I was involved in when we became friends. You were beautiful and perfect and I couldn't hurt you that way. Couldn't ruin your life."

"Tell me the truth. It's over?"

"I write songs and run a recording studio and a men's club. That's it. Even quit smoking, although I might have a jelly bean addiction." He raked long fingers through his hair. "That stupid kiss put you in danger. The best laid plans and all that."

"You punched that guy so hard he went flying." I laughed.

"I was drunk. It seemed like the right thing to do."

"Would you punch him again?"

He didn't hesitate for a second. "I'd do a lot worse today." He twisted away and strode toward the door that led to where Paul was positioned. "We can turn around if you want."

I walked up behind him and put my arms around his waist, leaning against his back. "I'm a good listener. And you promised me Half Moon Bay and a great meal."

"I did." His body had tensed, as if he'd expected the worst. But he'd told me everything and it had almost broken my heart to hear his story.

"When your dad got out of jail he just kept doing what he used to do?"

"Yes. Only he was worse than ever. I had to turn him in."

"Do you ever talk to him?" I took his hand and brought him to one of the chairs.

"He calls, but I don't pick up."

He sat and rubbed his face, his body hunched over in pain—the kind of pain that lives in your head and your heart every minute of every day. When my grandparents died together in a car accident, I'd felt that pain. Now most of my memories were good ones.

I moved behind him and began to massage his shoulders and neck. He moaned with pleasure as I worked on a particularly bad knot.

"Oh god. You're so good at this. Please don't stop."

"My brothers and father played touch football whenever we were together. Mom, Caitlyn, Kathy and I were put in charge of bandaging, icing and making sure they hadn't sprained a muscle or gotten a concussion. They'd sit there and grunt and groan, but we knew they appreciated it. Caty was a world class swimmer, the only real athlete in the bunch."

Vic groaned again, rolling his shoulders and sighing. "Your hands are gold."

"You must have a masseuse at the Gate Club."

"I never have the time to go."

"That's complete crap. You can set your own schedule. Who's the whiner now?"

"Ha!" A familiar voice drifted in from the galley.

"See what I mean about Drew being nosy?" Vic laughed, twisting to snake his arm around my waist and pulling me so I was in his lap.

"Hey!"

He grinned, rubbing his hand up and down my arm. "Am I in danger of being attacked?" he asked, his wicked smile sending my brain to the rear guard and my body to the front lines.

"No, but it looks like I might be."

His eyes burned with a yearning to connect. "Only if you give me permission."

"I'm not about to dive over the side and swim back to land, so I have no choice but to accept your conditions. You're a pirate who stole me away on his ship."

His boyish grin brought a sweet twinge to my chest. "I always wanted to be a pirate. Can I be Long John something?" He scanned my body with a sultry expression.

"Everything is sex with you."

The low rumble of his laughter vibrated through my belly, sending all kinds of wicked tingles dancing around my body. "I'm a straight man and you're a beautiful woman. I shall begin my attack now. Give me a heads up if I'm in danger."

He kissed my neck, working his way up to my ear. His warm breath smelled like grape leaves and wine. I sighed. Heaven.

"You okay?"

"Perfect." I snuggled a little closer, pressing into his lap with my hip, surprised to find him growing hard.

"Um..."

"Sorry." I started to rise, but he held me tighter.

"I like you here."

"I'm getting that impression." He kissed the corner of my mouth. "You smell like a Mediterranean banquet."

"I was just thinking you smelled delicious too," he said, burying his nose in my hair as I threaded my fingers in his dark locks. He nibbled on my earlobe. "I want to taste you everywhere." His warm words teased my ear, sending a wave of shivers skimming over my skin.

"I..."

Before I could finish my sentence, he was kissing me and kissing me, only allowing me time to gasp in a breath before his mouth was on mine again. Vic demanded and my body submitted, allowing him free access without a hint of unease, despite my earlier plans. I melted in his arms, turning soft as he grew hard.

"You two are going to miss the sunset," Paul called from the galley.

I groaned and Vic pulled me closer. "Sunsets are overrated."

"It's rare to have a night so free of fog," Paul added.

I pulled away and stood, my knees a tiny bit shaky. He saw it, steadying me with a hand on my hip. I smoothed down my hair and straightened my sweater. "I'm only here for the food and the sunset, remember?"

10

We slipped on our leather jackets, stuffing hats and gloves in the pockets. I led Sloane to the deck where we'd get the best view. Paul was already stretched out on a lounge chair, coffee in hand.

Paul had turned the engine off as soon as we were out of the major shipping lanes. Running with sails alone was ideal, the peace the crew and I experienced with only the sound of wind and water renewed my often-sagging spirit. I'd stand alone on deck and wonder at the courage of the ancient explorers, relying only on stars to guide them, the wind and the currents to power them, their minds and hearts to steer them forward.

I tugged Sloane closer and she came willingly, sharing the pleasure and peace a California sunset could bring when all you saw was the green sea and the painted sky.

"So perfect. Thank you all for letting me board your amazing ship." She turned to Paul. "Who's piloting the boat, captain?"

"Drew's a licensed pilot, but he prefers to putter around in the galley," Paul said.

"I heard that!"

"It's true."

"Besides the point, love," shouted Drew. "I do not putter. You make me sound like an ancient galley drudge."

Sloane smiled. "If it makes you feel any better, I'm the land version of a galley drudge. Cooking and creating dishes feeds my spirit. We all need something like that to keep us sane."

"The sea is the place where I feel free and easy," Paul said. "I can forget the stress of my job and everything else when I'm sailing."

"What do you do, Paul?"

"Drew and I own an antique store in the Castro District. Fortunately, we have the best employees in the world. They run the shop when Vic wants to take out *Adagio*."

"So, you don't own a boat?"

"Oh no. It's always better to have a friend with a boat than own one of your own." We laughed together at the old adage I'd told Sloane earlier. It was true. Maintaining *Adagio* throughout the year cost me more than maintaining The Zone. But the peace she brought me was worth every penny.

I patted Paul on the shoulder. "These two bums have been urging me to take a trip to Tahiti, Australia and New Zealand. It's been one of my dreams to make that sail."

"It sounds like heaven. I've never been to any of those places."

I wanted to ask her if she'd go with me, but that was me being impulsive again. I had to play it cool. Stick to my plan. Nudge Sloane into my arms, then convince her she didn't want to be anywhere else.

"Paul and Drew's store is amazing. High end and unique."

"I'll have to stop by."

"Remind me to give you our card," Paul said.

"We'll make a reservation at Bel Cielo this week. There's still time, right?" Drew shouted down.

"Yes. And I have faith in Vic. He'll find a way to keep us open." Sloane sighed against me.

I tried hard not to tense up as she snuggled closer. Right now, it didn't look good. The engineer's report was due any day and I'd have to tell Sloane soon that I'd heard back from Andrew. Renewing the restaurant's lease with the same rent was off the table. The other two stores would not be allowed back in at all.

Frank loved to throw his power around. Especially if it meant fucking with something I was working on. I looked at Sloane's hopeful face and wanted to strangle my father. I was stuck in a deep crevice without a fucking rope. Sloane was relying on me, but she was going to end up being one more person on my list of people I'd let down.

I was never ruthless enough for Dad, forgiving enough for Mom, smart enough to save Damien's dad or a loyal enough son to ignore my father's crimes and not turn him into the cops. And now Sloane... Disappointing Sloane would be the hardest blow to take.

I only had weeks left, but all I could come up with was to keep hounding my uncle until he got Frank to cave. The only other option was not an option at all. I would not go to the prison and beg.

"It's so lovely." She turned in my arms, resting her head on my chest. "This is a peaceful place and we both needed some peace."

"We'll be docking at Half Moon Marina in about three hours. Would you like dinner?" Paul asked.

I tilted her head with a touch of my finger. "Sloane." My voice was hoarse, my body hungry.

She smiled and leaned forward, kissing me quickly, then using her teeth to pull on my bottom lip. "Maybe we can eat later?"

"Later sounds..." My mouth was a desert. I cleared my throat. "We'll let you know if we need anything, Paul." I made a couple of go away gestures behind Sloane's back. Paul slid quietly past us, taking the ladder to Drew after a discreet thumbs up.

When he'd gone I lifted Sloane, urging her to place her legs around my waist. She squeaked in surprise. "What are you doing? Put me down."

"No."

"That's it? No?"

"I'm a pirate, remember? What are pirates known for?" I squeezed both cheeks of her ass.

She buried her head against my neck, the edges of her mouth curling into my skin in a soft smile. "Making people walk the plank?"

"No planks on *Adagio*."

She met my gaze, her dark eyes reflecting the fairy lights on deck. "Spectacular sword fights?"

"No weapons, unless you count the knives in the galley and my Swiss army knife."

"Keelhauling?"

I laughed full-out. "Wow. You have a vicious imagination."

"I like the action-packed shows on TV when I have time to watch. Dangerous dragons, treacherous Vikings and creepy cowboy cyborgs."

"No rom coms?"

"They never seem to get it right."

"Ah, but dragons really do exist."

She pointed toward the north star. "Watch the skies, pirate."

Despite her protests, I carried her through the galley and into the salon, allowing her body to slide down until she was standing again. I kissed her cheek, then trailed my lips along her jaw to below her ear.

"Don't move."

"And if I do?"

I stroked the line of her neck, then slid the tips of my fingers under the top edge of her tee shirt. "I was planning on ravishing you like any true pirate. But if you try to escape I may change my mind."

She narrowed her eyes. "Can I ravish you too?"

Her words were a caress to the groin. "Anytime. Anywhere."

"Then I'll stay. For now."

I walked with as much cool as possible considering the state of my cock, closing the door that led to the galley. When I returned I kissed her, drawing it out to let her know how much I wanted her. "Your mouth is so sweet. I want to spend days and days and nights and nights kissing you."

"There's a poet inside you." She giggled.

I laughed. "You wouldn't say that if you heard my song lyrics."

"I want to hear them." She pushed my jacket down my arms and I let it fall to the floor. Her jacket was next. She peeked at the ceiling. "Do you think they'll hear us?"

"They're probably up there making out like teens. The motion of the boat makes everyone horny."

"First the bike, now the boat." Sloane giggled as I turned slowly, scanning the room. "What are you doing?" she asked.

"I've had so many fantasies involving you on *Adagio*. I'm trying to pick which one I want to try first."

"You're usually so impulsive."

"This is an important decision." I kissed her again, harder this time. "God, you're beautiful."

"You're beautiful too, Vic." Sloane placed a hand on my heart. "Here." I shook my head and went back to scanning, but she shifted position so she was in front of me again. "Why don't you believe it?"

I shrugged and did what I could to lighten the mood. "I'm just a horny pirate."

"Planning to ravish me."

I grinned and kneeled on the floor, lifting her shirt and unbuttoning her fly. "These. Off."

"A bossy pirate." She made a show of kicking off her shoes and unzipping and wiggling out of her jeans.

Still kneeling, I nuzzled her sex through the silky panties, taking in a deep breath before standing. Sloane moaned and I slid my hands up to her waist, backing her toward the bar. "Aren't you going to beg for mercy?" I asked.

"I never beg."

Oh, and I loved a challenge. "Mmm Hmm. You're going to beg tonight."

"Pretty confident for a guy who can't decide where to fuck his captive."

A shudder ripped through my horny self. "More dirty talk. Now."

"Only if you beg." She lifted my hand and slid a thumb into her mouth. I had to close my eyes as she sucked.

"You're asking for torture. Arms up." She did as ordered, all the while laughing and sighing at my antics. I took my time sliding the tee shirt off, enjoying each patch of flesh as it was slowly unveiled.

Her lacy purple bra matched the tiny bit of fabric covering her pussy.

I swallowed hard, trying to keep my over-enthusiastic dick from forcing me to throw her to the ground and ravish her at turbo speed. Wait a minute... Pirate. Captive. I lifted her again and she wrapped her legs around my hips.

"The couch is over there." Sloane pointed, as if I didn't know where the couch was.

I kissed the line of her jaw, pulling her closer and softening my tone. "Baby, this isn't your kitchen and you are not in charge." Lowering Sloane onto the bar, I stepped between her legs, pushing her thighs wider. She was breathing heavy, so I kissed her. Soft. Sweet. Hoping to help her relax, I nuzzled her neck and cupped one of her beautiful breasts. "You can tell me to stop."

Her nipples were hard but her eyes were a tiny bit deer in the headlights. "Isn't this a bad height? I mean, you're tall but—"

"Let the nerves go. This isn't our first time."

"Me? I don't get ner—"

"This is the perfect height for what I have in mind." I pulled down the cups of her bra, exposing her full breasts, then kissed the delicious curves. My body was on fire, her sexy energy seeping into every cell. I kissed her mouth again, not so gentle this time, using tongue and lips and teeth, stroking her back and arms to soothe her body and mind. I needed her all in, no doubts. No second thoughts.

In a way, it was our first time. This wasn't Sloane getting her fill so she could walk away clearheaded. Or me taking the edge off with a woman who used me in the same way. This was so much more and it was hitting us right between the eyes.

When we were together, we fit. We were more than us

alone. I'd heard this happened with couples but never believed it was something I'd ever feel. Not that she thought of us as a couple.

Not yet.

I stroked my hands up Sloane's silky thighs then licked a path along her neck to just below her ear. I rimmed the edges with the tip of my tongue, nibbling her lobe.

She purred. "I like that."

"Tell me what you want." I licked her nipple, teasing it with the tip of my tongue.

"Vic." Sloane threaded her fingers in my hair and yanked me close, arching her back to bring her chest to my mouth. I used my teeth.

"Oh, god. Vic."

I lifted my head. "You're mine tonight, JT."

"JT?"

"You're a juicy Italian tomato." I went back to my fun.

"I might have to... Oh... Have to kill you later."

"Later?" I stilled, smiling against her soft skin.

She pushed my mouth toward one of her nipples. "Not now."

I suckled each nipple, loving the soft whimpers she made. When I moved my knuckles over the thin purple fabric of her panties, targeting her clit, she opened her legs wide and pressed her hand against mine. No doubts now.

"More."

"Juicy and sweet. Makes me want to lick you everywhere." I peeled off her soaked panties and dropped them to the floor.

I spread her legs, dipped my head and blew on her throbbing sex. "Tell me I can call you JT."

"Oh god. Call me whatever... Whatever..." Sloane jerked as I licked her sex over and over, avoiding her clit, waiting for that first *please*. Her body arched, but I held her in place, trapping her exactly where I wanted her.

Damn it, she got me hard faster than anyone. I might not last through what I had planned.

"Vic... Please..."

I grinned. "Keep begging, captive, and I will rock your world."

11

Vic played my body like his Les Paul. Gentle strums and sudden flicks of his tongue. Deep humming tones that brought intense pleasure. His mouth and tongue and teeth sent lightning from my breasts to my sex, while his fingers... Oh god. His callused fingers slid into my pussy again and again. His thumb teasing my clit with the gentlest of strokes, never enough.

I cried with pleasure. I fucking begged. "Press...press harder."

"Hmm?" He licked my nipple and pinched the other.

I gasped from the pain. So good. "I want..."

"Say it."

"Please, Vic." I tried to arch my body closer, but he'd trapped me in place. Open and vulnerable and wanting so much more.

"Talk dirty."

"Fuck you."

"That's my girl."

He sucked harder on my nipple, his long skilled fingers

tormenting my sex. My body burned as I breathed in the scent of sea and sex and Vic. Glorious Vic.

He peeked up at me, mischief glittering in his eyes. "Keep begging."

"You ass." I gasped again when his fingers found a spot inside, curling and stroking, curling and stroking. Playing me like one of his songs.

I tried to squirm. "Please. I'm so close." But he was relentless. Teasing me to the top then backing away just a tiny bit—enough to drive me fucking crazy.

He stepped away to get a good look at the woman he was torturing, watching his fingers move in and out. "Your pussy is perfect."

"And suffering."

Vic laughed and pulled my upper body closer, pushing my thighs farther apart. He buried his fingers inside as we watched together. "Squeeze me."

It brought me so close I almost screamed.

"What do you want, beautiful Sloane?"

"I need you." I pulled at his waistband. "Please."

His smile was wicked and so fucking hot. He bent his head. The first lick over my clit destroyed me. The next brought me over. I spasmed around his fingers, his mouth now attached to my clit and sucking hard. This time I couldn't hold back the scream.

Vic was out of his pants in record time, slipping on a condom then lifting me and pressing my back against the wall. He plunged into my cunt without finesse, but I was on board in every way. Vic filled me like no one had before, stretching every inch, a perfect fit. He stilled for a moment, then moved out and back, each entrance a hard one, each exit excruciatingly slow.

My body was hungry enough to consume him whole.

Hitching my legs tighter around him, I thrust back. "Faster. I want it hard."

"Tell me dirty."

"Fuck me harder!" I should have begged for this sooner because Vic pounded into me with all the pent-up horniness he'd accumulated by playing my body and not letting me touch his cock. "Yes. Oh god."

I exploded with pleasure at the same time he groaned and slowed, thrusting once. Twice. Shuddering then relaxing with a long exhale. I'd grasped his thick hair in the process and noticed a few strands still tangled around my fingers when I moved them to his shoulders.

Well, he deserved it. Dirty pirate. For the first time I noticed the mirror behind the bar. I was grinning.

He stumbled backwards and lowered me to the ground, holding the condom when we pulled apart so there wouldn't be any accidents.

I leaned against the wall of passion, breathing hard. When he came back his large cock was still semi-erect, his body... Whoa. His body was glistening with sweat, and ripped and...

"You gonna stop ogling me?"

"Nope." I glanced out the window. It was dark as sin. "Let's go outside."

12

W e were back on the deck, still naked except for two large blankets. Sloane had said she wanted to look at the stars, but our bodies were practically letting off steam. We chose a lounge chair and she curled up in my lap. "You run hot," she said. "My personal sauna."

I stroked her shiny hair and tightened my caress. "Must be my Scottish side."

"I'd like to see you in a kilt."

"Hairy legs and all?"

"Especially the all, Long John."

"I didn't hurt you, did I? Went a little wild at the end." Her pussy was so tight and her small body seemed too delicate for a large guy like me to be manhandling. I'd been hesitant from the start to slam into her. Until she'd begged me.

Sex with Sloane was not just hot as fuck, it was fun.

Sloane twisted so she could see my face. "What if I promised to make it worth your while if you wore a kilt for me?"

"Will ya cook me some bannocks, lass?" She rolled her eyes. "My accent sucks." She nodded.

We laughed together. "I had something else in mind."

"I'm listening."

She kissed me, a sweet, delicious answer. She kept shifting her weight, a situation my cock was excited about. I tried to move her to the side. "Will you stop wiggling?"

"Not up for another go?"

I placed her hand over the section of the blanket my cock was currently tenting. "You always set me on fire, but I'm guessing you might be a little sore." I kissed her knuckles and winced. "Your fingers are ice cubes."

"I bet if I stuck them between your legs…"

"My balls would shrivel up."

After a few more minutes of stargazing, we snuck into the galley, gathered more of the delicious appetizers and a bottle of wine, then took the starboard stairs to the large bedroom below.

"Where were you going to sleep if I'd decided I didn't want Long John in my bed?"

"My gear is in the port hull."

"Really?"

"*Adagio* comes with two bedrooms and four beds on that side. My office on this side is another bedroom, but I never use it that way. In good weather we sometimes sleep on deck or in the salon. I can easily sleep over a dozen."

"So, the pirate captain gets the entire starboard hull?"

I nodded. "I value my privacy. I've written a lot of songs in these rooms."

"Can your crew scuttle a frigate?" Sloane tried using a pirate accent.

I laughed full-out, then pulled her closer. "That sounds dirty."

"Everything sounds dirty to you."

"I'll scuttle your frigate." I'd lowered my tone.

Her eyes widened. "It does sound dirty."

"I wrote you one of my dirty songs."

"You didn't."

"I'll sing it to you later."

"Now."

"No. You have to be naked and in my bed when I sing it."

"You have to be naked too."

"Not a hardship."

She giggled. "A hard ship."

I groaned. "That was really bad."

"I want to be really bad. Wild."

Sloane let the blanket fall to the floor, her nipples pebbled, her skin still bumpy from the cool air on deck. She pointed toward one of the chairs beside the table. "Let me feed you."

"Feed me?"

"Sit." She nudged me with icy fingers into one of the chairs by the small table, tore off a piece of pita and dipped it in the bowl of hummus. She faced me now, holding out the delicious morsel. "Keep your hands down. I'm feeding you."

I opened and Sloane slid the piece inside. I chewed slowly as she watched. I swallowed.

"I like to watch you eat."

"I like to eat you." Her breasts were at the perfect height for my mouth, so I leaned forward, taking a nipple. My hands went to her hips and I moved her toward me, forcing her to spread her legs so she could straddle my thighs.

Sloane's sexy little exhale had my dick growing harder.

She sat on my thighs. Trailed her fingers over my belly. I grabbed her wrists. "Just to let you know, those icy fingers are not going anywhere near my dick until they warm up a little."

I sucked her thumb into my mouth using my tongue the way I had when I sucked her nipple. I released it with a scrape of my teeth and a kiss on the tip. The index finger was next.

"That feels dirty too."

I finished with the index finger and guided it to her nipple, moving it over the wet nub. She closed her eyes. "You ever masturbate thinking of me?"

"Maybe."

I closed her thumb and index finger around her nipple. She pinched her body hard enough to quicken her breaths. "Did you beg the imaginary me the way you did the real me?"

I sucked on her other breast, then moved her fingers over. She played without guidance this time, pinching then twisting.

"I didn't beg."

"I counted seven times."

"Because you made me say please."

"And you did. Clearly. No mistaking your words." I kissed her neck, licking the mark I'd made earlier. "You begged."

"You think you're so smart." She sprang up. Her eyes glittered with mischief. "I'm going to make you beg."

"What happened to feeding me?"

"I'm hungry. You can wait." She kneeled and spread my legs, my cock pointing directly where I wanted it to go. "Be prepared to beg." She smoothed her hand over my belly. God, I ached for her. "I'm taking revenge."

"Sloane..."

"Shush. I'm torturing Long John."

When a beautiful woman threatens to use her mouth and tongue on your cock, you don't argue.

With both her hands on my inner thighs, she licked from root to tip. I grunted but didn't close my eyes. I wasn't missing a fucking moment of this. Sloane smiled, a study in wickedness. She grasped the base and squeezed, then licked the head, swirling her tongue along the rim. She smiled up at me. "You want more?"

"Fuck, yeah."

"Beg for it."

I'd never had a problem asking for what I wanted, but I wasn't going to beg. "Open your mouth and take me inside." I'd tried to make it more like a demand, but I was trembling slightly and my tone might have held a pleading note.

She giggled and lowered her head, lifting my balls and sucking one into her mouth.

"Oh...fuck..." I sucked in a breath and hissed it out slowly, digging my fingers into the arm of the chair. "So good..." was all I could croak.

She pumped my dick with her small tight grip, keeping her fingers pressed against the large veins, her other hand stroking the inside of my thigh. Her tongue continued to play with the sensitive sac, moving to the other ball to do the same. I was crazy with lust and had to be inside her right now.

"Do want me to suck you in? Swallow you down?"

I tightened my jaw to choke out the single word. "Yesss."

"Then say please eight times."

Fuck it. "Please. Please. Please. Please. Please. Please. Please. Pleaaaase."

"Good pirate." As she moved from my balls to my cock with her hot mouth, I threaded one of my hands in her hair. I fucked her slowly, carefully, testing her limits, speeding up when I saw she could handle my size. When Sloane opened her throat and swallowed, I just about lost it.

"I don't want to come like this."

Dragging her teeth along my flesh, she pulled away and grinned. "Is there something else you want?"

I stood, bringing Sloane with me to bed. I lay down and urged her to crawl up until her pussy was right over my face. She hesitated at first, but when I pulled her closer and sucked on her delicious clit, she moaned and begged again.

She tasted like honey and cinnamon, juicy and sweet. Like Sloane. My Sloane. A powerful yearning to protect, love and possess this generous soul for all time slammed into me with gale force winds.

I lifted her down my body so she straddled my groin. "Take what you need."

"Like this. I want to see you." Sloane sounded vulnerable, her emotions jumbled, her body on the edge.

She lowered her slick heat onto my body and we moved together. I took her gently at first, our breaths coming as one, our bodies in sync. When she was close she leaned down clutching both shoulders. "Harder."

"Anything for you." I thrust my dick balls-deep over and over, giving her the pleasure we both craved. She gyrated to meet each thrust, and we broke apart together, our heartbeats pounding out a perfect rhythm as she collapsed on top of me, both of us sweaty and sated beyond words.

As we breathed in loud bursts, I stroked her warm skin, holding her tight. Like this, I thought. Like this.

When I could move, I disposed of the condom, pulled down the sheet and blanket and urged Sloane against my sweat-slicked body. She was boneless, smiling with a catlike grin. "Long John gets a star from Zagat's."

"Only one?"

"He has to earn the rest. It takes a very long time."

My next kiss was a little bit a desperate. How could I keep her? Make her love me? When we were together, I felt whole. Strong. As if my life had meaning and hadn't been a waste of time.

When she kissed me back, hope, the brutal spirit that enjoyed kicking me in the balls over and over, grew in my soul. Sloane was a symphony composed of heart and desire. I would cherish and care for her if she'd only agree.

I hugged her close, knowing tomorrow I'd have to let her go again.

I missed her when she wasn't around, looked for her to pop in unexpectedly, always disappointed when she didn't. In my dreams, the future I'd once dreaded was filled with giggles and snarky comments, delicious food and passion-filled nights. My life was beginning to make sense, but only when she was with me.

Sloane was a sexy, vibrant, earth-shattering song I needed to sing to survive.

I stored those melodies and harmonies in my head for later. First, I'd love her into oblivion.

THE DAY after Sloane's and my trip to Half Moon Bay, Uncle Andrew called and told me to come in.

"The structural engineer's report has been delivered and I'm sorry to say the news is bad." I'd invited Uncle Andrew to sit and offered him a cup of coffee I'd made all by myself. He sat but declined the coffee.

Prick.

"When did he do the inspection?"

"Two days ago."

"Seems pretty fast."

"Look, I know you want to help the neighborhood residents and all that, but the building's structural integrity is in question. The three stores and four apartments will be leveled and rebuilt. I've already hired an architect who says we're looking at eight or nine months."

"Eight or nine months?" I glared at my uncle. "You've already hired an architect without consulting me?"

"At the request of your father. He wants to use the same firm Damien used." Damien had purchased the building that butted up against Bel Cielo when he decided to build a gallery for Cassandra attached to her art studio.

"I see."

"The three businesses and apartment tenants will be reminded in a timely manner that their rental properties must be cleared out by September thirtieth. That's six weeks, making it exactly sixty days from the first notice. I'm certain they'll be able to find something similar somewhere in the city. Especially the restaurant. Restaurants are closing at an alarming rate."

"It's part of her family history. Their legacy."

"Time to move on. The woman has no choice."

When Uncle Andrew left, I stared out the window for a few minutes, thinking about Damien, and how he'd helped his woman save her business. What else could I do to help Sloane?

Slowly a plan took root, a crazy plan. An expensive plan. But what the fuck was money if it couldn't be put to use to help people? Gio's grandmother's words came back to me. I wouldn't be a monster. I'd put Blake to work digging up information. I'd call Damien, honeymoon or no damn honeymoon.

Damien and I talked for a good hour. He was on board

with my idea and said Blake should draw up the paperwork as soon as possible. Relief brought my heartbeat back to a normal speed. My next call went to Blake, then Lori. I needed to get moving on this right away. We needed people we could trust. People who loved Sloane.

They wouldn't be hard to find.

13

He wasn't at the club or answering his phone or my texts, so I looked up the address and took a ride share to In the Zone Studio. He hadn't come by the restaurant for two weeks and I'd only spoken to him twice after the *Adagio* Affair, my new name for our long night together.

Something was up but I wasn't one to leave the water to boil out and ruin the pot. I faced problems full-on, then dealt with whatever the situation was as quickly as possible.

During the ride to the studio, I smiled, remembering the way we'd laughed together, the way he'd touched me and brought me pleasure again and again. We'd enjoyed each other several times on our short voyage and each time it had felt more like making love than having sex. I hadn't wanted this. In fact, I'd wanted the opposite. But Vic had burrowed into my heart, dragging in music and sexy smiles and long slow kisses, making a home for himself that looked to be permanent.

He was alone in the studio, picking out notes and chords on a baby grand piano. I'd always pictured a recording studio to be a small, crowded place, but this room was large enough for a ten piece band and a small chorus.

His smile was warm but lacked the energy that usually fed it. "You're just in time."

"I couldn't find you. Where have you been?"

He didn't stand to hug me. "I've been working on something special—something I can't get out of my head. The band is showing up any minute now. You'll get to meet them." He pointed toward the pizza boxes and beer, water and soda bottles on a nearby table. "Dinner. Help yourself."

I glanced around at the guitars hanging on the walls, the drum set, the music stands, microphones and stools of various heights. A set of glass windows covered the top half of an entire interior wall, the high-end equipment on the other side lit up and waiting for the touch of a skilled engineer.

"You own this place?"

"Yes. I'm happiest here." He glanced at me, then away. "Or I used to be."

"It's amazing. How often do you work here?"

"I stop by whenever I have time. That's less and less lately." He noticed my frown. "Not because of you, but the other. You know, the businesses."

"Do you rent out time?"

"Yes. You'd be surprised if you heard some of the names. But mostly I loan it to other musicians I trust not to trash the joint. Studio time is expensive. I try to help out."

He patted the piano bench and I sat beside him, relieved beyond words that he was okay. He slipped his hand to my nape and kissed me, sweet and lovely. When we pulled apart he rested his forehead on mine, leaving his hand where it lay. "I missed you."

"You didn't call. I thought—"

"I'm sorry. It's been a bad couple of weeks."

"Anything I can help with?"

"Just forgive me."

"Done."

His fingers danced on the keyboard as he played a couple of runs.

"What kind of music do you like?" he asked.

"Anything. My parents listened to everything from The Beatles to Metal to Country."

"But what do you listen to?"

"Not much. I put some rock and roll women on when I exercise. Like Pink and No Doubt and Florence. It's a channel on a streaming service."

"Do you sing along?"

"No."

"Well, you're required to sing along when we're playing on break, so warm up your windpipes."

"This isn't a break. You haven't started the session yet."

"If I say it's a break, it's a break." His magical fingers played a couple of Pink songs and a Pat Benatar favorite of mine and we hummed and sang along together, Vic adding some harmony once in a while. He had a husky, mellow voice that could soar into the stratosphere but still sound soothing and sexy. Perfect for the clubs he played. I managed to stay on key, which was my main goal. While we sang, he smiled, like all was finally right with the world.

But something was off. His mind was somewhere else.

He sighed a long sigh and kissed my cheek. "That was nice."

"Will you come to Mangia Monday with me?"

His expression changed. "Can we hang out in your room with the door locked?"

"My parents, my two sisters and my twin brothers will be there. Tony Jr. has to work."

"Guess we'll have to stay here, instead." He kissed me hard this time, biting my lip, then moving down to suck hard on my neck.

"Are you giving me a hicky?"

"Hmm?"

"Victor." I pushed him away. "I'm seeing my family tonight. I'll have to explain."

"You don't want to have to explain about me. I get it."

"That's not it. They'll force me to bring you next time. Unless you come tonight."

"You can wear a turtleneck."

"It's hot."

"You're hot. Spicy. God, you taste so good." He kissed me again. This one felt desperate. "If my band wasn't coming I'd fuck you on this piano. Nothing better than sex and music combined."

"You would, huh?" I smoothed my hand over the black finish. "Doesn't look too comfortable. My ass is delicate."

"I could make you love it."

"I love everything when I'm with you."

His face paled. "Today, right?"

"Vic..."

"We could start on the bench." He pulled me into his lap and wrapped his arms around my shoulders, burying his nose in my hair, his long sigh despondent. "You smell so good and feel so good. Stay with me."

I touched his face. "What's wrong, Vic?"

"I hope—"

"Hey, who's the bird on your lap, Vic?" A deep voice with a southern accent.

I smiled. "Looks like the band is here."

14

I introduced Sloane around, trying to snap out of the doldrums. After everyone had some pizza and beer and a few laughs, I sent Sloane into the next room with Howie, our amazing sound engineer, and passed out the sheet music for the song I'd been working on. Sloane's song. The working title was "A Peaceful Place," but titles changed constantly. By the time the song was finished, the title might be completely different.

I ducked my head and slipped on my guitar while the band ate and drank and listened. When they finished eating I sang it through again. The guys followed the music, sometimes strumming a chord here and there, sometimes beating out the rhythm. When we worked a song, I listened to their suggestions and sometimes made dramatic changes. But in my heart, I knew this song was what it was. My benediction to a woman who made me see outside myself and my own problems. Who brought me a peace I'd never experienced before. Who gave every bit of herself to others and needed my arms as much as I needed hers.

With Sloane I wasn't a disappointment or a fuckup. I

made her laugh. I brought her pleasure. I gave her all I was and it seemed to be enough. I loved her, and whether she loved me or not, my feelings would never change.

We ran through it together four or five times. When I glanced at the booth to tell Howie we were ready to start recording tracks, Sloane was standing at the window, tears running down her cheeks.

She mouthed three words and all the fucked-up shit in my head dissolved in the music-filled air. I mouthed the same words back.

We started recording tracks, beginning with the drums, the bass and the piano—together first, then separately. The lead guitar and rhythm guitar came next, then the lead singer. At first, I thought it shouldn't be me on the test demo because this was a song born to be shared with the world. I'd find the right singer to get it on the charts, but as I worked the number I grew possessive. It was an intimate letter from me to Sloane and maybe that was what it was meant to be.

I glanced at the booth for another reaction and was surprised to see her on her phone with a worried expression. I raised my hand to stop the recording and went to see what the problem was.

"It'll be a couple of hours before I can get there, Ma."

"What's up?" I whispered.

Sloane held up a finger. "I'll do my best." She ended the call. "Family trouble."

"Can I help?"

"I'm fine. I'll catch a ride share."

"I'll drive you wherever you have to go."

"I can't mess up your session."

"Shut up. Where do you need to go?"

"Do you think you could drop me in San Rafael?"

"Of course." I returned to the others. "Stay as long as you like and work on whatever. Just make sure to close up the right way. I don't want the alarm company calling me again."

"Stay off his lap, Sloane. It's a dangerous place." Howie called out.

"Have fun you too!" Someone else shouted.

"Fun is not what we'll be having," Sloane mumbled on our way out the door.

I was quiet until we got in the Tesla and I started driving toward the bridge. Thank fuck I brought the car today. "Your parents don't live in San Rafael, do they?"

"I'm going to the police station."

"Turning yourself in for assaulting me?"

She didn't crack a smile. "My nephew is being held and no one else can pick him up."

"Didn't you say you have three brothers and two sisters?"

"Kathy the cop is at a concert, Tony Jr. is working and the twins just go nuts on the kid when this happens. His mom is Caty, but she isn't well."

"His dad?"

"He's supposed to be with his dad this week, but Larry is not the most reliable guy. I think he leaves him alone a lot. Mom asked me to deal with it."

"Are you asked to deal with a lot of family shit?"

"It's okay. I'm the calm one."

"You're the calm one?" She cracked a smile but didn't reply. "How old is your nephew?"

"Thirteen."

"Thirteen is a tough age."

"He'll be at the station with a female cop or a social worker. They don't put him in a cell."

"He's done this before?" She nodded. "What's he in for?"

"He calls himself an artist of the people."

"Graffiti." She nodded. "Where does he practice his art?"

"This time it was a city bus. Last time it was the side of the high school. The time before that... I think it was an overpass on the highway. Mom almost fainted when she heard. Ang was ready to kill Larry, the kid's dad.

"Which high school?"

"Central."

"That's okay. My friends went to Parker. We hated Central."

"You're not helping."

"Let me talk to him."

"He won't listen to you."

"What's his name?"

"Chad. No one seems to be able to get through to him. The split between his parents has been hard. Not friendly. And now Caty..."

"How ill is ill?"

"It's a heart thing."

"Fuck."

"No kidding. She's seeing the best doctors and just got put on the transplant list."

"I'm so sorry." We were quiet for a few minutes. "What does Chad enjoy doing besides painting city property?"

"Before Caty and Larry split he played soccer, but I never got the impression he was mad about it. He's always liked to draw. Manga stuff especially."

"Does he draw using a computer? Graphic design?"

"He likes that, but he has sketches posted all over his wall."

"Have you spoken to Cassie about him?"

"No... But that is actually a great idea. She's starting classes for kids, only I think it's for older kids."

"Has he ever been sailing?"

"You can't think of rewarding his bad behavior with a boat excursion."

"Paul, Drew and I would put him to work. He'd scrub the deck, peel carrots in the galley, practice tying knots until he formed calluses. Learn the ropes...literally. My father used to make me help scrub our boat from topsail to bilge. Not fun, but when it was done he let me take the helm when we were out on the ocean. Best times I ever had with Frank."

"Where is your father?"

"I told you."

"I mean which prison?"

"Atwater."

Her eyes widened. "Oh." She turned away, embarrassed. It was a high security federal prison.

"It's okay. I'm used to that look."

It took about forty minutes to get to San Rafael. They brought him out— a scruffy kid, small for his age. Sloane moved to sign the paperwork while he stood there staring at his beat-up sneakers.

"Do you know where your dad is?" I asked.

"Who're you?"

"Vic." I held out my hand.

He looked from me to Sloane and back to me. "You screwing my aunt?"

"Chad!" Sloane held her pen in the air. Guess she hadn't finished signing.

"Apologize," I said.

"I don't have to do shit for you."

"Apologize to your aunt. The one who comes out in the middle of the night so you don't get taken to some boys' home where the seventeen-year-old bullies eat an artistic kid like you for breakfast. You'll be lucky if you keep all your teeth. Now apologize."

"You know a school like that?"

"I went to a school like that."

He took a step back. Maybe he figured I'd been one of the bullies. "What're you gonna do if I don't apologize?"

"If it were up to me, I'd send you right back to Officer Randall. You're obviously not learning anything by getting rescued all the time."

"We can put you in a cell and you can wait for your father to come in the morning." Officer Randall was enjoying the show.

Chad's eyes narrowed as if he were working out some kind of strategy. He turned to Sloane. "You wouldn't do that, right? Mom'll flip and she's been so weak." His expression had gone from angry brat to puppy dog cute. A master manipulator already. The kid was heading down a narrow path with a cliff on one side and poison snakes on the other. I knew that path. I'd walked it for years.

"Your mom's not here. I'm here. And I'm waiting." Sloane was tapping her foot. I'd be sweating if I were Chad.

I winked in her direction then started counting down for dramatic effect. "Five, Four, Three, t..."

"I'm sorry."

"For what exactly?" she asked.

"For spray painting the bus and making you come to get me."

"And?"

"Saying that thing."

"What thing?" she asked.

"You know."

"Say it in a whole sentence."

"I'm sorry I asked if he was screwing you."

"Thank you. You're forgiven on all counts."

We started walking toward the car. "I'm starving."

"I'm taking you to Nana's," Sloane said. "You'll get food there."

"I'm at Dad's this week. When he gets home he'll be pissed if I'm not there."

"Does he leave you alone a lot?" I asked.

"A couple days. Not too often. I'm learning to cook."

"If you want to learn how to cook, ask Nana or me."

"I don't really want to learn. I just want to be able to eat something other than microwave crap."

He seemed to realize what he'd just said to his executive chef aunt. Sloane picked up on his fear. "You'll help me cook something when we get home."

"No...really. I can have a peanut butter sandwich or something." A man after my own heart. "But can't we stop at the diner?"

"No. Nana's worried."

"Ooookay." He came to a halt beside the Tesla, eyes wide and glittering with interest. "This is yours?"

"Yep."

"Sweet."

"Thanks."

"How fast can she go?"

Sloane opened the rear door. "None of your business. Get in the back."

"This car isn't designed to do high speeds, that's not the point, but I have a scrambler you might like to see."

"A BMW? Will you give me a ride?"

"No."

"Oh." He slid into the back seat and was quiet for the next fifteen minutes as we drove to Sloane's parents' house. "Guess I should apologize to you too."

"Sounds like a plan."

"What's your name again?"

"Vic."

"I apologize, Vic, for asking if you're screwing my aunt Slo."

"I'll forgive you. This time. But if I hear you disrespect your aunt again, you'll be scrubbing out heads for the weekend."

"What the fuck does that mean?"

"Boat bathrooms," Sloane explained.

"You own a boat?"

"A catamaran."

"Holy shit. You must be rolling in it."

"Chad!"

"You with your mom next weekend?" I asked.

"Yeah."

"Maybe I'll pick you up. Take you to work with me."

Silence. "You're not one of those creepy guys into boys, are you?"

"Chad!"

SLOANE'S FAMILY home was situated in a great neighborhood at the end of a cul-de-sac—a large two story with a Spanish tiled roof. Sloane told me to pull around back so they could enter through the rear door. Chad got out first, trudging toward the house with a dejected but resigned expression.

"Please park it." She pointed to an open space to the right. "Over there is fine."

"It's one in the morning."

"My parents will be up. They'd like to meet you."

"Tonight?"

"Sure. We'll even feed you." She leaned over and kissed me, short but sweet. "C'mon." I did as she asked, parking and getting out of the car with a great deal of trepidation. I must have looked a lot like Chad. "You're not being thrown to the wolves. I promise, you'll like them."

"Hmm." No words came to mind.

"What is it?"

"Nothing. I'm good." I smiled as broadly as I could and kept it plastered there when she opened the door and we stepped into her home.

"Sloane! Thank you, sweetie." A small woman with a shock of wavy red hair and an enormous smile hugged Sloane tightly to her chest. A tall dark-haired man stood off to the side, also smiling. "How did you get here so quickly?" her mom asked.

"Victor drove me. We were at his music studio near the Haight when you called." She took my hand and pulled me closer to her parents. "Mom. Dad. This is Victor. Victor, these are my parents."

I extended my hand to the petite woman. She and Sloane were obviously mother and daughter, except for the hair color and maybe the nose. Sloane's was longer and straighter. "It's great meeting you."

"I'm Emma." Instead of shaking, she clasped my hand warmly between both of hers. "We can't thank you enough."

"It wasn't any problem at all. My mother lives nearby and I have a house on her property." I could go there tonight, but I'd probably end up sleeping at the club as usual.

The man wandered over. "Antonio. Tony," he corrected. He was tall and broad shouldered and his thick dirty blonde hair and straight nose made up the rest of the puzzle.

"It's a pleasure to meet both of you."

Her dad was sizing me up the way fathers of daughters were supposed to do. "Where did you two meet?"

"Dad. No third degree. I told him I'd get him something to eat. All we had was crappy pizza at six."

"I like that pizza."

"I didn't see you eat any of it."

"I was busy."

"I have pasta fahjol," her mom offered, smiling.

"Great." Other than the pasta, I had no idea what the fahjol part was.

"Perfect." Sloane helped me take off my coat. "It'll only be a few minutes. I'm hungry too. Where did Chad disappear to?"

"Sulking in his room no doubt."

"He said he was starving."

Her father nodded. "I'll get him down here."

"Would you like whiskey or wine or coffee?" her mom asked.

"Coffee's best. I'll be driving."

"Coming right up." Her mom started preparations and Sloane led me into a family room off the kitchen. She pulled me onto the couch next to her.

"I told you they'd like you and you'd like them."

"We just met," I whispered. "They may hate me when they see my table manners. What's fahjol anyway?"

"F-a-g-i-o-l-i." But she still pronounced it fahjol.

"Oh, the bean and pasta soup. Fah-gee-o-li?"

"Fahjol," she repeated with a beautiful accent, laughing, then crawling into my lap and snuggling against my chest. "It's the shortened New York version. My Grandparents lived there for the first thirty years after they came to the US."

I glanced toward the kitchen. "Your parents might see us."

"How do you think they had six kids?" She pouted and

moved into a more acceptable position—for her parents' sake.

The clomp of footsteps on the stairs signaled the appearance of Tony and Chad a moment later. Emma called out that the meal had been reheated and we sat down to steaming bowls of pasta and bean soup with shaved cheese on top. Freshly warmed bread, a dish of olive oil and herbs for dipping, and a bowl of assorted olives, slices of tomato and tiny balls of mozzarella cheese had been placed on the table as well. I finished the bowl of pasta *fahjol* faster than anyone else, except maybe the kid.

"Would you like more, Victor?"

I hesitated, but noticed Sloane rolling her eyes. Did that mean I should or I shouldn't? She answered for me. "Yes. Give him another bowl. He only eats one good meal a day and that's when he comes to the restaurant."

"No one cooks for you at home?"

"I live alone in the city."

"Didn't you say…"

"I don't stay in Marin too often." I left out the part about the bad memories.

Two large males entered the kitchen from the rear door. I had to do a double take because they were so much alike I thought I might be going crazy. They each kissed their mother on the cheek and greeted their dad, then sat at the table. This time Tony got up to serve the food, since Emma was still eating.

"Brought home a friend, Slo?" number one said, looking me over.

"Nice ride." Number two smiled in my direction.

"Thanks."

"The smiling one is Angelo and the disagreeable one is Joey," Sloane said, frowning at the first speaker.

I reached across the table. "Vic." We shook. Nobody tried to break any fingers to prove how macho they were, although these two could have done some damage. They were around my height, but with a broader build. Joey, the one who'd spoken first, had a thin scar from his ear to the corner of his mouth. A knife wound maybe. I hadn't noticed it at first, but now that I'd seen them close up, they were pretty easy to tell apart.

"And what do you do?" Joey asked.

"Victor's a..."

"I asked Victor, Slo."

Sloane grunted but shut up. Okay, this was not the friendliest greeting, but these two were out to protect her. I smiled at Joey, glad she had brothers who stood up for her. "I compose music. Run a recording studio."

"He also owns The Gate Club." Sloane frowned. "It's for men only."

"Really?" Her mom looked at me, her frown identical to Sloane's.

"Been in my family for almost two hundred years."

"The Gate Club?" Joey narrowed his eyes. "You're not Granger. I've met him. Arrogant prick."

"Joey!" His mom looked embarrassed.

"It's okay. I've called him the same. I'm the other owner."

"Hanley," Angelo said, puzzling it together.

I nodded, waiting for the rest. Exactly what I'd tried to avoid, especially at this first time meeting with Sloane's parents.

"Your dad's in jail," Angelo said, leaning forward. I wasn't surprised they knew the story. Angelo was a PI.

"Yes."

"This isn't your business." Sloane rested her hand on

mine in a gesture of support. I resisted the urge to thread my fingers between hers. I might need to defend myself.

Angelo ignored her but didn't continue.

Joey picked up where his brother left off. "You turned him in." Joey scratched his wrist. A tattoo of something written in Italian curled around to the inside.

"Yes."

"You had nothing to do with that shit?" he asked.

"Boys. Another time." Emma's expression was full of compassion, the way Sloane's got sometimes. I liked her mom already.

"Damien Granger is one of my closest friends and his dad was like a father to me." That information hadn't been in the news.

"You did the right thing." Angelo smiled before popping a small black olive into his mouth.

"Must have sucked." Joey tugged at his shirt collar exposing the snake tattooed on his neck. He hadn't cracked a smile once. "How did you two meet?"

"Joey!" Sloane's face was turning red, her hands fisting.

He raised his hands in surrender. "Take it easy, little sister. You never bring guys home. We're doing our job, right, Ma?"

"No topic is sacrosanct in the Gabrielli kitchen," Angelo added.

"We met at Cal," I said.

Her father placed two bowls on the table in front of the twins. "Enough. Eat."

"Sure, Dad." Angelo grinned. Joey dug in without another word, and the inquisition ended.

Sloane gave me an apologetic glance. "I'm sorry. They usually aren't so bad the first time."

"You're our baby sister." Angelo shrugged as he dipped a piece of crusty bread in the olive oil.

"I'd probably be the same if I had a younger sister."

"Any siblings?"

"No." I couldn't completely hide the envy in my voice. I pictured Sloane bandaging me along with the others after a wild game of touch football, or all of us gathering at the kitchen table—talking with people who'd been there for each other their whole lives. This was a real family, not the cold, judgmental, dysfunctional mess I'd always thought of as family.

The twins rose and cleared the table, putting everyone's plates in the dishwasher. I brought Sloane's and mine. "If you or your dad are in the area, stop by the club. I'll show you around. Buy you lunch," I offered.

"Trying to get on our good side, huh?" Joey's expression was suspicious.

"Can't hurt to try."

Angelo lowered his volume. "Keep her happy and you'll have no trouble from us."

Joey glowered. "Hurt her and—"

"I get the picture."

Angelo ruffled Chad's hair, receiving a scowl in exchange. "You still smearing paint across Marin?" Chad nodded, still looking sullen. "Where's Larry?"

"I don't know."

The room was silent. Seemed his dad wasn't too concerned with the kid's welfare.

"We'll be talking tomorrow after you get a good night's sleep, got it?"

"Sure, Ang."

"Take a shower and hit the sack, hellion."

Chad trotted up the stairs, the food having revived him.

"Joey and I are heading out. We just wanted to check in," Angelo said.

"Love you!"

"Love ya too, Ma."

"Drive safely," Tony said, smiling with pride at his sons.

"Always, pater." Joey and Angelo were grinning as they left through the mudroom, now in a much better mood than when they'd arrived. The positive energy surrounding the Gabrielli kitchen had a healing quality. Even I felt better.

Two noisy engines started up. "Old pickups they won't part with," Sloane explained.

"What do your brothers do?"

"Joey runs a gym, although he's not happy with the set up there. Seems the owner is in debt up to his earlobes and the place might close. Angelo's the PI. Lost his wife three years ago to cancer and sometimes helps with Chad. He travels a lot. Both twins get called in to fight forest fires when they need bodies."

"They live half a mile from here," Emma said.

"They live together?"

"Yeah. When Angelo's wife passed he fell into a bad depression. Having Joey around to cheer him up was an enormous help," Tony said.

"Joey cheers people up?" I whispered to Sloane.

Everyone laughed. "Once you get to know him," Emma said with a pat on my arm.

I glanced at the wall clock. It was almost three a.m.

"I've got a long day. I should try to catch some sleep."

"You're welcome to stay in the guest room."

"Thanks, but I'll go to the club. Thanks again for the delicious meal and the hospitality."

"Come over for dinner Monday night. That's family night."

"I don't know…"

"Nonsense."

It was impossible to say no to this lovely woman. "If it's okay with Sloane."

"Of course, silly." Sloane took my hand and walked me out to my car.

"Come back with me. I have something we need to talk about."

"What we both need is sleep. I'll see you tomorrow at the restaurant. We can talk then."

I gave in, knowing she wouldn't sleep at all if I gave her the bad news in the middle of her parents' driveway. I'd get to her place early tomorrow, ask that we go up to her office and then explain everything. Tell her I still wasn't giving up.

I pulled her close. "Were you mouthing what I thought you were mouthing at the studio?"

"Mmm hmm. Fuck off asshole."

"Same here." I kissed her deep, pressing my body into hers, wanting to brand her as mine. She gave back the same, and we parted, vowing to see each other tomorrow.

15

The building management guy knocked on the restaurant door at nine a.m. Really? I concentrated and came up with the name. Flint. "Hello, Mr. Flint. We're not open this early. Is there something I can help you with?"

"I have a letter from Gate of the Bay to be delivered personally to you and the other two lease holders. Do you know when the clothing resale shop opens? I can't wait around for hours." He was acting a little flustered.

"I'll have one of my staff deliver it for you if that will help."

"Thanks, Ms. Gabrielli, but I'm afraid it has to be delivered by a representative of the firm."

A cold shiver ran down my spine. "Could I have mine please?"

"Here you go. Sorry it has to be this way, but the engineer's report was clear."

"The engineer's report?" The engineer and the inspector hadn't spent more than ten minutes in my restaurant and even less time in my office upstairs.

"Oh. I thought Mr. Hanley would have told you. My cousin works security at The Gate and he says Mr. Hanley's here almost every day."

"Mr. Hanley didn't tell me the results."

I tore open the envelope and read through the notice twice. The building housing the three stores and the apartments upstairs would be torn down and rebuilt from scratch due to structural damage. Nothing was described in detail, but it was official. I was out on my ass on the thirtieth of September with no hope of returning before April of next year.

I clutched at the doorframe, my knees having gone a little weak. "I have to get back to work, Mr. Flint."

"Sure, sure. I'll go to the deli next."

I locked the door and lowered my body into the nearest chair, placing the notice on the table. Everything I'd worked for would be gone, all because of Mr. Frank Hanley and his fucking company. My eyes filled with tears, but I quickly wiped them away.

Vic. Vic hadn't told me the results. Hadn't told me his efforts had failed. When had he known?

I took the stairs two at time. I'd left my phone in the office.

"The Gate."

"Mr. Hanley please."

"He's not available."

"This is Sloane Gabrielli."

"Oh, hello, Ms. Gabrielli. I'll wake him up. He got in late."

I was biting my lip so hard I was sure I was doing damage, mulling over all the choice things I was going to say to Vic. But I would not fall apart. My employees needed my strength and I wasn't going to let them down.

"Hey. Good morning."

He sounded drowsy, but I'd be waking him up. "You bastard."

He paused, putting two and two together. "Sloane..."

"Don't even try to make an excuse. When did you know?"

"Two days after we got home from our trip on *Adagio*."

"You're a shit for touching me after that."

"I..."

"You're a coward too. Had to send your minion to deliver the news."

"I was coming over today. I thought we could have gone to your office. Damien and I—"

"Don't ever contact me again." I ended the call.

He was at the front door of the restaurant forty-five minutes later. He must have broken all speed limits getting here. "Don't let him in, Gio." I was on the phone with a storage unit company. Everything was so expensive. I might have to borrow money from my parents. I hated doing that.

"He looks pretty upset. He's pacing back and forth in front of the restaurant."

"Tell him I'll call the cops."

"How can I tell him if I don't open the door?"

"Open the door and tell him."

Victor was six foot and Gio was only five foot six and didn't stand a chance. "You have to listen to me," Victor said.

"You should listen to him. He's really been trying to help," Lori said.

"I can get a frying pan," Gio suggested.

I held up my hand to settle my staff. I pointed toward the ceiling. "Upstairs. This is just between us."

Once in my office I shut the door. "You're upsetting my staff even more than they are already." I'd had to call a special meeting, even calling in staff members who weren't scheduled for today. They took it pretty well, especially after I promised them I would open again in another location as soon as I could find a place. I'd had my eye on a couple of spaces, thinking I might be able to open a second location, but now I needed a first.

Vic cut off what I was going to say next. "The first inspection wasn't done properly. I've arranged for two more building inspectors to check the building out and write reports. I don't think it needs to be rebuilt."

"You and I both know this is bullshit, so please, just leave."

"Blake has sent all the information to your lawyer. You can ask him. Also, Damien and I are joining forces on a project that might make things much easier for you."

"I can't trust a word you say." I turned away and stared out the window that overlooked Mission Street. How often had I sat at my grandmother's kitchen table in just this spot and watched the people and the cars go by? "Get out or I'll call the cops. I have connections."

"So do I."

"Of course you do. Do you bribe the commissioner?"

"Let me explain."

"For more than two weeks you've acted like nothing has happened at all. You lied. You wanted to fuck me on your fucking piano." She wiped away tears. "I took you to meet my family."

"I wanted every minute I could with you. I love you."

I walked as close to him as I could manage so he'd have no chance to tell me he didn't understand what I was saying. "People who love each other don't withhold vital information that could break their partner's heart." I choked back a sob. "They don't take what isn't given with an open heart. If you'd told me the news that morning, I probably wouldn't have wanted you to touch me at first, but I'd have come around, because you'd been honest with me."

"And now?"

"I can't trust you. And I'd like you to leave, please." I returned to the window, turning my back on Victor. I'd made the mistake of letting him into my heart. Again.

"Sloane… Please."

"Don't make this any worse."

He sighed in a huff. "I'll be back to help."

"I don't want your help."

"I'll be back anyway."

16

Plan B was still up in the air. Plan A was a clusterfuck.

"You're going to make space. This is an emergency."

"But we're full."

"Then clear out one of my units and truck everything to my garage. I'll make room at my house."

I paced back and forth in front of the window that overlooked the bay, trying to calm my mind and not think about the look on Sloane's face when she told me she couldn't trust me anymore. I'd fucked up every goddamn thing the way I usually did. There was no excuse for what I'd done. Yeah, I'd worked it out logically, finding the best time to tell her so I'd have some control over how she'd react. But a relationship wasn't logical or rational and you couldn't control a fucking thing about it. It was explosive and soothing, filled with exquisite pleasure and punch-in-the-stomach pain. A few nights ago I was almost part of a family, and today I was more alone than ever.

A black pickup truck drove into the club lot and parked.

The twins had arrived. I thought they'd be here sooner, but it must have taken time to spread the word. I glanced at the coffee pot and shook my head. It wouldn't help. I shifted my gaze to the liquor cabinet. No. I'd have to face the beating like a man. I deserved it.

I sat behind my desk, grateful for the barrier despite knowing it wouldn't do me any good. This really sucked.

The intercom buzzed.

"Sir..."

"Yeah, I know. Let them up. And call Blake. I'm probably going to need him to mop me off the floor." Blake was pretty good with first aid. We'd been in plenty of school fights together.

"Sir, should I call the police?"

"No." I winced. "Unless you hear a gunshot."

I eyed my dish of jelly beans, taking a handful and popping a few in my mouth. A sugar rush would have to suffice.

A moment later the door opened and the two brothers wandered in, taking their time, looking at the art on the wall and peeking out the window at the view. One of them wandered over to my keyboard and I tensed up. I loved that keyboard. Mom had given it to me when I was nine years old. He picked up the music on the stand in front of the instrument. "You write this?" I nodded. He put it back and I started breathing again. I really should make copies of new compositions.

The two men seemed larger and more muscular than they had in the small kitchen at Sloane's parents' house, but maybe it was their posture, or the tight tee shirts they wore.

"Hanley," Joey said, sitting in one of the ugly chairs. It seemed to fit his broad body better than most.

"Joey. Angelo." Angelo only nodded. He didn't sit.

They stayed silent, glaring at me in a markedly intimidating way. I waited, keeping my expression neutral. One of us was bound to talk eventually.

"At least you're not making excuses," Angelo said.

"I'm an asshole. There's no excuse for that."

The comment surprised them. "What are you going to do about this situation?" Joey asked.

I explained Plan A. Plan B was still iffy, so I'd only mention it if I thought they intended to kill or torture me.

"It's a start." Joey popped a couple knuckles. I tried not to listen.

"Sloane called you?" I asked Angelo.

"Nah. She called Caty, who called Kathy and she called Joey."

"Really?" I looked at the twin with the scar and the glowering expression.

"Joey's always the one the sisters call."

Must be the enforcer of the family.

"So, you have a gym here?" Joey asked.

"You want a tour of the club?"

"Yeah." Angelo stood.

"Okay, great."

"Especially the gym." Joey's expression might have been more terrifying if I hadn't shared a meal with his family. They weren't assassins. They were here because they loved their sister, a woman I'd lied to and hurt. Hey, if roles were reversed and I had a sister, I would have...maybe sent Damien.

It wasn't that I couldn't fight. Damien, Blake and I had beaten up several bullies back in school. Had trained together for years in martial arts. But playing a piano or a guitar with broken fingers or wrists or elbows was pretty much impossible, and music was what kept me sane from the time I'd played my first scale.

We walked and they stayed close. I pointed out the golf course, the pool, the spa and the archery range, the tennis courts, restaurant and bar, avoiding the gym for obvious reasons. But I couldn't stall forever. Luckily no one else was in the gym.

"You box?" Joey asked, rolling his shoulders.

"Yes." I was pretty good, but I'd have no chance against this guy. He was built like a heavyweight right out of the ring.

"You want to have a go?"

"Why not?" I changed in the locker room and returned wearing workout clothes and high-end boxing shoes. I might not be quite as large, but I was fast and I intended to give this guy a run for his money. For a couple of minutes anyway. "You want shoes? We have extra. Sparring gloves too."

"Thanks."

I lasted ten minutes, getting in a few good punches that had him nodding in what might have been approval. After I blew a jab to his chest, he punched me in the gut and uppercut me on the chin. My head snapped back and I went flying, landing on my ass. I shook my head and groaned.

Angelo patted Joey on the back. "You done, bro?" Joey had landed quite a few other punches but thank fuck he'd been holding back. As it was I'd be sore for days.

"Yeah, I think I'm done." Angelo helped Joey off with his gloves then helped me up, but it was Joey who gently lifted my chin to look at the damage. He shook his head. "You're strong for your build and fast on your feet, but you need to pay more attention to how your opponent shifts his weight. I wasn't being subtle. If you'd been watching, I never could have hit you so many times." He helped me off with my gloves and sent Angelo for ice. "You're gonna have some ugly bruises."

"I'm getting used to Gabrielli-inflicted bruises. Your sister's already assaulted me."

"Yeah?" He chuckled. "I'll have to ask her about it."

Angelo patted my back right over one of my new bruises. I held in the wince. "Don't give up. We think you're good for her."

"Even though you hurt her." Joey's voice sounded more like a growl.

"I didn't mean to hurt her. I thought I was protecting her, but I was protecting myself."

Joey slapped the bag of ice on my chin. "That should help."

"Ow. Thanks."

"We've asked around. People respect you, especially your employees," Joey said.

"They stick around for years. Sure sign of a good boss." Angelo looked like he was going to pat me again, but I stepped aside. He grinned.

Sadist.

"I've recently taken over as co-owner. I haven't done all that much..."

"Yeah, but they say you've been running the joint with Granger for years."

"And what about my crazy family? No objections there?"

"You handled it right. You protected your mom and stood up for your friend," Angelo said.

Joey rolled his shoulders and took another look at the gym. It was beautifully outfitted, with all the latest exercise equipment. Frank and Uncle Mike, Damien's dad, had never been cheap when it came to club renovations. "Amazing facility."

"Thanks." An idea popped into my muddled brain. "We haven't had a proper boxing coach for years."

"No?"

"And our sports facilities manager is retiring next month."

"Are we discussing a full-time position?"

"Yes."

"And what would the manager be responsible for?"

"He might be asked to do some coaching. I have someone working the golf course, the range and the pools, but whoever filled this position would be in charge of the gym and the courts and the archery range."

"Are there benefits?"

"Great health benefits. Three weeks off paid vacation to start. Lifetime membership comes with the job. You know anyone who might be interested?"

"I might know someone." Joey scratched his light stubble. "Would this manager have a crew or is he solely responsible for maintenance, ordering supplies, etc.?"

"We have four assistants on staff already taking care of that end."

"So what would I... What would the new manager be doing?"

"Making sure his team does their jobs but also putting in time as a personal trainer. A coach. Group classes. Pretty much whatever he thinks would pull in new members and compete with other similar clubs. If your sister has her way, we may be building a new locker room, gym and spa for women. Maybe expanding in other ways."

"What about a class for teen boys?" Angelo asked.

"You're thinking of Chad."

"Yeah. You have an art studio, right?"

"We do. Does he like any sports?"

"Snowboarding. I take him out, but it's an expensive hobby."

"Damien and I have shares in a ski resort near Tahoe. We might be able to help you out."

"I wouldn't be able to pay you much."

"If I need a PI, I'll ask for a discount."

"You got it." He grinned.

"I'll have to discuss the job offer and the art classes with Damien. We have independent artists reserving time in the studio so we might hit a snag with scheduling."

"You have time to talk about all this now?" Joey asked.

"How about over lunch?" I sniffed under my arm. "After I shower."

"Does the job include lifetime membership for the employee's brothers and father?" Angelo asked.

I laughed. I was starting to like these two, despite my throbbing chin and bruised ribs. "I might be persuaded if you could help me out with something else."

"Nothing nefarious." Angelo draped an arm over his brother's shoulder. "Your skills finally came in handy, bro."

"Vic here hasn't offered me the job and I haven't accepted. I want to get the details."

Ang rubbed his chest. "Think of my pecs. They need serious work."

"You box too?" I asked Angelo.

"Nah. If I'd been in the ring with you, you woulda kicked my ass."

"You look like you're in good shape."

"I climb. Hike."

"On weekends he drags his fancy camera to the top of

the Sierras or the Cascades to take pictures. Mom wants to strangle him."

"She wants me to take headshots and baby pictures." The brothers laughed and I felt a stab of envy.

"Hey!" Blake had finally arrived, moving into the room with his usual grace. I introduced him. "Except for the size, I see the resemblance." He looked me over. "Not as bad as I thought it would be."

"They took pity on a man with a broken heart."

"Cut the violins and stop sitting around on your ass. I'm sick of all the whining."

"How's our Plan B?"

"We hit a snag, but Damien and I are working it out. You take care of Plan A."

"We heard all about Plan A, but what's Plan B?" Ang asked.

"Tell us over lunch. I'm hungry." Joey frowned.

"I want a ringside seat when Sloane finds out what you're doing," Blake demanded.

"You will, but make sure to bring your coveralls."

"What?"

"I'm putting you to work." I glanced at the brothers. "Maybe all of you."

17

My side of the block had been orange-coned off all morning. Was this the beginning of the end? We were due to be out in four days, but if they were going to bring in heavy construction equipment this early we'd have trouble when our trucks arrived tomorrow. I turned away from the window, exhausted and depressed.

I'd had to say goodbye to most of my staff, the hardest thing I'd ever done. I'd given them a hefty severance and there wasn't a dry eye in the bunch. Most of them were family to me, and I'd spent hours on the phone, getting them interviews at other restaurants. Gio and Lori had stayed on to help with the packing, which was invaluable, and I was bringing in a moving company and had lined up a storage unit. It was costing me more than I could afford, but I'd had no choice.

Lori brought me coffee and the newspaper, leaving them at a window table—her way of telling me I needed a break. I complied with her silent suggestion and leafed through the paper. Gentrification had hit the news again, with an ad for a protest in Golden Gate Park on October sixth. Maybe I'd attend. There was also an ad for Gate of the Bay Realty touting its newest apartment building complex. I folded the paper and pushed it aside.

I spent too much energy every day trying not to think about Victor. I missed him and hated that I missed him. I did everything I could think of to keep from missing him, including chanting over and over in my head that he'd lied to me. Left me to flounder like he had at Cal.

Only I knew deep down he'd been trying to protect me from the hurt of seeing the end of my restaurant. He'd hurt my pride by not being honest, fed into my own insecurities about losing the restaurant and disappointing my family. Brought my control-freak bristles to full attention.

It was better if we ended it here. I'd be busy 24/7 trying to find another place and he had his work, work he'd put aside to spend time with me. I couldn't afford to fall in love, not with my responsibilities. Who would see to Caty and Chad? I'd learned a valuable lesson in all that had happened with Bel Cielo. Dreams can be crushed in a heartbeat.

But I'd had other dreams too, and Vic had made them real. He wasn't the kid in college who'd made choices he hated in order to survive. Now he was living his dream, defying his father. Yes, he'd taken the trusteeship, but he'd done it to save people's jobs and his mom's income. I wish he'd made a different choice, but I understood his motives.

I leaned back in the chair and closed my eyes. I wanted more than anything to feel safe the way I had in Vic's arms, to feel loved and desired. To trust him again. Only that meant opening my heart to him, and I was a fucking coward when it came to love. Caty had seen it and called me on it.

Be wild, Slo. Take him and let him take you. Open your heart and let someone in.

Vic called me every morning and every evening. I didn't take the calls, but I foolishly listened to the voicemails. Sometimes twice, just to hear his voice. They usually made me cry.

I love you. Please pick up.

I fucked up, I know. Give me a chance.

I'm going to make this right between us.

I'd tried to shut the door, but Vic's large foot was jammed in too far. The intimacies we'd shared were embedded in my heart. His music warmed my soul. His quirky smile lightened my spirit.

How could I let him go?

The rumble of a truck pulling up in front of the building had me wiping my eyes and craning my neck to get a good look. It was a small moving company truck, not construction related equipment at all. Blake, Vic's friend, jumped out of the passenger side while the driver came around the front of the truck. It was Vic and he was wearing navy blue coveralls. I almost dropped when I saw the twins pull up in their two pickups. Also in coveralls.

Vic looked good enough to eat. But what was this about? Did Frank's realty company want us out even earlier?

I opened the door with Gio and Lori at my back. They didn't look overly concerned. "We're here to help," Joey said, a hint of amusement in his usually serious expression. Vic waved, then jogged off, ducking into the thrift store.

"You're wearing Dickies coveralls." Those two wouldn't have been caught dead dressed like that yesterday. "What the fuck."

"Nice greeting, sis. What do you think?" Angelo opened his arms and turned around slowly.

"Yum," Lori whispered beside me.

"I never knew these things were so roomy." Ang grinned. "Especially without any clothes on under them."

Lori laughed but I ignored Ang and turned to Joey. "What do you think you're doing?"

"Helping you pack and move. That's the plan, anyway."

"So, you've switched teams?"

He gave Lori a slow once-over which she seemed to enjoy. "No way that's ever going to happen." He winked at her and Lori leaned against the door frame, giving him an even better perspective.

Gio slapped her shoulder. "Have some respect for yourself, girl." Lori shoved Gio back, but I wasn't worried. They were as close as siblings.

"You dope. I'm not talking about sexual preferences. I'm talking about taking orders from Victor." I folded my arms.

"He's offered me a job."

"He what?"

"I'm going to manage the club sports facilities Wednesdays through Sundays. I'll make twice what I make working six days a week at the other gym. I'll be giving private boxing lessons too."

He sounded really excited about the prospect, so I didn't want to shoot him down. "You didn't think to ask me before just showing up? I've hired a moving company and reserved a storage unit."

"Um..." Lori looked guilty.

"What?"

"Blake cancelled them," Lori said.

"And you've turned traitor too?"

She grinned. "You won't believe what Victor's done. Not just for you, but for the neighborhood."

"He's covering the moving expenses for all three stores," Angelo said, pulling me in for a hug. "No worries."

Joey frowned. "Least he can do after breaking your heart."

"He didn't break my heart!" I snapped, turning away and changing the subject. "What about my deposits?"

"Blake has a check for you."

I huffed out a breath and scanned the restaurant, trying hard to digest this change in plans. "Do you have any idea how to do a move like this?"

"Victor and Blake have done it before. We've promised to follow orders."

I glared at Victor, who was back and standing off to the side. "The musician has packed a moving van? I find that highly unlikely."

Blake looked at the ground then at Victor. "Uh...yeah. It was mostly fine art, but he knows what he's doing. My dad owns a couple of moving companies. That's where we got the truck. I helped out some summers."

"You only brought one. We're not going to fit everything."

"A lot of your stuff isn't going into the truck," Blake said, grinning.

"It isn't?"

"Nope. Look over there." Blake pointed across the street and my mouth dropped. "Vic and Dame bought the building. They've worked like dogs getting the restaurant renovated—you know, the one that closed a few months ago. Lori, Gio and your sous chef helped out with ideas. Basically, we're moving your shit across the street."

"Yeah, the truck is for the stuff you're not going to use. You can donate it somewhere," Angelo said.

"He's really trying to do the right thing. So go thank him. I don't think he's slept for a few days." Lori gave me a quick hug then nudged me in Victor's direction.

I turned back to the restaurant across the street. "I... I don't know what to say."

Gio brought out a ladder and began to unscrew the Bel Cielo sign.

"Will the sign fit over there?" I asked. It was the original one my grandparents had designed.

"Yep. We've got it all set up. With everyone helping, the restaurant should be able to open in around a week or two. Of course that's up to you, Chef." Gio was grinning like a chimp.

"A week or two?" I was expecting months. Months of searching for a place. Months of setting up and trying to find customers. Months of regret. "And the other businesses?"

"We're helping the Kriegers tomorrow and the sisters the next day. Everyone will be out before the deadline," Blake said.

"Are they moving across the street too?"

"The Kriegers are on the opposite corner, but the thrift shop is moving around the corner and half a block down. It's still a great location. And there's more parking too." Blake handed me a folder. "This is the paperwork for your new place."

"Mom and Dad are coming to help you set up the restaurant tomorrow," Ang said.

"Mom and Dad are in on this too?" Ang and Joey kissed my cheeks, then smiled the exact same smile. They'd never looked more alike. I felt a little light-headed. "I think I should sit down."

"I got you." Victor snaked his arms around me, holding me up. I clutched at his collar and he held me tighter. "I'll always catch you."

"You're a sneaky pirate," I whispered.

"Pirates usually are. Don't you want to see your new place?"

"I... I do."

He steadied me. "You okay?" I nodded. He took my hand, checked for traffic and we jogged across.

The space was much larger, with wide windows covered in shades and curtains. Beautiful curtains in a subtle print sheer enough to let in the sun when the shades were up. The tables were polished maple, the chairs matching but with different colored inlaid cushions that looked hand-made. The main part of the restaurant was set up for families, but the tables in the back section sat two and four, the lighting more romantic. The gas fireplace would add a lovely touch and there was even a small area near a classic brick wall where a guitarist or a duo could set up and perform.

The bar area was in the front and off to the side with high swivel chairs but also high tables where people could stand and chat over drinks. People waiting for their reservations could be placed near the door with plenty of space for seating.

The kitchen was much larger than my old one, with new high-end appliances.

"This place is enormous. The rent—"

Victor kissed my cheek. "I know the landlords. You'll be paying an extra one hundred dollars a month for a lifetime lease."

"Instead of five thousand more," Blake added. Mr. Flint had told me to expect that amount.

"I want you to be happy more than anything in the world." Victor lifted my hand and kissed my knuckles.

Gio strolled inside and flicked a switch to pipe in music, acoustic and relaxing.

I turned in place, trying to take it all in. "I love it. Thank you."

Ang and Joey gave me one of their sandwich hugs. It was like being stuck between two boulders. Gio and Lori tried to do it next, but they were small and it didn't have quite the same effect. I turned to Vic, who was waiting on the side.

"I'm paying you back. Every penny."

"My grandfather's bequest was just sitting around earning interest, and Dame is my full partner, so he had to shell out half. We both agree the building is a really good investment. We're renovating the rest of it too. The large apartments on the fourth floor have been offered to the families who lived in your old building with only a fifty dollar increase in their monthly rent. You still have an upstairs apartment if you want it, although there's a large office behind the kitchen that's already part of the restaurant."

He took my hand and led me to a set of three elevators, pressing floor two. "Dame and I will make our money back on the two floors of offices." He led me around the three mid-sized offices on the second floor and the full floor office on the third. They needed paint and some patching, but otherwise looked to be in good shape. "We'll need to upgrade security and electric, but they aren't bad."

"I'm glad the apartment tenants won't have to walk up three flights of stairs." Some of them were elderly.

"Sloane." His tentative touch had me turning toward him. "I'm sorry."

"I'm sorry too. I didn't let you have your say. I didn't listen. I don't know why I'm so hardheaded."

"Maybe it balances with your soft heart."

"My soft heart? Look at all you've done."

"Not enough. We'll go to the rally together. Find out

what else can be done. Dame and I are committed to protecting the neighborhood that means so much to our women."

"Am I your woman?"

"If you'll have me."

I wanted to say more, to tell him all the things in my heart, but the moment was ruined when the elevator doors opened and Blake barged in. "We should get to work. It's going to be a long day." We took the elevator down together, Blake smiling when he noticed we were holding hands.

"Blake is moving his dance studio next door to Bel Cielo."

"And I'm paying full price, although I'm hoping for a free meal once in a while. I know the owner of the best Italian restaurant in the city."

I laughed. "The Kriegers will love you too. Amazing pastrami."

It took Blake, Victor and my brothers half the day to safely unhook the appliances, wrap them in protective blankets and get them onto the truck. I'd called up three shelters that also ran soup kitchens and between them, they said they could take all the large items off my hands.

At the end of the day, my restaurant was empty. Most of my upstairs possessions were packed into the two pickup trucks and would be taken to Mom and Dad's so I could sort everything out. I'd decided against taking the apartment, figuring Victor could use it for additional income.

The next two days were even crazier with Victor, Blake, Ang, Joey and a few extra guys Victor had hired from the shelter packing up the other stores and moving everything to their new locations. Mom and Dad showed up exactly at seven a.m. to help me set up my new kitchen, oohing and aahing over all the appliances.

"This is top of the line. How did your musician know what to buy?" Dad asked.

"My sous chef, Poppy, spends a lot of time fantasizing about her future kitchen. She even went with Victor to buy everything, since she knows my kitchen habits. She's now determined to find herself a rich man so he can buy her a building with a restaurant and the best appliances on the market."

Lori laughed. "Poppy can be pretty focused. She'll do it if anyone can."

I wanted to argue with Vic about footing the bill, but I couldn't get him to budge. Pride wasn't always practical. Better to pay Vic back in my own time than feel I was putting a drain on my family or ruining my credit rating.

Vic finished before me on the third day and was waiting by his car when I came out, looking sexy as shit wearing sneakers, jeans and a skintight black tee.

His smile gave me the pleasant kind of goose bumps and tightened my chest at the same time. "Thank you."

"I love you, babe. I couldn't let my asshole father ruin your life." He rubbed his neck and I made a note to give him a massage later. "I'm going to see him tomorrow. We have things to work out."

"I thought you'd sworn never to visit him."

"I've been chickenshit about it, but he's always been a bigger than life presence in my world. I need to see him as he is. Close the book on the past."

"I'm proud of you." We were both exhausted, both mulling over what tomorrow would bring. "Do you…"

"What?"

"Do you want me to go with you? To the prison?"

"Why would you do that?"

"I care about you. I… We have a history, right?"

His soft laughter didn't reach his eyes. "More than that I hope. But I have to do this on my own. I've been a coward. Put it off for too long."

We were six feet apart, but it felt like miles. He met my gaze, his eyes no longer showing the confidence I'd grown to love. "Will you give me another chance? I'm stumbling around in the dark without you to hold onto."

He opened his arms, hope shining in his eyes. I stepped into his embrace, leaning my cheek into the hollow beneath his shoulder, breathing in my favorite scent. "I've missed you so much."

He held me tight, dipping his face into my hair, taking me in the same way.

"Sloane." He pulled away a little then gently tilted my head so he could see my eyes. We kissed, mixing passion with forgiveness. "Love you, JT."

"Who's JT?" Ang asked as he ambled over.

"I thought you left," I said.

"Nah. Lori, Joey, Blake and I are going to grab dinner. Wanna come?"

"No thanks, I'm beat." I shook my head.

"But who's JT?" he asked again.

My PI brother was a dog with a bone. "Don't you dare," I growled softly to Vic.

"It's our secret," Vic whispered, never taking his eyes from mine. Vic was a wise man at times.

"Must be one of those cutsie names couples give each other. Just don't get it tattooed on your ass," Ang said. Blake and the others had wandered over.

"Is there a cutsie name on your ass, Joey?" Lori asked, the insta-chemistry between them still crackling even after three days of hard work.

"Feel free to find out, Red."

"Nothing on his ass except hair," Ang said, earning him a smack on the shoulder from his scowling brother.

Vic leaned in to put his mouth near my ear. "I'll give you a ride home before the fighting starts." He walked around to the passenger door and held it open for me. I glanced down at my clothes. "I'm filthy."

He smiled. "There is absolutely no way in hell I am leaving you here, even if it means another bruise."

"My brothers will drive me."

We looked over. They were still arguing.

I sighed and slid into the pristine passenger seat. When he got in beside me and started the car, I buckled up and automatically placed my hand on his thigh, the usual spot I rested it when he was driving in the city. When we were on the Embarcadero, he twined our fingers together, but stayed silent. Rational thoughts built walls inside my mind, while deeper feelings battled to dissolve those walls. I was a mixed-up mess.

"Can I come up?" His voice was hesitant. Vulnerable. We were two blocks away and I was exhausted. "To shower and sleep. Nothing else. I... I need to hold you. I'm only half human without you beside me."

And he was seeing Frank tomorrow. "Pull into the garage."

We walked upstairs, only noticing when we got to the third floor that we'd been holding hands the entire time. So easy to fall into familiar habits. We smiled, sharing the joke as I unlocked the door. Vic lowered his long body onto the couch, his forearms on his thighs, his hands hanging between his knees. He was stressed to the max. "You go ahead and shower. I can wait."

"Are you hungry? You must be. I'll cook something."

"I thought you were tired."

"I'll make something quick. Come into the kitchen. I'll put you to work."

"You're putting your trust in the wrong guy." His eyes widened when he realized what he'd said. "I mean in the kitchen. Not... Not anywhere else."

"The kitchen aside, I do trust you. You wanted to spare me. But I'm one of those control freaks who likes all her information up front."

"I can make adjustments."

I donned an apron, washed up and prepared chicken piccata with some leftover creamy polenta. Victor made the salad. It took almost as long as the rest of the dish, but it came out just fine. I opened a pinot grigio and warmed up a few rolls. Victor inhaled his portion.

"Have you been eating at all?"

"Of course."

He was in his tee shirt and jeans, but it seemed his face was thinner. "You've lost weight."

"Have I? I don't know. How's Chad doing?"

"He's excited about the upcoming art classes. Thank you for that."

"Everyone needs an artistic outlet. I can't wait to see his work." I gave him a look he interpreted correctly. "When Damien gets home, I'll speak to him about changing the club's bylaws. It's an expensive proposition to admit women. We'll have to build a new wing."

"But it makes sense."

"It does. I'll clean up. You shower first."

We showered separately and crawled into bed, me in a tee shirt and panties and Victor in a pair of clean boxers he'd stowed in his bag. "Never know where I'm going to be sleeping," he explained.

I curled my body closer, relaxing into his large, comforting presence. "This is nice."

He sighed and draped an arm around my waist. "Better than nice."

I yawned. "Perfect."

He held me closer, burying his nose in my hair, but not taking it further. He wouldn't have turned me away if I'd wanted to make love, but our bodies were already spent, and our hearts were in a fragile place. I kissed his cheek, then turned so we could spoon the way we usually did.

I fell asleep at ten and woke at seven. Vic was already awake and staring at me, playing with a lock of my bed hair. I'd turned during the night so now we were facing each other.

"I've missed this so much," he whispered. "Waking up beside you gives me the courage to face today."

I scooted forward, kissing his mouth, letting him know with my body what was in my heart. "Make love to me." I could give him more than courage. I could give him hope.

He kissed and stroked and licked me from head to toe, always gentle, always seductive. By the time his cock slid inside my sex, I was soaked and aching for him. But he took his time, bringing me slow, loving me with his skill and his soul. Playing me until we cried out together, then easing me until we lay in each other's arms, panting and smiling.

Vic pushed sweaty strands of hair out of my eyes. "I love you. Always."

He rose to get ready for his visit with Frank and I got up to make coffee. We kissed on the threshold before he left. I felt as if I were sending him off to war.

18

I put my shoes back on after the scan, the metal bench hard against my ass. I found a more comfortable chair then waited, thumbing through old magazines. They'd taken my phone and any item they thought could be used as a weapon, including my pen. Andrew showed up a few minutes later. I scowled in his direction. "Why are you here?"

"Your father asked me to come. Maybe he's concerned you'll punch him."

"He's not worth the energy." Although the thought had crossed my mind.

"He loves you, Vic."

"If that's true, he sure as hell never knew how to show it."

He stared at my yellowing bruises. "More war injuries from your lover?"

"Her brother."

"What did you do to fuck up *this* relationship?"

"I got roped into a trusteeship I never should have accepted."

"Too late now."

"No. It isn't."

"This way." A tall overweight guard led us along dim hallways that still echoed with decades of shuffling ironclad footsteps. Even though we were passing by offices and meeting rooms used by the staff, the passage still smelled of disinfectant and made my shoulders slump with an oppressive weight. The world was a safer place with my dad locked up, but this bleakness was more disturbing than I'd imagined.

So was his appearance. He'd lost the weight he'd gained after being released two years ago and his skin had a grayish pallor, matching his hair. When he saw me he smiled, but as always, it didn't touch his cold blue eyes. Eyes the same color as mine. His hands were cuffed to a bar in the middle of the table and he was wearing the usual prison coverall. "Victor."

I sat in the seat across from his. "Frank."

"It's like that, is it?"

"What do you expect? You killed Uncle Mike. You hurt Mom."

"I went a little crazy, I admit." He shrugged with one shoulder. I'd been here thirty seconds and I already wanted to punch him.

"Will you ever own up to what you've done? To the people you've hurt? Damien looked up to you."

"Damien should have followed orders and not tried to fuck me around."

I had no response. Frank was a violent narcissist. A sociopath. Poison. He'd never change.

Frank leaned back in his chair and smiled, making a stab at pleasant, something he'd never mastered. "You're looking good. Is the transition to trustee going well?"

"What do you think?"

"I thought you'd come around if I put you in charge. Gave you some real power."

"But you didn't put me in charge. You handcuffed me into following your orders from a distance."

"You have nothing in your life. I was trying to help."

"I have The Gate, my music and..." I left it there. He didn't need to know about Sloane. "Give the trusteeship to Uncle Andrew or sell the businesses."

"You signed a contract, son."

My jaw tightened at the reminder that I was related to this asshole. "I'm handing in my resignation today. I have a conflict of interest. I've become a competitor in the real estate market." I pushed a paper across the table. Andrew snatched it up before Frank had a chance to look at it.

"You're contracted for three years. If you renege, I can sue you," Frank said, eyeing Andrew as he read through the document.

"He can't hold the position of trustee of Gate of the Bay if his company is purchasing buildings in the same city." Andrew was looking at me with a small amount of respect. Will wonders never cease. "Your buddy drew this up?"

"My lawyer. Blake."

"Right. Blake. He did a fine job."

"His company?" Frank looked at me as if I'd grown horns.

"Dame and I are partners in City Block Realty."

"City Block Realty?" He looked to his brother then back to me. "You've gone into business with Damien?"

"Yes. I suggest you make Unc here your trustee." No response. He was still in shock. "Or here's another option. Damien will pay a fair price for Franklin Art Acquisitions if you're interested in selling. He and I are looking to expand our new business partnership and may be able to take a couple of buildings off your hands, particularly if they're in the Mission District."

Frank's eyes turned to slits as his face reddened. This always happened when he didn't get his way. "Your mother counts on that income to maintain her style of living."

"I talked to Mom. She owns the estate and the property. She can sell it and travel the world—live in a very comfortable and more reasonably sized home when she gets back. Plus, I can help her out if she needs it."

"You signed a contract!"

"How many fucking contracts have you broken? Like your wedding vows." I leaned closer, whispering, "I know more than you think I know. I have lists the feds might be interested in. Items that were sold and never reported. Stolen items."

"You had a hand in that as well."

"You forced me into it when I was a teen. Threatened me when I wanted to quit." I crossed my arms and smiled. "Blake is certain I can get a deal with no jail time for coming forward."

"What is it you want?"

"You to leave me the fuck alone. Hands off. Find someone else to harass."

"Think of all the people who will lose their jobs if you resign."

"I have." I rubbed the back of my neck, wishing for a particular petite blonde to soothe the ache. "If they apply to me for a position, Dame and I will do what we can for them, but it's on you and not my responsibility."

"Is this all to save the restaurant of your latest lover? Does she taste as good as her food?"

I stood, leaning over to grab his collar and strangle him.

Andrew pulled me back. He must have told Frank about Sloane. Shit. "If you mention her again, I'll pay the guards twice as much as you pay them. You'll be eating cat food and sleeping with a six-foot-five-inch dom." That wiped the arrogant sneer right off his face. "When people call you a big asshole it'll have a whole new meaning."

He'd tried to stand as well, but the cuffs pulled him back. "This isn't a game, Vic. It took me years to build those firms."

"Years you could have spent being a husband and a father."

He grunted and hunched over in his chair, looking more like the father I'd dealt with for most of my life. Quick to anger and strike out. Quick to assume the worst. Quick to find fault.

"Grow up, Victor. Life isn't a fairy tale. You always were a dreamer."

I thought about Sloane and the way she'd made me believe in myself, and this time his words rolled off my shoulders. Ten years ago, I might have gone out and downed enough whiskey to make me pass out. But not today. Today my dreamer qualities seemed like a good thing, because they fed my music. I leaned closer so there could be no doubt how serious I was. "The first time you hit Mom was the day I wrote you off."

"I hurt your mother, but I've apologized. She and I have reconciled. She understands why the stresses of my work and my imprisonment in 2014 weighed heavily on my mind. I wasn't myself and behaved badly."

My stomach knotted with anger. I couldn't look at him. I needed to get out of there before I said or did something...impulsive. There were times to use your head and times to use your heart. This man wasn't worth the effort or the consequences a punch in the nose might bring about.

He hadn't noticed my struggle for control. "I'm glad you're finally putting your business degree to better use. I'll be interested to see how City Block Realty does in the cutthroat San Francisco market."

His tone was sincere. Like I'd finally done something he could get behind. Like my music was a hobby and this was where I could make some real money. "Do what you want with the businesses. Just don't look to me to run them. I'm done."

I stood and started to walk out. The guard at the door shifted to the side to open it for me.

"Victor!"

"Yes?" I stopped but didn't turn around.

"I'm proud of you." He sounded surprised.

I froze for a moment. How many times had I wanted to hear those four words? I turned and stared at my father as if he were speaking Sanskrit. "I can't remember you ever telling me that."

"You've just forgotten. I've always—"

"Save it." My nails were biting into my palms. If I stayed any longer, the chain I'd strung around my anger might break. "Don't call me again."

I was shaking as I got behind the wheel of my car, at loose ends with nowhere to go. My usual haunt came to mind, so I drove into the city and parked in the garage under the studio. Here I could work out the fucked-up feelings my dad always brought on. At least I could try.

As soon as I opened the door my breathing came easier, my muscles loosening, my mind relaxing to the rhythm of the steady beat of my heart. The coffee pot was empty, but clean, so I got it going then walked to the table and shoved aside the graphic novels my engineer had been reading. He loved his Manga.

My phone rang with Mom's tone. I hesitated, then answered. "Mom?"

"Hello, sweet boy. How are you?" She'd always called me that when we were alone, never with Dad around.

How to answer. Fine didn't really cut it. "I'm working in the studio this afternoon." Not what she'd asked exactly. "How are you?"

"Busy with the usual things."

I was never sure what she did all day. "I saw Fr... I saw Dad." I couldn't call him Frank when I was speaking to Mom.

"And?"

"I quit as trustee."

"I'm sure that didn't please him."

"Have you really reconciled?" *With that monster* was what I wanted to tag onto the end of the sentence.

"Did he say we had?"

"Yes."

She sighed loud enough for me to hear. "I'm pleasant to him when I visit. Let him do most of the talking. He talks about himself. His past achievements. His plans for the future. All having to do with his businesses. He apologized once, saying he'd been at his wits end and had lost his sense on several occasions. He promised he would never hurt me again. He'd promised that before of course." Her voice broke.

"Mom, you don't have to talk about this."

"I want to. I have not reconciled with him. I'm not a complete pushover. He'll never step foot on my property again and if I have to, I will get an order of protection against him."

"I should've known not to believe him."

"You deserve a better set of parents, but I'm afraid Frank and I are what you were blessed with. I'm so sorry my fear almost destroyed your life. You're the most courageous young man I've ever known. You did something I should have done years ago. Mike might still be alive if I had. I understand why you don't... Why you don't..." She choked back a sob.

What the fuck had I done? Mom had been as much a victim of Frank as I was. "I'm coming over. I'm sorry, Mom."

"No. I've been video chatting with friends and they'll be calling in a few minutes. Two college friends I've kept in touch with on social media. Sorority sisters. I've poured out my heart to them and they've done the same. It's all very hormonal, but cathartic too. They suggested I continue to *call you until you picked up the damn phone.*"

She'd used a slightly different tone on the last part of that sentence, ending her phrase with a soft laugh. When was the last time I'd heard Mom laugh?

"They're moving to Napa so I'll be able to see them often."

"I'd like to meet them."

"I tell everyone about my son the composer. I'm so proud of all you've accomplished. My friends are fans of your music and would be thrilled to meet you, if you can find the time." She was quiet for a few moments. "Tell me about your new friend."

"Sloane?"

"Are you two serious?"

"She's the one. There's no one else."

"And does she feel the same?"

"I fucked up, but I think I made a start at fixing it. This

morning... This morning things were perfect, but I have a long way to go."

"Frank never admitted to being wrong, unless he wanted something."

"I almost hit him."

She laughed again. This time a little louder. "Punching someone in the penitentiary is probably not a good idea."

"Andrew held me back."

"Well at least he was good for something."

I played a few bars of his strident theme song on the piano.

Mom laughed. "I love you. I'll leave you to your music."

"Love ya too, Mom."

I walked to the table and spread out a large sheet of notation paper, staring at the unmarked pages as an artist might see a blank canvas or a choreographer an empty dance studio. I'd often compose online with special software or sitting in front of the piano playing with chords. But tonight I wanted to work free-form. To design my music on paper, hearing it only in my heart until I sat down with an instrument.

Music had always lived in my soul, music stirred up then reborn using keyboards, strings, drums, guitars—whatever conveyed the message most clearly. Quiet rainy days and bustling rush hours sang their unique songs, not with words that were spoken but with chords and crescendos, rhythms and resonance. Even a rest—a silence between phrases— was a holding of breath. A skip in your heartbeat. A precious moment that warned the listener the music might not come again, yet also held a promise of more.

I worked for hours, although it seemed like minutes, my focus shifting from darker to lighter, more joyful melodies. When I looked up it was six p.m. Crap. I'd told Sloane I would call. Blake too. I glanced at my phone. One call from Blake. Two from Sloane. I called Blake first, thinking the conversation would be short.

"Is everything okay? We wondered what happened with your dad. Your mom called. She was worried."

"I spoke to her."

"And your dad?"

"I'm a little shaken but fine. It was good I went."

"You need anything? Where are you?"

"The Zone."

"I'll bring over some food."

"I'm really okay. You must be tired. How did your move to the new studio go?"

"It went really well. No snafus. Sloane and her brothers helped."

"Good." I rubbed my eyes. I'd been giving them a workout.

"Did you tell Sloane where you were going today?"

"Yes. No secrets anymore."

"She knows about you and Damien and the art?"

"Yes. That was tough to come clean about. But Sloane sees the world with clarity. She doesn't let emotion drag her under like I do."

"You turned him over, Vic. That took a set of steel balls."

"Or a cold heart."

"Fuck that. You're all heart."

"It's funny but... A weight lifted today. It's over. I've cut myself off for good, so whatever happens now is all on me. Thanks for helping me out with the paperwork."

"You saved my ass more times than I can count."

"I only wish you weren't such a damn nag about shit. And stop calling at seven in the morning, you tool."

Blake barked out a laugh. "Someone's gotta kick you in

the butt, although Sloane is pretty much a master." I laughed as Blake yawned. "I'll see you tomorrow. Don't stay up all night."

"Can't promise anything."

He ended the call.

I made another pot of coffee, then moved to the baby grand and began to play my newest compositions. I began with "In my Arms," a song inspired by our night together and our lovemaking this morning. Much of my music was influenced by jazz and blues, but this piece was more an acoustic indie ballad. Perfect to perform at the various clubs I played. Maybe I'd release it as a single, see if it garnered any interest.

Lyrics were not my strong point, but I played it all the way through several times, changing the rhythm in one section, adding words in another.

Music was magically fluid. That's why one artist could perform a song and another could make that same piece his own. I was surprised to find my cheeks were wet, so I stopped and leaned away from the piano, searching for a napkin, ending up using the bottom of my tee shirt instead.

"Please don't stop playing."

I looked up and smiled. "I didn't hear you come in." Despite my somber mood, my heart beat a faster rhythm as soon as I saw her, my chest warming at the mischievous gleam in her eye.

"I can be very sneaky too. I brought lasagna from the restaurant. My first meal in the new place. The staff and I pigged out. We won't be opening to the public for at least a week and we wanted to start experimenting a little."

"With lasagna? How innovative."

"This was comfort food day."

"I'd better be your first customer."

"Your daily reservation is set in stone."

"Thank you." I wanted her to think of me as family and wondered if she had any idea that she'd already become family to me. Maybe this offering was a start.

She left the food on the table and sat beside me on the piano bench. "Your music is beautiful. How long have you studied?"

"I was eight. I started late but took to it like Mozart took to Haydn." She looked at me curiously. "One of my grandfather's expressions. He played the piano." I continued, my fingers expressing what my words never could. "I'm calling it, 'In my Arms.'"

"What's it about?"

I did a few dramatic runs over the keys, giving my mind a moment to work out what to say. "I was inspired last night and this morning." I glanced at Sloane. "You're blushing."

"I'm not."

"Fine. You're not." I kissed her cheek. "Thank you, for letting me stay. When I'm with you I feel as if I can face anything." I switched to her first song. Singing along.

"It sounds so different when you play your music without the band. More intimate. I like it better this way." She rested her hand on mine as it moved over the keys, smiling as I did a slow run up the scale in a minor key I'd always thought was sexy. "I confess, I'm a little bit in awe of your talent." She sighed. "Guess I'm a fangirl."

I shrugged. "Born this way, as you were born to cook amazing dishes."

"It's in the genes."

My dad's final words kept dancing around in my messed-up head and now my fucking cheeks were wet again. I stopped playing and tried to turn away, but Sloane held my chin and wiped my face with a tissue she'd fished from her bag. "Seeing your father can't have been easy. I'm here for you."

I stopped playing and she scooted closer, pressing my head into her chest and holding me tight against her body. If it had been anyone else, I would have felt ashamed. Unmanned. But not with Sloane.

"I hate everything he is and everything he's done. But he's my father and early on he was a good one. I thought for a long time it was my fault he turned away from Mom and me. I wasn't the son he wanted. I wasn't enough. But it had always been him. He wanted more from life. No one was enough."

Sloane kissed my wet cheeks, then trailed her lips to my neck. I sat there frozen, my cock growing hard, but my mind telling me if I made a sexual advance she might pull away. I ached for her body, but I wouldn't survive her leaving me. I had to be patient and let her choose.

I closed my eyes, opening my heart to the peace she offered me.

"Play my song again," she whispered against my ear.

Sloane rested her head on my shoulder, her warm breath teasing my neck, her arm snaking around my waist. I continued to work on the piece, pausing to change a phrase or two, asking for her opinion. She gave her opinions without hesitation, just as she lived her life. Open and authentic. No BS or hidden agendas.

When I finished, she crawled into my lap and straddled my legs, threading her fingers in my hair. "I missed you when you left this morning. I want you again." Her kiss was deep, brimming with passion. Our mouths danced together, humming our pleasure, one rhythm, one sweet, sweet song.

"Is your wild side coming out?" I asked.

"Caty used that word."

"She did?"

"She wanted me to..." I laughed. "To go wild. Everyone thinks I take on too much. So I'm taking a page from your book. Didn't you say something once about making love to me on the piano?"

"Fucking was the word I used."

Her laugh was husky. "Even better."

Standing with Sloane in my arms, I pushed the container of lasagna aside and lowered her ass to the table. "Give me a minute."

I pulled out the mattress I used when I slept at the studio and placed it on the rug in the studio office. It was small, but we'd fit just fine. Also, we could close the door. My engineer had a way of showing up at odd hours.

Locating the condoms took another minute.

"Was that a mattress? I thought—"

I kissed her, a brush of lips to quiet her questions. Spreading her knees and drawing her arms up so her hands rested on my shoulders, I kissed her again, this time deeper. I loved that she rarely tensed when I touched her, always eager to know where I'd take her next. Her fingers dug into my hair as she kissed me back enthusiastically.

I moved my kisses to her neck, spending time on the spots that usually brought a small gasp or a soft moan. I bit her nose and she giggled.

Sloane was wearing a dress. A mid-thigh print with a tight bodice. "I'm guessing no bra."

"A discerning lover."

"Panties?"

"You'll have to find out."

I nuzzled her neck. The sweet scent of honey brought back the taste of her sex. Blonde curls, damp with her juices. Soft warm skin, a perfect pink—liquid honey and female musk. My dick swelled to a painful size. I groaned. "Tell me what you want." My voice was rough. Needy.

"Everything."

She smiled and I kissed it away, this time wild and deep. A claiming more than a seduction. I pressed my forehead against hers, both of us panting our desire. "I'm aching for you," I said.

"Take what you need. I won't break." She bit my lower lip hard and pulled on it.

"You don't know wild."

"Make me feel everything." Her eyes were blazing with heat and need. My plans to take my time and make love to Sloane went flying out the skylight and into the foggy night air.

"You're mine." I licked the spot where I'd left my mark.

"Yours." She breathed out the word in a long sigh.

I'd closed the piano, so I placed her on the end where I played and spread her legs, her feet resting on the fallboard that covered the keys. No panties. Fucking perfect. I moved the dress aside so I had a perfect view of her delicious pussy, already seeping juices. "One day I'm going to put you here while I compose."

She laughed. "The view inspires you?"

"And the scent and the taste." I leaned forward, clutching her thighs so she couldn't bring them together, then blew on her flesh. Her body shivered. So did mine.

19

V ictor held me captive, licking my sex, thrusting his tongue inside as if he were fucking me. I leaned back on my hands, trembling with desire. I needed to come. Now. "Vic. Please."

"Shh."

"Don't fucking shh me." He plunged two fingers inside my sex as punishment, only it wasn't punishment at all. "More." I yanked on his hair.

"Behave." He laughed, nipping at the inside of my thigh.

"Never." Suddenly I was in the air, then up against the wall, the fly of his jeans grinding against my very sensitive flesh. His cock was fully erect beneath the fabric. "Oh god."

"You wanted more."

I wiggled my hands between us and fumbled with his zipper. He laughed. "Hold on." He raised my hands to his shoulders, freed his cock, slid on a condom, gave me the pirate-about-to-ravish look and thrust inside me balls deep.

"Ohhh." The groan erupted from deep in my belly.

"Damn. You're so... so tight." He closed his eyes, breathing rapidly through his open mouth. He filled every inch of my sex, his cock throbbing inside me, heating my body with his own fire. I squeezed him as hard I could and he moaned and bit my shoulder. He knew just what I needed as he moved his body slowly in and out, using his fingers on my clit.

I was so close. "Victor. I'm…"

He kissed his name from my mouth, fucking me like a male only interested in his own pleasure. But he worked the angle that brought me screaming to orgasm, groaning when I splintered, calling his name.

He hadn't finished. "Come again for me."

"I can't."

"You will."

He rubbed my clit with his guitar-calloused fingers as he continued to fuck me, and I came again, this time the spasms rocking my body so hard I bucked against the wall with my head.

"Shit. Ow."

He rubbed the back of my head as he carried me to the mattress, managing to lower me to my back without collapsing on top of my limp, sated body, or losing the condom. If I hadn't been a boneless lump from coming twice I might have been impressed. He thrust a dozen more times before stilling. His shudder strong, his body coated in slick sweat.

A few minutes later, he found the strength to deal with the condom and return with a cold beer for us to share.

I was sprawled across the bed, barely able to keep my eyes open. "We celebrating?"

"When I have the energy, I'm going to heat up the lasagna." He collapsed on the mattress, closing his eyes and looking like sleep was the only thing on the menu.

"In a microwave?"

"Mmm hmm."

"You don't have an oven?"

"Not something you usually find in a recording studio."

"Microwaves are the placebo of the masses."

He laughed so hard he had to clutch at his belly. "We'll eat it cold."

"I suppose I can cross piano off my bucket list now." I frowned. "Although we didn't have sex on it. Not really."

"Oral doesn't count?" He was lying on his back, his arm over his eyes, his beautiful naked body just asking for my touch. I stroked his chest. He smiled and peeked at me.

"Oh, it counts. It's almost my favorite thing."

His grin was wide. "I'm not against having another go."

"I won't check it off the list, then."

"Get dressed. We're going to my place."

"Can't I just watch you get dressed first?"

"No."

He threw my dress at me which I slipped easily over my head. I pulled panties from my purse and hopped on one leg then the other to get them on. He arched a brow. "I took them off in the car."

"I'm only going to take them off again."

"If I'm in the mood."

"When aren't you in the mood?"

I laughed. "Where's your city apartment?"

"Near the marina where I keep *Adagio*. You can hear the waves at night."

"Gotta be foggy there."

"Can get foggy in Marin too." He shrugged.

"But do you have a house in Marin?"

"In Tiburon. I'm never there. It's on my mom's estate. I can't show up without bumping into her."

"And why wouldn't you want to see your mother?"

"Long story."

"We should go there."

"Sloane..."

I pouted and swayed closer. "I promise to give you total control if you take me to your home in Marin. I want to meet your mom."

"Total control at my house?"

"Mmm hmm."

His smile twisted in a mischievous smirk. "Help me straighten up. Can't let the band jump to conclusions."

"Yes, sir, Captain."

Vic moved around the room, shutting down equipment, turning out all the lights and setting the alarm. I bagged up the lasagna.

"Wait, my shoes are over there."

"I'll toss them in my backpack."

"What? Why?"

He picked me up and swung me around so I was perched on his back.

"Vic!"

"I'm keeping you close. No running off."

I giggled. "You're carrying me to the car like this?"

"Mmm. Hmm."

"But my skirt is up to my ass."

"Then it's a good thing you're wearing panties. Don't want to flash the neighbors. If you wrap your legs around my waist the dress should hang a little better."

"You. Ass."

"Your ass, JT. Your ass is a thing of great beauty."

"You want it?"

"If you're offering," he said, taking the stairs at a quick pace.

"You'll have to earn it."

"And how can I do that?"

"I'll let you know."

"Fair enough."

The night was foggy, the air cold. Even with my jacket on, I was shivering. Vic cranked up the heat in the car and tossed me a blanket he'd fished out of the trunk. In another few moments I was cozy and warm.

After a half hour drive over the bridge and up and around several hills, we motored down a long driveway, parking between an ultra modern home and an enormous Tudor style mansion. A lovely woman stepped through the double doors of the larger home and I saw the resemblance immediately. She was tall and slender, her dark hair cut in a fashionable style. She wore a cream sheath dress with blue accents and a matching blue cardigan. She walked quickly down the path, her eyes never leaving her son's. "Victor." She stepped in to hug him, her hands going to his shoulders. "I'm so glad you're here. Andrew called to tell me everything that happened."

"Mom." He hesitated before returning the hug, but when he did she slumped with relief, her smile warm and her eyes beginning to glitter with tears. She hugged him harder.

"It's okay, Mom. I'm here." He kissed her cheek and held her more firmly as she buried her face in his shoulder.

After a few moments, she stepped away. "I've missed you."

"I'm sorry I don't come as often as I should. I'm not the best son."

"I know you're busy." She seemed to see me for the first time. "Hello." She wiped her eyes and extended her hand. "I'm Elaine. Victor's mother."

"Mom, this is Sloane. Sloane Gabrielli."

"Hello, Mrs. Hanley." I shook her hand. It was smooth and elegant, but she wore very little jewelry. No wedding band.

"Call me Elaine. Please come inside. It's cool tonight."

"We can't, right now, but..." Victor started to say.

"We'd love to." I took Victor's arm and began to move toward the house, nudging him along.

"Wonderful." She walked ahead, smiling.

"Complete control, remember?" he whispered.

"This is your mother. You can spend some time with her. If the number of phone calls are anything to go by, she worries about you."

"But later, you are my captive."

I moaned silently at the vision. "One hour. We can spend one hour with your mom."

He grumbled under his breath, then took my hand and led me through the front door and into a room his mom called the sitting room. No gathering in the kitchen for this family.

"Would you like coffee, Sloane? Or a glass of wine?"

"Do you have scotch?" Victor asked, winking at me.

"Yes, but I thought—"

"I'm teasing, Mom. I'll have a beer."

"A beer is fine for me too," I said.

"Are you hungry?"

We looked at each other at the same time and laughed. Between everything that had happened, we'd forgotten the lasagna in the car. "We brought lasagna."

"Oh. I... Thank you." She looked at me curiously. Neither of us were carrying anything that remotely looked like a bag of food.

"Vic left it in the car." Vic laughed and rose. "Have you eaten?" I asked.

"No. I wasn't really hungry."

"We'll heat it and make a salad." I popped up. "Point me toward the kitchen, please."

"But you're our guest," Elaine said.

Vic was back with the bag. "She's an amazing chef. Owns her own restaurant."

"Really? Are you related to the chefs at Abbiocco? I believe their names are Gabrielli."

"Mom and Dad are better than me, but I'm learning."

"Don't listen. Her food is delicious."

It took me twenty minutes to heat up the lasagna and oversee Victor's salad. Elaine watched her son with a mixture of pride and amusement as he chopped carrots and tomatoes, tossing in dried cranberries and pumpkin seeds with an extra flourish.

I located half a loaf of sourdough bread and put Victor on garlic bread duty next, making him peel and mash each clove, mix it with butter and olive oil, then place it on a flat pan in the oven. He decided he liked slicing and smushing things and was so proud of his achievements he'd eaten a third of the bread before we even sat down to eat together at the kitchen table.

Elaine finished off a good-sized portion, beaming with joy at having her son home again. We helped clean up then sat down to chat a little more before saying goodnight. The tension tightening Vic's muscles before we arrived had fled along with some of his guilt. Elaine was in heaven, listening to every word he said with rapt attention.

"We'll be right next door if you need anything," Vic said, giving his mom a kiss on the cheek.

"Victor." She hugged him hard and this time he didn't pause before wrapping his arms around her.

"I love you, Mom."

"I'm proud of you, dear." She turned to me. "Thank you, Sloane. For the delicious meal and…" She looked at her smiling son. "…and everything."

"Will you please come to my house for dinner one night? I'd love for you to meet my family. Vic can drive you over."

"Thank you. I would love to come."

Vic and I walked down the drive, cutting off along a pathway that led to the smaller more modern house. The main room was circular, with large windows that faced the bay and the ocean and a fireplace in the middle of the room. The kitchen wasn't enormous like I'd imagined, but then Victor was hardly ever here. Sliding doors led to a patio and a pool with a few lounge chairs stacked on the side.

"I didn't have a chance to get it readied for our stay. I'm sure there's no food in the fridge."

"We can raid your mom's kitchen."

"True. And I always have wine and beer."

"Some view." The bridge and the city sparkled in the distance.

"It's nicer with you in front of it."

He was checking me out. "You ready to ravish me, Captain?"

"At least five times a day."

"Arrogant ass."

"You doubt me?"

"I might put you to the test tomorrow."

"I'll be putting you to the test tonight, I think."

"Dirty pirate."

"I don't plan on wasting one minute." He pointed to the staircase. "Up."

"No." I folded my arms and tapped my foot, lifting my chin in fake defiance.

A sexy smile spread across Vic's face, his eyes darkening. He bent and lifted me with a quick swoop. "I believe punishment is in order."

"Mercy." I giggled, pretending to pound on his chest.

"Drama queen."

20

The phone buzzed exactly at nine. "Blake?" I rubbed my face, shocked at the late hour. I was always awake by six. "What is it?"

"Playing hooky?"

"I'm at my home in Marin."

"Was that a tremor I felt or are you actually next door to your mother?"

"We had dinner with her. Sloane provided the lasagna."

"The world-famous lasagna I have yet to try? Did she run to Elaine complaining about your behavior or are you two back together?"

"Door number two." A naked Sloane was stirring beside me. I had to get off this phone and take care of more pressing matters. "Why did you call?"

"I am the bearer of magnificent news."

"Spit it out."

"You always spoil my fun."

"Spit it out now."

"Renovations are moving along at a faster clip than we'd projected. You'll be able to put the offices on the market within the week and the apartments will be ready in five days tops. The electrical upgrade is finished, as well as the windows. Now it's just a matter of new paint."

"Have you changed professions?"

"Please, how could I ever give up law? Lawyers are so admired."

I noticed a faint echo. "You're calling from the dance studio, aren't you?"

"I had a break and wanted to choreograph a new routine for the upcoming dance extravaganza. You and Sloane have to come. These kids are amazing."

"If we can get away, we'll be there."

"Great. If Damien and Cassie are back, I'll wrangle them too. Damien's one of the Dance With Your Heart program sponsors."

"You've told me several times."

"Interested in helping out?"

"Of course. Just tell me how."

Sloane rolled onto her back, one of her arms curved under her head, the other across her naked belly. Her nipples were hard—a temptation I couldn't imagine resisting. I paced away from the bed, hoping to avoid a painful hard-on. "Can you email me the info?"

"Already sent," Blake said.

"Thanks."

"See you at the club later?"

I peeked back at the bed. Sloane had turned onto her side, facing me, her heavy breasts nestled against each other. I turned my back on the vision. "I'm not coming up for air until tonight. Maybe tomorrow."

"You two have fun."

I ended the call, silenced the phone and tossed it to the side.

"What was that about?"

She was checking me out, her gaze lingering on my semi-hard erection. Her voice had that morning roughness I loved, adding inches to my aching cock. "Give me an hour or so, then I'll tell you." I stroked my dick and enjoyed her lusty gaze as she watched.

"Impressive, LJ. Why don't you come a little closer?"

"Do you remember that song I mentioned? It's not meant for anyone's ears but yours."

"Why is that?"

"It involves some of the things I'm going to do to you right now."

She giggled and rolled to her back, tossing off the sheet and widening her legs. "Do your worst. Or should I say your best?"

Her beautiful pussy was glistening. "You're wet for me already."

"Sing." I waited, trying to pull off a stern expression. "Please, Long John."

I crawled up her body and began, taking it slow, with kisses, licks and nibbles in between the verses.

You were tipsy with the first kiss, almost killed me with the next,
But the third, sweet Sloane, had my mind and body screaming for your sex.
I tried to be persuasive, bringing out the Wilson Charm,
But you saw through all that surface shit and forced me to reform.

You said fuck off very clearly, but I'll work to change your mind,

And before this night is over you'll be mine.

I'LL TAKE my time kissing every inch of silken, scented skin.
    Using tongue and lips and teeth to make you yearn for sin.
    Two fingers will I slide inside your juicy, throbbing heat.
    You'll cry out "Victor please," and I'll lean down to eat.

CAUSE MY DICK is hard and your pussy's wet
    The music of your cries I will never forget.

I'LL RIDE you like a man on fire and you'll beg me for more,
    You'll flip me over and ride me too, cause you're the woman I adore.
    When we're spent and cuddling tenderly between the cozy sheets,
    I'll kiss your mouth and hold you close and sing my love to sleep.

YOU SAID FUCK off very clearly, but I worked to change your mind,
    And before the night was over you were mine.

MY VOICE HAD CAUGHT a little on the last line. Silence reined for the next thirty seconds. Suddenly she was hugging me, her belly laugh warming my senses. I had to kiss her, I couldn't hold back. Impulsive or not, sometimes you just had to jump in the deep end.

"That's the best gift anyone ever gave me," Sloane said,

wiping her eyes. "Makes me feel all sexy and sultry and not like boring practical me at all."

"You're all things to me."

"Am I yours? Really? And are you mine?"

"I want you in my life forever. But then you'd have to agree to be stuck with me."

"You mean I'd be stuck with a beautiful man with a beautiful heart and a beautiful soul?"

"Who's that guy? If I catch him near you, I'll..."

"Shut up, silly, I love you."

"Do you love me enough to marry me?"

"You're proposing? Now? Naked?"

"You're naked too. And I intend to spend at least two-thirds of my life naked beside you and over you and inside you. Seems like the perfect place to propose. I'm afraid I don't have a ring yet, so maybe you'd rather have the more traditional proposal? Or one of those skywriting planes? I'd have them write, *Marry Me you Juicy Tomato*."

I whacked him with a pillow, but he snatched it away and tossed it to the side. "You've turned me into a kid again."

"You're stalling."

"A few months ago, I would have said proposing naked in the middle of sex was a half-assed impulsive proposal and that you couldn't possibly be sincere."

"And now?"

"Now I know you say what's in your heart and you mean every word. This is the perfect place to propose."

"So, is it a yes or a no? A maybe would be okay too." He sat back, his gaze full of yearning.

I lay back, pulling him onto my body, cradling him between my legs. "Can we marry on *Adagio* at sunset?"

"Whatever you want."

"Then yes, Captain. I'll marry you." I rolled over so I was

on top, trying to assume a serious expression. "You know you're marrying someone who works long hours? I'll be at the restaurant late most nights."

"You can put me to work. I'm sure Gio will love bossing me around."

"I can't have you in my kitchen, but maybe you can play sometimes for the customers?"

"Of course. I have other musician friends trying to get work who sing and play a hell of a lot better than I do."

"Perfect. Only don't you ever sing that song."

"No worries there." He smoothed his thumb over my bottom lip. "Your mouth is sexy and wet and luscious and..."

I leaned up and kissed him, because he would have gone on for way too long. "What's the title of my dirty song?"

"'Before the Night is Over.'"

"I was yours. And I am." I glanced at my phone. "The day is starting and you did make an arrogant statement regarding your prowess."

"We can't count what went on between midnight and seven?" I asked.

"I'll think about it."

"I'D BETTER GET TO WORK." I spread her thighs and plunged my tongue inside her sweet heat. Sloane gasped, then moaned when I used her juices to tease her clit. I plunged two fingers deep, swirling them around then finding the spot that made her whimper. God, I loved that sound.

"Oh, Vic, more."

"What, baby?" I sucked her clit into my mouth and fucked her harder with each stroke. She screamed her pleasure, her body spasming and coating my hand.

I picked her up, limp and sated and carried her to the shower.

"I love my horny billionaire," she whispered, biting my neck.

"Sexy chef." I set her down as I leaned over to turn on the water.

Her ass was so fine. I wanted to bite it. Hard. Mark her as mine over and over.

Mine.

I'd never felt this way about a woman. Never wanted to spend more than a week or two with the same one. But I'd protect and love Sloane for the rest of my life.

"Why are you grinning like that?" She poked me in the ribs.

"You. Are. Mine."

"I love the sound of that."

I kissed my lovely captive, crushing her lips and easing my tongue inside her sweet mouth. As I picked her up and carried her into the shower, despite her protests, I knew there would never be a time I'd want to stop kissing her, touching her, holding her. I'd do everything in my power to make her happy, because she gave so much love to everyone around her, especially me.

With Sloane came a real family, but even if it were just us, I'd still feel a part of something so much bigger than myself.

"You're grinning again."

"Get used to it."

21

The rally was amazing.

"That's the mayor. How did you get the mayor to come?"

"He's a fan."

"You're using your celebrity?"

"My celebrity? I'm only the composer. Most people don't know what I look like."

"You do know there are fan pages on social media all about your music? I've seen plenty of pictures."

"Do you follow those pages?"

"No. They're filled with pictures of you and your old girl-friends."

"Ha. We'll have to announce our engagement."

"What are you going to say when they ask how you proposed to me?"

"I'll say it was private. Very, very private."

"Oh yeah, that won't peak anyone's interest." He had lived up to his word, making love to me five times that day, then giving me a break the next. Vic Hanley was an impressive specimen.

"All I care about is your interest, JT." He nuzzled my ear.

"Stop strutting around like a peacock."

"The most beautiful woman in the world is going to marry me. I get to strut all I want."

"I'll have to disagree with you there, Vic. Watching you strut may send the crowd home and we don't want that." Damien draped an arm over Vic's shoulder, but Vic pushed him away with a laugh.

Damien and Cassie had returned from their four month around-the-world honeymoon trip two days ago and had promised to meet us here at the Save the Mission Rally. They were tanned and relaxed and looking extremely happy. I'd never actually met Damien, but I'd seen him coming in and out of the studio/gallery. He was one of those men women had to look at twice—very tall with a commanding presence that shouted out danger, the kind of danger some women enjoyed very much.

Not my cup of tea at all, but exactly the right guy for Cassie.

"Introduce me to your lady, Victor." Damien's voice was low, his gaze intense.

"Dame, this is Sloane Gabrielli, chef extraordinaire. Sloane, may I introduce Damien Granger, the world-renowned reprobate."

I extended my hand and we shook. "And I thought Vic held that title."

"There can be more than one," Cassie said, smiling and snaking her arm through her husband's.

"True." I smiled at my friend.

"They're quite the pair, these two," Cassie said. She was tall, with thick dark brown hair pulled back in a ponytail and dark eyes that seemed to glitter with mischief today instead of the sadness I'd seen before Damien came into her life. Her brother, Graham, had been her business partner, both of them determined to make the art studio a success. But Graham had died, and Cassie had been left alone with nothing but bills. She was an amazing artist and also the designer of the blue, long-sleeved Save the Mission tee shirts we were all wearing.

The police commissioner was speaking now. "How do you know the commissioner?"

"Damien convinced him to come out in favor of our project." The two men smiled at each other and Cassie shook her head. I didn't want to know.

"Blake has set up the Mission Restoration Foundation and we've gotten quite a few hefty contributions already. Damien is the CEO and I'm the tech whiz of course. Dame is pulling in the CFO of one of his companies to take over the duties of Treasurer. Blake is obviously taking care of our legal department. If either of you want to sit on the board of directors, let us know."

"I would," Cassie and I said at the same time.

"Our plan is to see what we can do to restore buildings that might be in need of repair rather than seeing them purchased by companies intending to tear them down, rebuild and charge ridiculous rents. Some of the buildings on the block right now have some historical elements and wonderful character that will be lost forever."

I was so happy Damien seemed as enthused by the project as Vic.

"Who wants a beer and a burrito?" Blake had arrived. We all raised our hands. "Then follow me."

MY THREE BROTHERS were lined up at the door looking very

stern, my sisters and parents nowhere in sight. This was a total psych, but Vic didn't know that. They'd done this kind of thing with one of my old boyfriends the first time he'd come over for dinner. He'd made some excuse and beaten a path back to civilization in record time.

Vic was keeping his cool on the outside, nodding to Joey and Angelo, then extending his hand and introducing himself to Tony Jr., my oldest brother. Tony shook his hand but didn't drop his steely-eyed gaze.

"What makes you think you're good enough to marry our sister?"

"Yeah, dating is one thing, but you have to pass the Gabrielli Standard of Excellence which involves running the gauntlet and a touch football game and—"

"Guys! Would you stop already? Vic and I are engaged, so cut the crap." Angelo could have gone on for another five minutes.

"C'mon, Slo," Ang complained. "Don't mess with our fun."

"Do you want to get invited on the catamaran or not? We were planning on having an engagement trip to Santa Cruz next weekend." The toast would be just before sunset.

"You can sleep on board *Adagio* if you want. There's plenty of room for everyone," Vic said.

"My wife and three sons?" Tony Jr. asked.

"The youngest is seven," I added, not wanting Vic to think he was bringing babies aboard.

"Bring them. Kids love sleeping on deck. We'll make Chad the wrangler."

"What if it rains?" We were getting closer to the rainy season in California.

"I have a giant tent that covers the entire deck. And

worse comes to worse, Dame has a house in Santa Cruz for the landlubbers."

Because of the size of my family, and the number of friends I wanted to invite, we couldn't really get married on board *Adagio*. Mom and Dad suggested having the reception at Abbiocco and the wedding at the neighboring winery the restaurant was attached to. That sounded perfect, so all the dates and times and preparations were in place for a November wedding in Napa. We were lucky, because the winery didn't usually book weddings, but Mom and Dad had become close friends with the owners over the last ten years they'd run the restaurant and the owners were making an exception for me.

Elaine was helping out too, designing the floral arrangements and going with me, Mom and my sisters to pick out a dress.

I went with something very simple and sleek in ivory. Easy to take off was Victor's only request.

Vic had given me a beautiful ring as we ate together in a private corner of the new Bel Cielo—ruby and diamond in an antique setting. Paul and Drew had found it on one of their excursions to get items for the store, but Vic told me it was part of his pirate booty and that he chose a red stone because of the juicy tomato thing. I found out the next day Mom had told him that red was my favorite color and ruby my favorite gem.

Mom and Dad gave me congratulatory hugs, then did the same to Vic. He looked a little surprised but, hey, we were a touchy-feely clan. Mom put her hands on her hips and glared at her sons. "You boys had better behave tonight. We have a full house and I insist you follow Sloane's orders."

"Ma!"

"I mean it. This is a special Mangia Monday for Sloane

and Victor and you lot had better not do anything to embarrass them."

"Mangia Monday is going down the tubes," Angelo grumbled. Angelo and Tony stalked out.

"Get the barbeque primed, boys," Dad called out.

"Sure, Dad."

"Are they ever going to grow up? Tony Jr. is thirty-five!" I complained.

"They're men, dear."

I narrowed my eyes at Vic, but he kissed me so sweetly on the cheek, I couldn't find it in my heart to say anything.

Joey had hung behind. "Is Lori invited to your engagement party?"

"It won't matter because you won't be there," I said, still angry at my brothers.

Joey scowled, but Vic led him away with a hand on his shoulder. "I'm inviting you. And yeah, she'll be there."

"Thanks, bro." Joey went to punch Vic in the shoulder, but when he saw Vic wince, he laughed and jogged after our brothers.

"You shouldn't brown-nose those jerks. It won't help. They'll continue to torture you every Monday."

"Maybe I don't mind. I missed out on sibling torture sessions when I was a kid."

He looked so adorable, with a lock of hair flopping over one of his eyes and his gaze on the usual chaos going on in the Gabrielli kitchen. He wasn't looking at them with the same sadness he had the first time he'd met everyone. No, this time affection colored his gaze.

"They're part of your family now." I slipped my hand in Vic's. "Let's go say hi to my sisters."

"Sure."

We slid past the chaos and out the sliding glass door to

the patio and back yard. Caty, Kathy, Chad and Elaine were sitting together and chatting.

"Mom?" Vic waved.

"Hello, dear." Elaine rose and gave him a warm hug. He hugged her back a little more enthusiastically than he had the other time I'd seen them together. "Don't look so surprised. Emma and I have become good friends and I now have a permanent invitation to Mangia Monday."

"Of course you do. You're family now." I hugged my future mother-in-law and she grinned, her quirky smile so much like Victor's I was shocked at first.

I introduced Vic to Kathy, who was holding her baby girl. They exchanged greetings as Vic sat next to Chad. "How're things with you?"

"I showed my work to Mrs. Granger yesterday. She liked a lot of it. Said I had a great eye for color and form. Not sure what form is."

"You'll learn."

"Thanks, Vic, for giving me a chance."

"You'll call him Uncle Vic like you do Joey and Ang and Tony."

"I don't call Ang Uncle Vic." I smacked Chad playfully upside the head. He and Vic laughed together.

"I'll bring you to the recording studio next week if you're interested."

"Are you serious?"

"Yeah, sure. Sanity is recording a couple of songs Friday night. If you do well in school this week, I'll take you over."

Chad was bringing home weekly reports from his teachers. So far, so good.

"No one will believe it." Chad sighed.

"No problem getting an autographed vinyl or CD."

"Hey, Vic. You wanna help us with the barbecue?" Ang asked, looking all innocent.

I sent my brothers a glare that could have frozen a hot spring, but Vic squeezed my hand. "It's fine. I'm pretty sure they won't be putting me on the spit. Joey likes his job and the rest like coming to the club." He'd spoken loud enough for them to hear, just so there was no confusion.

Dad stuck his head out the kitchen window. "Don't you risk my membership!"

Dinner was wonderful and noisy with everyone talking. Vic and I walked the perimeter of the property when cleanup was over just to get some peace and quiet.

I hugged my love around the waist and whispered, "I'm going to have you cooking whole meals before you know it."

"It's a nice dream, but it will never come to fruition."

"Why?"

"I still mess up the coffee."

"How?"

"My mind is on everything but how many scoops I'm putting in. I lose count."

Rising onto my toes, I draped my arms over his shoulders and whispered, "I'll have you trained in no time at all."

Vic slid his hands to my ass and pressed me closer, his breath warm against my ear. "I'll be doing the training in this relationship."

"Not in the kitchen."

He grinned. "Yes, Chef."

"I'll start you off with chopping onions."

"You'll pay for it later."

"I'm counting on it, LJ."

∾

THE WEATHER WAS perfect for the sail, and as much as I wanted to savor time alone with Vic, the family and friend engagement party on *Adagio* was exactly right. Everyone chatted and laughed. Dad argued pleasantly with Drew about how to season hunter's stew and whether a particular vintage of cabernet was worth the money they'd paid for it. The twins had gathered around Paul as he gave them a quick run down on piloting the high-tech craft. They'd been looking forward to hoisting the sails, but *Adagio* had the latest tech and hoisting on this cat had gone the way of walking the plank. Joey still watched Vic with a wary eye. Big brothers of little sisters were a different breed.

Damien and Cassie joined us with many tales to share. Cassie was still a little surprised Vic was about to settle down.

"You're a great guy, Vic, but not the most...um..."

"Yeah, those days are over. I'm a one-woman man."

"I whipped him into shape," I said, pulling him closer.

"Like heavy cream." Vic smiled like the cat who licked it up on a regular basis.

Dame laughed. "It's worth every whisk, right?"

Vic stared at me. "God, yes."

"I'm happy for you, man," Damien said to his long-time friend. "I wish I'd been around to help."

Vic grinned at Cassie. "No he doesn't. Don't listen to the idiot." He turned back to Damien. "Thanks for stepping up and agreeing to the partnership."

"Yes. Thank you," I said.

"We've been partners since we were thirteen. Might as well make it official."

Damien and Cassie were regular customers now, recommending the restaurant to all their Graham Gallery customers. Business had dropped off slightly at first, but it was picking up again. I'd be hiring more staff soon. The Kriegers and the Garcia sisters were also happy with their new locations.

My mid-thigh red dress had gotten many compliments and Vic had already taken me aside.

"As hot as you look in this dress, I can't wait to peel it off your beautiful body." He kissed me seductively and it flashed in my mind for a moment that maybe we should send everyone home early.

"I could pretend to be sick."

He grinned. "I'm the luckiest fucker on the planet."

Vic said the nicest things.

Damien led the toast in his slightly British and extremely classy accent. "To Sloane and Victor. May Victor's music and Sloane's delicious cuisine feed the love they have for each other the way it has always fed their souls. We wish you the best in life, but as long as you have each other, the best is already yours. To Sloane and Victor."

The toast was perfect and I was a little teary-eyed at the end. Victor kissed me with all the love in his heart and I returned it full force. The sun set only minutes later and as my grandparents had said on their first night in California, the sunset created *un bel cielo.*

Later, when everyone had either been dropped off on the dock or were settled in their beds, Victor stripped me out of my dress and I rid him of his hand-tailored suit. We made love at first with heated passion, but for most of the night our connection simmered with a tender devotion, each touch and kiss leading to a deeper communication that would see us through tomorrow's troubles or next year's joys.

When he slid inside my body bringing me quickly to a powerful climax, my pleasure wasn't only physical. I was loved and in love with a man who treasured me, who saw me as I was and loved me for it. My heart sang with love, his music now a part of me forever.

"You are the most pliable captive."

"Sometimes the captive falls for the pirate," I said, sighing against his firm chest, wrapped inside his strong arms.

"Have you?"

"I'm afraid so."

"Mmm. How do you feel about the admiral and the cabin girl?"

"I might be able to fight off the admiral as long as the pirate rescues me."

"You can count on me." He stroked my hair, his eyes glowing with happiness.

And I always would.

THANK YOU FOR READING *SIMMER*. If you liked Sloane and Victor's story, check out Blake and Anya's story in *Split*.

Or Damien and Cassie's story in *Stroke*:

https://www.gayleparness.com/contemporary

Sign up for my newsletter to find out more:

http://eepurl.com/cLWAmD

split

MARIE BOOTH

SPLIT TEASER - MARIE BOOTH

GATE SERIES BOOK 3

Split: Gate Series Book 3

In the midst of a nightmare, Blake ruined his dance partner's dreams. Now it's up to him to urge her back onto the floor, and maybe into his arms.

Anya has managed to leave the long ago disaster in the past where it belongs. She's happy with her new life, so Blake can take his fancy dance shoes and stay the hell away.

Chapter 1
Blake

Anya's body twisted in rhythm as she whipped her head with every quick spin and smiled her lovely smile so every judge would mark us high.

I concentrated on the movement of my hips, the quickness of my legs and feet, the flow in the movement of my arms, the posture that marked me as one of the top salsa dance partners in the world.

We'd won the last two national competitions, but the

IBDC in Sydney was like roping a star in the sky for ballroom.

The lifts I'd choreographed were complicated, yet we'd worked them for uncountable months to make them look easy to anyone who didn't know the strength, balance and precision required. The competition was in three weeks and we'd already booked our flights and hotel and even shipped our costumes.

Nikki, our coach, a slim, petite woman, smiled when we finished. "Bella, Anya dear." But watch your footwork in the quickest section."

"Oh yes, thank you. I will."

Nikki turned to me. "You're tilting your head too much on the second refrain. You mustn't lose focus simply because you enjoy the music." She laughed and we joined in. She squeezed my shoulder. "The lifts you created are spectacular and that section near the end stands out. "Bueno, Blake."

"Thanks, coach."

She sighed with pleasure and took a step back. "You're ready."

We thanked Nikki over and over for all the time and effort she'd put into coaching us. Before leaving the studio, she forced us to vow to get to the airport three hours ahead of time for our flight to Sydney.

As soon as the door shut behind Nikki, Anya jumped into my arms. I swung her around, then changed tactics and kissed her hard and fast. We couldn't stop smiling or kissing or talking about our trip just two days from now.

An hour later we showered and ate take-out chinese in my apartment, our bodies buzzing with adrenalin, hunger and lust as if we'd fought a battle. Despite dire warnings from Nikki about keeping our personal lives separate, we agreed our dancing had improved since we'd become lovers. Anya and I were more in sync than ever, more focused, more connected.

It wasn't unusual. Dancing a sensual, sweaty, intimate experience. Many dance partners slid between the sheets in their rare time off.

She was demanding that night, not interested at all in slow seductions or extended foreplay. Five minutes after finishing our moo shu crab and the spicy General tso chicken dish I was inside Anya's perfect body whispering dirty words that made her wet, sweet phrases that had her laughing, soft promises of how we'd win the competition.

"I love you, baby." And I did, with every beat of my twenty year old heart.

Her smile was brilliant, her excitement electrifying the room. Her dream was coming true after years of excruciatingly hard work. "Let's go out and celebrate," she said, holding up a black number she kept in my closet. Low in the back and front, it showed off her gorgeous body to perfection.

"Tonight should be an early one." My practical side always kicked in when it came to sleep, food and scheduling rehearsals. Anya tended to let me organize her life, as long as the results worked out.

"You're too serious, Blake. Loosen up. I heard about a great club that just opened in Oakland. Let's go. I'm too wound up to sleep."

"If I didn't have to be in Marin tonight, I'd wear you out until you begged me to let you sleep." Pulling her closer I kissed her hard, taking every inch of her luscious mouth and making it mine.

"Mmm. Can we do more of that instead? Your mommy won't mind if we have a sleepover."

I had a class at UC tomorrow. "When the competition is over, we'll take a few weeks off, find a resort with a beach and relax."

"You and me?"

"You and me."

She sighed, kissed my cheek and swayed as she walked toward the door, now dressed in skin tight jeans, a colorful silky blouse and her favorite red jacket. "Fine." She turned and held out her hand. "Walk me to the train."

We shared another few kisses on the way, then said goodnight. We'd planned to have one last rehearsal tomorrow afternoon, then head to our respective apartments to finish packing.

Because of an accident on the highway, I got to my parents' house later than usual. Although I had my own apartment in the city, their house was more convenient to Berkeley and allowed me the ability to avoid the horrors of rush hour. Usually.

My seventeen year old sister, Val, was waiting for me.

"Can I use your car? Mine's in the shop."

I glanced at my phone to catch the time. Eleven p.m. Anya had texted she'd arrived home safe and sound. "No."

"Why?"

"It's a powerful machine and you don't have enough time on the road."

"But I have a party in Larkspur."

"Definitely no. Take the hybrid."

"That's Mom's car."

"It's only a year old and it runs great."

"But I want the Porsche. My friends aren't gonna want to show up at this classy party in a dumpy hybrid."

"You shouldn't be driving a bunch of your friends around. How many?"

"Two. Maddie and Crystal. Can't you take Mom's car?"

Her scowl was legendary. I held in the laugh with great effort. "When you're twenty-one I might think about lending you the Porsche."

She pulled out her phone. "Fuck you, Blake." Turning away, she stormed up the stairs in seventeen-year-old Valeria fashion. "Yeah, it's a no go. He's a douche," she announced to whatever friend was on the phone.

"Love you too, Shorty." Petite like Mom, Val hated it when I called her that, but she deserved it. Little brat.

Yawning, I emptied my pockets, dumping my keychain in the china dish on the table near the front door. Wincing when I bent down to lift my dance bag, I flexed my shoulders, still a little sore from the work out. Heat would help, so I locked the patio door, flipped the sign to occupied, and slid into the hot tub naked.

Closing my eyes, I allowed my mind to roam the enticing planes of Anya's body as my mouth and hands had a few hours earlier. Sex was a stress reliever after a long hard rehearsal, but Anya was so much more than that to me.

She was my future, damn my own career. I'd follow her to the ends of the planet and beyond, whether I worked as a dancer or a waiter or a lawyer like my parents. I had to end the day in her bed, her head on my chest, her soft breaths blending with mine.

Performing was great, especially when you won the title you'd worked so hard for, but my adrenaline rush took hold when Anya was beside me.

I toweled off and slid naked under the sheets, my muscles relaxed and sleep only minutes away. At three tomorrow afternoon we were scheduled for our last rehearsal before the competition. I set my phone for five a.m. I'd go for a short run before breakfast, then make it to class with time to spare.

But it was dark when I woke up next. Someone was ringing the doorbell. Dad went to answer it. I glanced at the clock. Three a.m.

Dad called out for mom in Spanish, his voice breaking. I pulled on a pair of shorts and took the stairs down two at a time.

Ten Years Later

Toweling sweat off my face, I hit end on my phone to stop the music. The choreography was still in its planning stages. Warm bodies in the studio to work the routines would make all the difference. Still, Vic's rhythmic, heart pounding music was making the process easy, and I was pretty sure Popup911 was going to love what I'd done with the tunes he'd be using on his first national tour.

Vic had done me a solid and introduced me to his client. The kid, real name Keith, had been open minded about checking out what I could do. I recorded a video to one of Victor's songs, standing in for P and using a few dancer friends as chorus. He called me five minutes after I sent him the video, practically bursting a gut with excitement. He told me later he'd watched the secret video another ten times. He even showed up just as I was closing to go over the moves face to face.

He was a natural dancer with a voice that could melt butter. Plus he was good looking and already had a few million followers on twitter. The Popup911 Tour was gonna break some attendance records.

This was my first big break as a choreographer.

Yesterday I got a call from an agent who represented several touring groups and singles. Keith had recommended me and the agent was anxious to see my work. I sent him a few videos and he called back, asking me to fly to LA, expenses paid. Some of the artists wanted to meet with me. I told him I had other commitments I couldn't break right now, but could probably schedule a meeting in two weeks. He didn't seem at all put off.

No way was I letting my classes down. We had a recital coming up and the kids were...well they were gonna blow some minds, that's for sure.

I grabbed a quick shower in the studio locker room before dressing in dark jeans, a black button down, boots and the leather jacket Val had gotten me for my last birthday. She always had great taste in clothes and enjoyed buying me shit online. Amazingly everything fit and looked great.

But I had to set her straight. My sister should not be buying my underwear. End of story. Only taking care of me made her happy and she needed every ounce of joy she could squeeze out of life.

I did a walk-through of the studio, shutting down lights and reassuring myself that everything was where it belonged. I locked the front door and turned.

A woman stared at me from across the street. A woman I thought I'd never see again. I raised my hand and started to call out, but she turned away and headed down the stairs to BART and Muni. In a daze, I stepped off the curb, but the sound of a car horn had me jumping back. Traffic was too heavy in this spot, so I raced to the corner and waited for the light to change. I took the stairs two at a time, but when I got to the station lobby, I had no idea which way she'd gone.

Could it really be Anya, or was she on my mind because

I'd been dreaming about her lately? It could have been anyone.

Split - Gate Series Book 3

Books by Marie Booth

Contemporary Romance Series:
The Gate Series: A steamy contemporary series centered around the members of an exclusive club in Marin County, California.

Stroke: Book One
Simmer: Book Two
Split - Book Three

Paranormal Romance/Urban Fantasy Series:

Steamy Bites Series:
Dying for a Bite: A zany vampire menage - M/M/F

Worst Holiday Ever: Releasing 11/15/18 A holiday anthology filled with funny tales of holiday horrors written by best-selling romance authors. Genres: Contemporary, Paranormal, M/F & LGBTQ

My contribution to Worst Holiday Ever: *Ringing in the Reefer* - set in the Steamy Bites Universe. Despite her husband's protests, a couple and her straight-laced parents make a Christmas eve visit to his relatives in Podunk. But more than a Christmas ham is being served as chaos erupts and family secrets are spilled. Paranormal M/F

Santa Cruz Shifter Series
Flying Hard - a m/m paranormal romance

The Theta Series: New York City is overrun with supernatural creatures all under the thumb of an archdemon known as The Director. Thetas - powerful psychics - are a new species, born of human parents, then forced into slavery. But a rebellion is in the air and the country's most popular theta female may be leading the charge.

Playing with Passion: Available now

Yielding to Pleasure: Available now

And if you like sweeter action packed paranormal romance... check out the eight book Rogues Shifter Series, the three book Triad Series, and the two book Rogues Inc Series written by the real me - **Gayle Parness.**

Book One - Rebirth - is **permanently free** at all vendors.

Rebirth - Rogues Shifter Series Book 1

ACKNOWLEDGMENTS

To my daughters and brother: You are my heart. Thank you for inspiring me every day.

To my writing family who've supported my crazy journey through thick and thin. Thank you for all your encouragement, feedback, and for keeping me on track.

To my amazing editor, Reina Robinson at Rick Rack Books: Thank you for your terrific advice and incredible amounts of patience. https://rickrackbooks.com/services

To Natasha Snow at natashasnowdesigns.com - I wasn't sure we could come up with another cover I liked as much as the first one, but that tomato...yes! Can't wait to see what we come up with for Split. Thank you for sharing your amazing gift with me.

Thank you to my readers, because you bring my characters to life in your own unique ways. I love to hear from you, so please feel free to contact me on my social media accounts or my website.

Sign up for my newsletter to get all the latest info on my upcoming books and to find out about sales, cool prizes and fun giveaways. https://www.mariebooth.com

http://www.facebook.com/MarieBoothBooks
http://www.twitter.com/marieboothbooks
https://www.instagram.com/marieboothauthor

Marie's a California girl who happily shares her life with two daughters and a big boned solid black rescue cat. She's currently working on her next Gate Series novel - Split - which will be out in Spring, 2019

Sign up for her newsletter to get info on her latest Contemporary Romance and Urban Fantasy releases. https:www.mariebooth.com

Follow Marie on Bookbub
http://www.bookbub.com/authors/marie-booth

Website: http://www.mariebooth.com
http://www.facebook.com/marieboothbooks
http://www.twitter.com/marieboothbooks
http://www.instagram.com/marieboothauthor